Gerald Hammond worked as an architect for thirty years before taking nominal retirement in 1982. He lives in Scotland with his wife and has three sons and four granddaughters. The author of over forty novels, he now divides his time between shooting, fishing and writing.

FINE TUNE

Jane Faraday never intended to compete seriously in a driver's championship for Formula One — and she certainly didn't expect to succeed. At first she only plans to enjoy the freedom of the circuit, put in a few fast laps and leave it at that. Then insidiously, the competitive world draws her in. Honing mind and body with single-minded determination, Jane's ability and beauty slowly bring success and widespread media coverage. But fame is a fickle and dangerous ally, and Jane has already made several enemies on the way up . . .

Books by Gerald Hammond
Published by The House of Ulverscroft:

DEAD GAME
THE REWARD GAME
FAIR GAME
SILVER CITY SCANDAL
THE LOOSE SCREW
MUD IN HIS EYE
COUSIN ONCE REMOVED
SAUCE FOR THE PIGEON
FRED IN SITU
THE WORRIED WIDOW
ADVERSE REPORT
STRAY SHOT
DOG IN THE DOG
DOGHOUSE
A BRACE OF SKEET
WHOSE DOG ARE YOU?
LET US PREY
HOME TO ROOST
STING IN THE TAIL
LAST RIGHTS
THE EXECUTOR
THE GOODS
PURSUIT OF ARMS

GERALD HAMMOND

FINE TUNE

Complete and Unabridged

ULVERSCROFT
Leicester

First published in Great Britain in 1998 by
Severn House Publishers Limited
Surrey

First Large Print Edition
published 2000
by arrangement with
Severn House Publishers Limited
Surrey

The moral right of the author has been asserted

British Library CIP Data

Hammond, Gerald, *1926 –*
    Fine tune.—Large print ed.—
    Ulverscroft large print series: mystery
    1. Women automobile racing drivers—Fiction
    2. Suspense fiction
    3. Large type books
    I. Title
    823.9′14 [F]

    ISBN 0–7089–4286–5

Foreword

Shortly after beginning this novel I realised to my horror that my slender experience as a constructor and driver was out of date by a matter of . . . good God! Could it be more than forty years? Well, yes, it could.

Some urgent research was called for and in this I was enormously aided by my friend Robin Grady and by Jon Baker. Despite their considerable help, or for reasons of the plot, some deviations from strict accuracy may persist. For these, may I be forgiven!

But this is a work of fiction and should be treated as such. In particular, the episode in the concluding race should not be taken to mean that I think that a certain famous coming together in Australia was deliberate. Certainly not. Perish the thought!

G.H. 1997

1

Wing Commander Faraday DSO, DFC glared peevishly across the glass-topped desk at the younger man. 'I'm too old to have a young girl, even a granddaughter, dropped into my lap. Knickers on the line, what'll the neighbours think? But if needs must . . .'

'It isn't absolutely essential,' the solicitor said. 'As you know, I was a close friend of Jane's father ever since our university days and our families stayed in touch.' He could have added that he would readily have married Jane's mother if her father had not jumped the gun. 'Jane would be welcome to a home with us, but with four of our own in the house . . .'

'No question of that,' the Wing Commander said gruffly. 'Family is family, after all.'

The solicitor felt that family duty was a poor substitute for affection but he decided to make the best of it. 'Splendid! And she needn't be a burden on you. Her parents had at least paid off most of their mortgage and there was some insurance, so she won't be penniless.'

1

The Wing Commander cheered up slightly. He was getting by, even managing to live in some style despite the effects of inflation on a largely fixed income, but he had a vague idea that raising a young girl might entail all sorts of unforeseeable expenditure. 'All the same,' he said, 'she's such a plain little thing. Well named. Plain Jane. Carrot hair in pigtails and braces on her teeth. Straight out of St Trinian's, if you ask me.'

Gordon Black, the solicitor, smiled. 'I would call her hair auburn rather than carrot. How long is it since you've seen her?'

'Must be several years now. My son used to meet me for lunch in Town now and again, but we hardly ever visited.'

'I think you'll find that it's been eight years at least. She may have changed a little in that time.' From the few papers on the desk he selected a colour photograph and passed it across. 'It's no more than a snapshot, but it gives you some idea.'

The old man studied the likeness. It showed a mid-teenager with auburn hair smiling shyly at the photographer. 'At least the braces seem to have worked. She has good teeth. But her nose is too long.'

The solicitor hid a second smile. The Wing Commander had a nose which he could point like a sword when the occasion suited. 'It's

2

not in the Cyrano de Bergerac class,' he said. 'In point of fact, most people's noses are too long. We prefer short noses because we admire youth. Children start life with short noses, so cosmetic surgeons are kept busy doing nose jobs.' He recovered the photograph and studied it. 'Somebody once said that a millimetre isn't big, except when it's on the end of a woman's nose. That's probably all that we're talking about. It gives her a slightly haughty look, quite undeserved.'

'Just as long as it doesn't spoil her chances of finding a husband.'

Gordon Black raised his eyebrows. 'I don't think she's very interested in matrimony.'

'They're all inclined that way,' said the Wing Commander. He would have gone to the stake rather than admit that his experience might be slightly out of date.

'Perhaps. But your granddaughter's not exactly run-of-the-mill. I have her school reports here . . . '

The Wing Commander shook his head. 'You *know* her. That's worth more than a lot of damn reports. Her father never spoke about her. Took her for granted, I suppose. Tell me about her. What is she really like?'

'A tall order,' said the solicitor, 'but I'll do my best. She's athletic. She takes a lot of exercise, but I think that it's only for the sake of fitness, because she doesn't give a damn about competitive games. She told one of my girls once that anyone who wasted precious time sending a silly ball from one place to another didn't deserve to have a life. According to the school, she's very gifted in mathematics and physics, has a natural understanding of computers and is an absolute duffer at everything else.'

It was the Wing Commander's turn to smile. It gave his age-raddled face a look of ferocity while at the same time handing back a trace of his earlier good looks. 'We never had computers in my younger days,' he said. 'Had to learn a bit about the analogue ones later, but they were only coming in as I was going out. Apart from that, she sounds a bit like I used to be.'

'So your son said. And yet I see her as a compound of her two parents. A mathematician and an aeronautical engineer, and they never bothered much about socialising. They were too wrapped up in their jobs and in each other. The girl's the same. She'll trot along with the others of her age but you get the feeling that she isn't really with them in spirit, she'd rather be alone, with her head in a book. And I don't mean novels, I mean heavy text-books. I have a feeling . . .'

'Go on,' the older man said. 'Feelings are

4

often worth more than facts.'

'It's not easy to put into words. But you asked what she was really like and I'm trying to tell you. I just sometimes get the feeling that she's seen through the frivolous lives that most of these young girls lead. She's going to go places but she doesn't yet know where, so in the meantime she's preparing her mind and her body, waiting for life to begin. She gets on well with one of my daughters. The others are rather in awe of her, but they like her. She helps them with their homework.'

'I thought that she was at a boarding school.'

'She is, or was. But she came to us for holidays and weekends and half-terms when her parents were away, and her terms didn't always coincide with theirs. She's been here since the accident.' The solicitor paused. 'As we've approached the subject,' he said, 'I may as well offer my views on her future education . . . if you want them?'

'Certainly I want them. I don't know a damn thing about educating young girls. Never even had a daughter, just the son. And a daughter-in-law, of course, but she was already over-educated when the boy married her.'

'I understand.' Black was beginning to like

5

the old chap. He had been a fine-looking man, years earlier, but the passage of time and loss of weight had slackened and wrinkled his skin. For all his abrupt manner he was polite and he seemed determined to do his best for his granddaughter. 'I think,' he resumed, 'that her present school has done as much as it can for her. Indeed, I think that they feel the same way. She's already ahead of her teachers in maths and physics — '

'That'll be all the books?'

'And her parents. She was always asking questions and they were very patient about answering them. Obviously, she's university material — in fact, I believe the local university would welcome her. Her mother lectured there, as you know, and was buddies with the Vice-Chancellor. The trouble is that she doesn't have the exam results she'll need to be admitted.'

'What do you suggest?'

'One of the best private schools is an easy bus ride from your house and they do take day pupils. Cranfield. You know the sort of place — they charge foreign royalty fat fees for educating their idiot offspring and take in the brilliant children of charwomen for free. They could bring her up to scratch within the year while still keeping up her maths and so on.'

The Wing Commander thought it over. His first impulse was to continue with the boarding school rather than have a teenager, all noisy friends and rock music, in the house, in and out of term-time. But she did not sound like that sort of girl and he really did mean to do his best for her. After all, she was his sole surviving descendant. As a female, she would not pass on the family name — except by single parenthood, and he hoped that she would avoid that particular method. It was a good name and one which he considered very suitable for anyone with a scientific turn of mind. 'You're probably right,' he said. 'I'll have to think it over.'

'Of course.' The solicitor looked up at the clock on the wall. Watches never worked for long on his wrist. Jane had tried to explain it to him once but he had only understood the first half-dozen words. 'We'll have to be moving soon, for the funeral. Jane won't be there, by the way. I thought it better not. She's been taking the death of her parents rather hard. So she'll stay with my wife at our home and we can collect her later.'

The Wing Commander nodded and struggled to his feet.

★ ★ ★

7

The funeral took place in a small church, built of flint with stone corners and margins, mostly Norman but with Early English windows added. The churchyard was shaded by huge trees and undulated gently, like a sea feeling the effect of a far distant storm — which, the Wing Commander felt, was not inappropriate. He stood with his bared head bowed, thin locks lifting in a faint breeze, and decided that he had no intention of being left to rot, but that this was where he would like his ashes to lie when the time came. The place was welcoming and at least he would have a few relatives nearby. His wife, of whom he had been mildly fond, had been lost in a plane crash over the sea years earlier. The nearest churchyard to home was huge and impersonal and he had been giving thought to cremation.

There was no proposal for a funeral meal, no suggestion of *come back to the house for a drink*. With the couple both dead and the nearest relative not out of her teens, it was not expected. The sprinkling of colleagues and the few personal friends shook hands with the old man and went on their ways, only too happy that duty had been done, formality appeased, and they could now set about forgetting a couple who few of them had known more than in passing and who had been tolerated as intelligent acquaintances rather than liked as friends.

The big Jaguar, chauffeur-driven, six years old but still glossy, followed the nearly new Volvo to the solicitor's house on the edge of a village. It had been a small house, added to in a rambling way so that it was now larger than it looked and, though never beautiful, it had a lopsided look which gave it a slightly eccentric charm. But it seemed filled by young voices which hushed momentarily and then resumed as Gordon Black ushered his visitor inside. The hall was cluttered. Black's wife, Estelle, was a tall woman who gave the impression of being competent and imperturbable. 'I've put sandwiches in the dining room,' she said. 'The rest of us have had a proper lunch. Are you sure that that's all you want?'

'It's as much as I usually take at midday,' Faraday said. He looked at Black. 'I hope that I'm not leading you into starvation?'

'Not a bit. And I must get back to the office soon. We'd better have a working lunch and tidy up a few details. Where's Jane?'

'Somewhere around,' Estelle Black said. 'With her head stuck in a book as usual, I have no doubt. I'll find her for you. And I'll give your chauffeur some nosh in the kitchen.'

The Wing Commander thanked her on both counts. The two men settled in a dining room half filled by a table extended by several leaves. The sandwiches were thick rather than dainty and filled with savoury meats. There was an inexpensive wine. The Wing Commander found that he had an appetite after all.

Gordon Black chose a sandwich but put it down on his plate. 'Another word of explanation,' he said. 'It may help you to understand your granddaughter. For her age, she's a remarkably logical rather than an emotional person. Or if she has emotions they're buried as being illogical and therefore of no importance. I don't know which. Confronted with any problem, she'll arrive at her own solution. It may not be conventional, but it's usually worth finding out what's at the back of it. Very often, it's sound common sense. But common sense can offend people.'

Wing Commander Faraday sipped wine to clear his mouth. 'What kind of things are we talking about?' he asked.

'Almost anything. Time, especially. She seems to feel that there's an awful lot to do in a single lifetime. As I said earlier, she doesn't know what it will be, but she's getting ready for it. Sometimes, ordinary courtesies get in the way — '

They were interrupted by the arrival of the subject of their discussion. Jane Faraday was tall for a girl and, as Gordon Black had said, auburn-haired. She was dressed in an inelegant school uniform and wore wholly unsuitable spectacles but her grandfather, who had had an eye for the ladies in his day, noted that her figure and skin were good. There might be hope for the girl yet. He was still thinking in terms of getting her married off.

He offered his hand. She had to switch the book that she was holding, with a finger to keep her page, into her left hand, but she took his in a firm grip.

'I'm sorry about your parents, my dear,' he said.

'Yeah,' she said calmly. 'It's a drag. But you've lost family too.'

'It seems that we're about all the family that's left to either of us. What are you reading?' She showed him the book. From the position of her finger it seemed that she had almost reached the end. 'Dunne's *An Experiment with Time*, eh? I had a go at it myself when I was younger. An interesting opening but, further on, the mathematics of it beat me.'

'It didn't seem to me like it was all that difficult,' she said, 'but all the same I don't know that I agree with his conclusions. Of course, it's all a bit old hat now — '

The solicitor, who had seized the chance to tackle his own sandwich, hastily emptied his mouth again. The Wing Commander was unlikely to take kindly to being patronised by somebody a fifth of his age. 'Your grandfather and I were just considering what's to be done,' he said. 'You know that we'd be delighted to have you here but, honestly, we don't have room.'

'I, on the other hand,' said her grandfather, 'have plenty of rooms. We thought that you should finish out the summer term where you are and then come to me. You can have your own bedroom — and a sitting room as well if you want such a thing. It's a nice house, fronting onto the upper Thames, and the boatyard nearby hires out canoes and things.' He was annoyed with himself to realise that he was speaking almost pleadingly.

'I don't suppose it matters an awful lot,' she said musingly. 'But . . . is there a health club nearby where I can work out?'

'About half a mile away.'

'That's OK, then. I like to keep fit without having to play a lot of fool games.' The two men exchanged an amused glance. *I told you so*, said the solicitor's and the Wing Commander's said, *You were right*. 'Uncle

12

Gordon,' she went on, 'will you go on acting as my solicitor?'

'Yes, of course. I was going to ask you whether that was what you wanted. Do you want me to sell the house for you?'

She shook her auburn head. 'No way. That's not what I want at all. It's my home. It's where I grew up. Wherever I live in between, I'll want to go back there. Could you find me a good tenant and see that the house and garden are well kept? Of course, I'd expect to be charged a fee.'

'Of course,' Black said cheerfully. He might have meant that of course she would be charged a fee or of course she would expect it. 'No problem.'

'And one other thing. Could you call the garage and ask Gunge to put Dad's car up on blocks and take the battery out of it?'

'Gunge?'

'He's the apprentice or dogsbody or something. He used to be called Ginger because he has red hair — yes, even redder than mine,' she added mildly as the two men smiled ' — and that was shortened to Ginge and it became Gunge, I suppose, because he gets landed with all the dirty jobs.'

'But is the car worth the trouble?' the solicitor asked. 'Wouldn't it be better just to sell it?' Jane's parents had neglected their road transport in favour of the light aircraft in which they had died together.

Jane removed her glasses, thereby improving her appearance, in her grandfather's opinion, about a thousand per cent. 'I don't think so,' she said seriously. 'I don't suppose I'd get more than about two pee for it, but it's a good little runner and I'd have to pay through the nose when the time comes to replace it. Anyway, it's the only car I know how to drive. Dad taught me on private roads and around the airfield.'

'That seems to settle that,' said her grandfather. 'So, when we've had our coffee, perhaps we can give you a lift back to school? I looked for it on the map and it's almost on our way home.'

'Well, all right,' Jane said. 'But could we go round by my house on the way?'

'I think we could manage that,' said the Wing Commander. 'You'll have to be navigator and bomb-aimer.'

His granddaughter looked at him askance at the mention of bombs but, evidently identifying the remark as elderly humour, made no retort. 'I'll go and say goodbye to Laura,' she said.

★ ★ ★

Jane showed the first sign of animation when they left the house twenty minutes later and she saw the Jaguar parked in the shade of a tree. 'That's real cool!' she said.

The old man decided to demonstrate that he also was with it. 'Groovy?' he suggested.

She frowned. 'No, not quite groovy. But definitely cool.'

Rightly interpreting this as expressing approval, the old man smiled. 'You like cars?'

She considered the question. 'I like any machine that's well designed and perfect for what it's supposed to do and manages to look good as well. This is designed to take you from A to B, comfortably. Machines respond predictably. There's no telling what a person will do next.'

'I see.' He indicated the chauffeur who was waiting beside the car. 'This is Henry Dodson. He's my chauffeur and gardener. Mrs Dodson keeps the house.'

'Do I call him Henry?'

'If you like.'

'How do you do, Henry.'

'How do you do, miss.'

'Can I sit beside Henry, Grandfather?'

'As long as you don't distract him while he's driving.'

The Wing Commander was slightly miffed. He had been looking forward to sitting with his granddaughter, perhaps even beginning to know this alien creature. But she behaved so sensibly, asking penetrating questions about the car, its performance, handling, fuel consumption and a host of other things, but always waiting for a straight and empty road in case Henry should be distracted, that he quite forgave her. After all, they would have years together, provided that his stupid heart managed to go on pumping away. He seized the chance of a quick surreptitious nap.

Guided by Jane, they joined the motorway, left it again, bypassed a sprawling industrial estate, turned off at a garage and service station and entered a dignified old town where they pulled up outside a well-kept house. The house was small by some standards, perhaps four bedrooms, but it had been built around the time of World War One, when dimensions were generous. The plot must have extended to more than half an acre, so that even after a large double garage was taken off it there was ample space for a lawn and flower beds and several trees. There seemed to be some sort of extension at the back. The garden and the trees were rather overgrown, which only added a touch of charm to an otherwise pleasant but undistinguished property. The garden, Faraday noticed, backed onto a golf course, which would certainly add a few thousand to the value.

Jane was sitting still.

'Don't you want to fetch something?' he asked her.

'I have all my books at school with me,' she said. After a minute, she sighed. 'Drive on, Henry,' she said.

★ ★ ★

The Wing Commander's house was a spacious late-Victorian villa. As he had said, it fronted on the river which, by mid-June, was bustling with traffic — yachts and cruisers, tourboats, rowing boats of every size and style and occasional light commercial traffic. Boys were to be seen, hazarding their lives in canoes in ways which would have given their mothers hysterics.

By the middle of the month, also, Jane was installed. Mr and Mrs Dodson were delighted to have a young person about the place to spoil. The Wing Commander was not sure whether he was quite so pleased but rather doubted it. His granddaughter sometimes presented a puzzle. She was a tranquil person and yet intense.

Jane spent several hours every day jogging to and from the health club and working out, he was given to understand, with great dedication; or she would hire a skiff from the boatyard and row with enormous energy in and out of the other craft. And during these activities, or while attending to minor tasks around the house or toying with one of the computers inherited from her parents, she would have on her head a Walkman radio or cassette player to which she seemed to be listening intently. This seemed strange behaviour in one who considered music to be a mathematical aberration and rarely watched television except for the news or programmes of instruction. Moreover, not a sound of popular music ever escaped from the earpieces. Sometimes the Wing Commander thought that he could detect the sound of a female voice remarkably like that of his granddaughter.

One day, finding the Walkman abandoned for the moment in the hall and being overcome by curiosity, he played to himself an inch or two of the tape and was surprised to hear some formulae which he recognised, from his aeronautical experience, as being those for calculating the airflow over an aircraft's wing. On his enquiring, she explained quite openly. Airflow was one of the many subjects that she found fascinating. Any fragment of information which she might

18

want again but might not remember she dictated onto the latest in a large and growing collection of audio cassettes, to which she listened in strict rotation. In that way, she explained solemnly, she could impress them on her memory without going to the trouble of memorising them.

The Wing Commander shook his head over what seemed to him an excessive dedication to the pursuit of knowledge, especially in one so young. For most of the time, he allowed his granddaughter to go her own way. But he was determined, despite the obvious signs that it would be an uphill struggle, that while under his roof she would acquire at least some of the social graces which her academically minded parents had disdained. So it was an inflexible rule that the two should sit down together for dinner at night. And there was to be no bolting of food. If she happened to finish early, there was no escaping. Polite conversation must continue for not less than twenty minutes. For much of the time he found that he was having to do more than his fair share of the conversing, but just occasionally they found a common chord.

Once, he asked her, 'Don't you feel the need to be with others of your own age?'

'Boys are silly,' she said.

'What about girls?'

'They're even sillier.'

Compared to her, he thought, it was possibly true. But it led to another thought. 'Weldon, at the boatyard, thinks you're hoity-toity.'

'By his standards,' she said loftily, 'he could be right. He's a slob. He swears. He uses the f-word all the time.'

The Wing Commander was amused. 'Does that make him a bad person?'

She thought seriously about the question. 'No,' she said at last. 'It makes him stupid.'

'Or uneducated?' he suggested.

'Could be. You mean, he doesn't have the right word so he puts that one in instead?'

'Right. Have you ever wondered why some words are considered rude?'

She looked puzzled. 'Because of what they mean?'

'Partly,' he said. 'But think a little deeper. Why, for instance, is it quite polite to refer to a posterior or a backside, marginal to use the word bum and definitely rude to say arse? Think about it.'

'I've thought,' she said a minute later. 'You'll have to help me. Is it something to do with languages?'

'It's everything to do with languages. If you thought a little more, you'd see that most of the unacceptable words are Anglo-Saxon. That suggests that, whenever there was a conquest, the inhabitants' older language was considered *infra dig*.'

'And so their word for any yucky activity became the rude one?'

'Right. But that in turn suggests that the designation of some words as rude or blasphemous is a human necessity. After all, there's no logical reason for one word to be acceptable and another with the same meaning to be anathema. They used to say, in the RAF, that there was a word that you were only allowed to use when your parachute failed to open.'

For the first time since he had known her, she laughed aloud. 'What word is that?'

'I'll tell you some day — when your parachute fails to open. But swearing and blasphemy aren't there only for when you hit your thumb with a hammer. There have to be forbidden words just so that the embargo can be broken. They're meant to shock.'

'To underline what you're saying?'

'And more. Otherwise there's no reason for their existence.'

'I see where you're coming from,' she said. 'You mean that by being shocked I'm helping to keep it alive?'

'Now you're cooking with gas,' he said.

'You're still a square!' But before going upstairs that evening she kissed him on the top of his balding head. It was another first. 'Good night, you old bastard,' she whispered. She could hear him chuckling until she was almost at the head of the stairs.

On another occasion there was a guest, Julian Berkeley, a man who to her young eyes looked almost as old as her grandfather. Jane sat quietly while her elders conversed, until the words 'civil rights' caught her attention.

'It seems to me,' she said, 'that the civil rights they talk about are mostly the right to be a real pain in the . . . the backside of society. Society itself has very few rights.'

Instead of laughing at her, Mr Berkeley nodded seriously. 'Very often it's as you say. But that's not the attitude that I would have expected from one of your tender years.'

She shrugged. 'It's how I see them. People who talk about civil rights are usually on the side of the baddies. It seems to me that people who step outside the law give up their rights under the law. Or that's how it should be. The world's full of people who want to stop other people doing things and I can sympathise with anybody who wants to get rid of the busybodies. But that's not what they're on about.'

'And top of the list of busybodies,' Mr

Berkeley said, 'I would put accountants. They set out to rule the world, but if you look into the figures on which they base their tablets of stone, you'll find that those tablets crumble. Your grandfather tells me that you're quite a mathematician.'

'She is,' said the Wing Commander.

'Somewhere along the way,' said Mr Berkeley, 'in the course of your further education, try to find a course entitled, 'How to destroy an accountant with three easy questions'. You'll find it invaluable in later life.'

A few days later, she realised that her grandfather was studying her across the dining table. 'What's up?' she asked. 'Is my head on crooked?'

'How long is it since you had your eyes tested?'

'Not long. March, I think.'

'Is your eyesight bad?'

'I'm slightly myopic.'

'No astigmatism?'

'No.' She took off her spectacles and looked at him. 'You're not sharp but I can see you.'

'I'm going to send you along to my optician tomorrow. Those glasses don't do a damn thing for you. He'll test you for contact lenses. If you can't tolerate them, at least let somebody choose more suitable frames for you.'

'Appearances are a drag,' she said. 'They don't matter.'

'Your appearance may not matter to you. But you're the one person who doesn't have to look at it. Do appearances matter on a machine?'

'That's different. It's a matter of design. But you can't design the human body. I wish you could. It's not very well thought out or put together.'

'There I agree with you,' he said. His arthritis was paining him. 'But you can do a lot about the body. You work to keep it in good trim. Why do you do that?'

She looked puzzled. 'Why do I? I suppose because I hate to see women with soft, flabby bodies and I don't want to get like that. And I want to live for ever.'

'An understandable ambition but I doubt if you'll attain it. Tell me, you wouldn't think much of a good machine in a hideous casing. Would you?'

'I suppose not. But I'm not . . . hideous?'

'No, of course not. But you could look so much better than you do.'

'Why would I want to?'

'To attract the boys, perhaps. And to make other women jealous.'

She pretended to yawn. 'Boys are another drag. I'm just not interested.'

He sighed. She was carrying him back sixty years or more. 'You will be,' he said. 'Boys are interested in girls all the time, that's how they're made. But some day you'll suddenly realise just how interesting they are. You won't expect it, but it'll happen. And that's when you'll want to look like an atractive woman, not a lumpy schoolgirl. So we'll start with the glasses and go on from there.'

The contact lenses were duly obtained — soft lenses which were regularly discarded and replaced. Jane admitted that they were comfortable. The Wing Commander even caught her looking at herself in the mirror and he realised that she had never seen herself clearly without her spectacles. Delighted with the improvement to his granddaughter's appearance, he was becoming caught up in a fresh interest, an elderly Pygmalion. At dinner the next evening he launched a fresh attack. 'Next,' he said, 'you have your hair done.'

'It's done,' she said.

'It's cut, after a fashion. Apparently by electric hedgetrimmer. There's a stylist in the High Street — quite good, I'm told. Go and get it styled. Say that you want something smart but easily kept.'

25

'I'd sooner spend the dosh on books. Or save it for when I really get going.'

The Wing Commander looked surprised. 'I didn't mean you to spend your own money. These were to be my treats. Did you pay for the contact lenses? I told them to send me the bill.'

'It's all right,' she said. 'You needn't look like I've stolen your rattle. If it makes you happy, I'll go to your old stylist. Don't worry about the money. Dad's insurances kicked through and Uncle Gordon found me a good tenant for the house.'

He hesitated for a moment and then decided to agree. Spending her own money would be part of becoming an adult. 'Afterwards, if you're really satisfied, go to the chemist and get a passport photograph taken,' he said.

'But I'm not going anywhere,' she said reasonably.

'Nobody said that you were.' He tried never to sound irritable despite frequent temptation, but he could hear irritation creeping into his voice. 'Do try to listen to what people really say. When you read, do you take in what the book says? Or what you expect it to say?'

She flushed. 'What it says.'

'Then do me the favour of giving me the

same attention. If you have a photograph of how you want to look, you'll never have to describe how you want it cut and have them usually get it wrong and still charge you the earth for it. You'll be able to say, 'Cut it like this,' and you'll have a good basis for refusing to pay if they make a mess of it.' It was a trick learned from his late wife.

'You're not so dumb,' she said.

It was those words that decided him to broaden his approach. While she was at the hairdresser he did some shopping of his own. He visited a bookshop where audio cassettes in the spoken word series were also stocked. Being only a casual reader himself, he asked the proprietor to select up to a dozen taped books by writers with good style. 'Not too many of them old-fashioned. I want plots to interest a modern young lady, in language which is lively but correct.'

'I know what you mean,' said the man. 'I have three daughters.'

'In the services,' said the Wing Commander, 'we'd have called that a self-inflicted wound.'

Jane returned to the house with her hair cut to a style which looked deceptively simple. Relieved of the weight, it had assumed a natural wave. The Wing Commander looked at her approvingly but decided not to hand out any flattery. Girls, in his remote experience, could get swollen-headed if complimented on their looks. He gave her a parcel of boxed cassettes. 'I want you to listen to these,' he told her. 'Alternate them with your own tapes if you like. But listen and learn.'

'Why?' she asked. She was always direct and he respected it.

'Because your English is awful and you'll need it. For University. And later. Do you still want to be an engineer?'

'I think so.'

'You'll have to make up your mind,' he said. 'He — or she — who hesitates ends up in the wrong job. Let me tell you that even engineers have to write good reports. And you may want to impress a prospective employer. Or you may end up as the wife of a diplomat. You wouldn't want to let your husband down by talking like a hippy teenybopper, would you?'

'I'll listen to your tapes,' she said with dignity, 'but only so's I could *be* the diplomat — if I wanted to, which I won't — and not be a hanger-on to one.'

'Good for you,' he said. He wondered how to approach the subject of clothes, but decided that enough had been gained for the moment.

There came a day of rain. Jane stayed at home. She was not afraid of being soaked but the rain might have damaged her precious Walkman. She read a few chapters and listened to a few minutes of P.G. Wodehouse while working her way through a set of Swedish exercises.

Soon she fell victim to restless boredom and a desire for fresh air. Rain was still falling but there was a covered way between the house and the garage, with roof timbers just within her reach. Looking round to be sure that she was out of view from the street or the windows, she put aside the Walkman and began a series of exercises. Squat down. Stand up and grab the timber. Chest to the bar, down again and repeat in continuous, fluid motion.

The next exercise would have entailed bringing her knees up to the bar, but her grandfather preferred her to wear a skirt around the house and she had relegated that exercise to the gymnasium at the health club ever since inadvertently giving the postman the surprise of his life. She picked up the Walkman and was about to put it in place, preparatory to returning to the house, when she heard a sound from the garage.

Anything was better than nothing. She went to investigate.

There were two cars in the garage. One of them was under a dust-sheet. The Jaguar's bonnet was up and Henry Dodson, socket-spanner in hand, was stooped over the engine.

'What are you doing, Henry?' she asked.

Henry looked up. He was a small man with thinning hair. He had a friendly smile despite protruding teeth. 'I'm going to fit a new manifold gasket, miss,' he said. 'Old 'un was blowing a little exhaust gas and the Wingco says he won't need the car again till Saturday. The manifold gasket's — '

'I know what a manifold gasket is,' she said. 'I know nearly all the theory. Dad used to do his own maintenance.'

'That'd be the aeronautical gentleman, miss?'

'That's right. He was an engineer — not a mechanic, a designer, though he wasn't above getting his hands dirty. He let me watch and he explained as he went along but he never let me help. He said it wasn't suitable for a girl and anyway if he did it himself he knew it was done right. Cheek, I thought it. What's under the dust-sheet?'

'It's a TVR, miss. One of the original Tuscans. An RAF officer who'd been a cadet

30

under the Wingco came to visit and the Wingco admired his car. So when the young man flew his jet into a mountain in cloud he'd left the Wingco the car. He'd been hoping to go racing, the youngster, so there's racing wheels and things. Didn't have any relatives. Sad, that! Would you like to see it?'

The name had meant nothing to Jane. 'Later, perhaps. Can I give you a hand, Henry?'

Henry straightened up and eyed her. 'I could find you a pair of overalls . . .'

'These clothes don't matter. It's high time I bought some new ones anyway, don't you think?'

Henry did think, almost as fervently as his master, but it was not his place to say so. 'All the same, miss, you'd best put on the overalls. And the Wingco won't be pleased if I let you spoil your hands. There's a pot on the bench. Rub some of what's in it into your hands.'

'What *is* in it?'

'My own mixture. Some just use soap — makes it real easy to wash off any muck afterwards. But that don't suit everybody's skin. So I mixes it with lanolin and things. Good for the skin and if you fills your pores with clean soap before you start, the dirty grease can't get in. Just wipe off the excess or you'll leave fingermarks all over everything.'

31

So Jane rubbed Henry's mixture into her hands and wiped off the surplus and they set about dismantling the manifolds. Among other things, Jane was taught the use of the torque-wrench. When the job was done, they checked the ignition timing in both the advanced and retarded positions, using a little light which they rigged up by dismembering a perfectly good torch. And, because they were enjoying themselves, they went on to check the tappet clearances and give the engine a loving clean and polish.

'Now I'll look at your UFO,' she said.

'TVR, miss.' With the flourish of a matador, Henry swept off the dust-sheet to reveal a long, low coupé in metallic red paint. Jane's first thought was that it was clean but for two pins she would lick it cleaner. The Jaguar had been cool, but this car was *groovy*.

She had to hurry to be ready for dinner, but at least when, with some difficulty, she had scrubbed Henry's mixture out of her hands they were left clean and soft and ladylike.

Next morning it was still raining so they decided to service the TVR.

2

As the new term approached, Jane herself broached the subject of clothes. School uniform was not a requirement at Cranfield. After some thought the Wing Commander approached a neighbour, a young matron with daughters of her own, who expressed herself delighted to go on a shopping spree with somebody else's money and somebody else's daughter. Her own daughters disdained their mother's help, making what she considered to be terrible mistakes and for which she was sure she was blamed.

As might be expected, the result was a compromise. Jane was equipped for school with her own choice, severe and adult garments more suited to the secretary of some tycoon, but she also brought home some smart and suitable leisurewear — most of the selections jointly agreed but one or two party frocks foisted on her by her mentor and of a style which Jane, who had no acquaintance with current styles, objected to as more resembling underwear and leaving the viewer in no doubt that there was a naked girl not very far underneath. These were consigned to hangers at the back of the wardrobe and not even shown to her grandfather.

Jane also returned with two suits of overalls. The Wing Commander had given qualified approval to his granddaughter's attendance on his chauffeur — the Jaguar had never run with quite so silken a smoothness nor with such remarkable economy of fuel — but this clear signal of intent worried him. 'You're still hell-bent on a career in engineering, then?' he enquired.

'Yes. Definitely,' she said.

He sighed. 'So be it. But promise me one thing.'

'I expect so,' she said. (He felt a momentary pang of satisfaction. A month earlier, she would have said 'Like what?')

'Promise me that you'll stay away from aeroplanes.'

'Time is free, go by sea.'

'You seem to be developing a sense of humour, at last,' he said, 'which can't be bad.'

'It must be those books.'

'Very likely. But I'm not suggesting that you never go by scheduled flights in passenger aircraft. Those are probably the safest form of travel. But promise me that you'll stay away from light aircraft. Any other form of transport, if you get into difficulties you can stop and sort it out, but with single-engined aircraft an engine failure can spell disaster. My wife was lost that way, I was nearly killed when the engine of a Harvard trainer conked out on me and we know what happened to your parents. Promise?'

'All right. I promise,' she said. She spoke reluctantly. She rather liked aircraft as machines but was sure that she could see areas for innovative improvement.

* * *

One other problem remained unresolved almost to the last day of the holidays. It turned out that the journey to Cranfield required not one but two bus journeys which failed to make a timely connection and, moreover, with a lengthy walk at either end. This prospect did not bother Jane much — she was quite prepared to make the most of the time, run rather than walk and spend the bus journeys in study.

The Wing Commander would not hear of such a thing. In particular, no young girl was to go on foot along quiet roads, and soon to be after dark, through any failure on his part. 'Henry shall drive you,' he said.

'What'll they think of me at the school if I turn up in a Jag with a chauffeur?'

'Do you really care what they think?'

'No, not a lot. In the Jaguar?'

'Of course. It's that or go as a boarder, my girl.'

Jane stopped objecting. He was not usually so firm. But it was not her grandfather's threat that changed her mind but the sudden realisation that there could be some distinct advantages to the plan. 'I'd rather go in the TVR,' she said.

He goggled at her. 'You've got a hell of a nerve!'

'But can I?'

'Persistent young animal! I suppose so. Occasionally. Time they both did some work, the car and Henry. We've had the TVR for several years and it's still hardly run in.'

For the first day or two, Henry Dodson was proof against her blandishments; but he was soon persuaded to divert onto a route, very little longer than the main road, which ran through open country where the police never penetrated or, if they did so, could be seen a mile away. There, they would exchange seats and she would drive the Jaguar, or sometimes the TVR, very carefully and quite illegally, while Henry Dodson advised and criticised. She bought a copy of the Highway Code and transferred its messages onto another cassette.

She made few friends at Cranfield. Her own shyness was unrecognised. In her own subjects she was far in advance of her peers. Potential friends went in awe of her intelligence, her clothes and of a girl who arrived daily by chauffeur-driven and shiny Jaguar or even shinier sports coupé. Perhaps the haughtiness of her nose was another deterrent. But Jane suffered no sense of isolation. She worked hard at her studies and for the rest of the time she was free to make the most of the gymnasium and of the computer room, where a dedicated instructor, delighted for once to have a pupil capable of identifying with the logic of the computers, taught her what he knew of programming and let her teach herself the rest.

The first snow of winter came early that year. It snowed over a weekend and on the Monday morning Henry hustled her into the Jaguar and set off early and with unusual haste. Their route led past a hypermarket which was open at weekends but stayed closed on Mondays. Henry turned in.

The vast car park would not be needed until the next day. The snow was unmarked. Henry pulled onto its pristine surface and stopped. 'Here's what most learner drivers don't get,' he said. 'They're taught to pass a test on a dry road in daylight. If they survive their first skid, they maybe know how to cope next time. If not, they're dead anyway.'

He drove, faster and faster. He demonstrated, when the rear wheels broke away, how to steer into the skid. Then he showed her how to induce a front-wheel slide and how to kick the rear loose to bring the car back under control. Later that day an amateur photographer took prize-winning shots of the floral patterns they were making in the snow, but they never knew it.

Then Henry stopped the car and made her take the driver's seat. 'Now, miss, drive.' Twenty minutes were enough to teach her a lesson that she never forgot.

When they passed the hypermarket again on the way home, the car park was swept, sanded and salted.

'Henry,' she said, 'I'll soon be old enough for a provisional licence. Do you think I could pass the test?'

'I've seen many a worse driver sail through, miss.'

'Really? What I'd like to do is to pass the test as soon as I'm old enough.'

'Then you'd better put your name in now, miss.'

'Good idea.'

'And, miss, perhaps it might not be a good idea to tell the Wingco.'

So she applied to take the driving test, but when at last the letter arrived she was still a week short of her birthday. Henry told her to phone in and say that she had 'flu. She was given a further appointment for a week ahead.

'That's on my birthday,' she told Henry.

'Just what you wanted, miss.'

'But it's at nine-fifteen in the morning!'

'You can do it, miss. There's a post office on the way to the test centre. Don't forget to tell the school you won't be in.'

The day approached and arrived. There was a small parcel from the Wing Commander beside her plate but she was too nervous and in too much of a hurry to open it. The old man had an appointment and had elected to drive himself in the Jaguar, so they left early in the TVR.

Henry pulled up at the post office. She dashed inside. It was pension day and she was at the back of a queue. She fretted her way slowly to the front. When she came out, she saw that Henry had attached new L-plates to the TVR. She took over the driver's seat, nearly stalled, but got to the test centre only a few seconds late.

The examiner, to her great relief, was later. He looked from her face to her brand-new provisional licence to the car at the kerb and

39

raised his eyebrows. He made up his mind that she would fail. In his experience, young girls in powerful cars were a prescription for disaster.

In a few minutes, Jane's nerves wore off. She managed a three-point turn. The day was dank, the road slick with the first wet after a dry spell, but she managed the emergency stop cleanly with only the slightest of slithers.

A minute later she was bowling along a clear lane at exactly the legal 30 m.p.h. when a stout woman pushed a pram off the kerb and into her path. She braked but with no hope of pulling up in time. Beside her, the examiner was making a mewing sound. She began to pull out but there was a lorry coming, much too fast. There was a side road opposite, her only hope. She pulled on the wheel. The front slid out but she tapped the throttle just as Henry had taught her and caught the incipient skid with a flick of the steering-wheel. The car came back under control. There was an obstruction a few yards into the side road, an excavation surrounded by tapes and cones, but by then she had stopped. She found that she was neatly parked at the kerb.

They sat, breathing deeply. The woman with the pram stopped beside the examiner's window. 'Road hog!' she shouted.

'Don't answer,' said the examiner grimly. 'Just wait until she's out of the way and then take me back to where we started.'

Jane drove, very carefully, wondering if she had gone wrong, while the examiner filled in a form. As she pulled up at the test centre, he said, 'Well, you can drive, no doubt about that.'

'I've passed?'

'Yes, you've passed.' He smiled suddenly, an almost unheard-of occurrence. 'It's a pity there wasn't a hedge. That woman reminded me of a *Punch* cartoon from way back,' he said. 'A man sitting in the hedge shouting 'Road hog!', just as she did, and the motorist replying 'Hedgehog!' Well, I thought it was funny at the time.'

Jane laughed politely. She only saw the joke later.

She drove back to her grandfather's house without the L-plates, singing out of tune. Henry declined to join in. When she opened her grandfather's present to her she found a pair of driving gloves.

★ ★ ★

Conversations between the Wing Commander and Jane usually took place across a meal table. At other times she was usually too

41

busy absorbing knowledge, putting an edge on her physical fitness or working out abstruse problems on one of her two computers. But one day in early summer he invited Jane into his study for what he called a 'chinwag'.

'I had a phone call from your headmaster today,' he said.

For no reason, she suddenly felt guilty. 'Mr Walker? Why? Have I done something?'

'Quite a lot, my dear, but nothing bad . . . that we know about yet. Except that he did say that you were politically suspect. Fascist or Marxist, he wasn't sure which.'

'I'm not political at all,' she said indignantly. 'I hope they all lose their deposits. All that happened was that civil rights came up.'

'And you said . . . ?'

'Much what I said to you and Mr What's-his-name.'

'Berkeley. No wonder they have doubts about you. But apart from that little *faux pas*, Mr Walker's been very impressed. He doesn't expect any difficulty with your exam results. What he phoned to say was that, with your science subjects, you could get into Cambridge without a doubt.'

'He said that to me. But I don't want to go to Cambridge,' she said, vehemently. 'I want to go to the university at home.'

'I thought that you were beginning to feel at home here,' he protested.

He looked so hurt that she was immediately penitent. 'Oh, I am at home. But this isn't really *my* home. It's just that . . . that . . . '

'I understand. The place where one was brought up always has a special pull at the heart-strings. But Cambridge would be a much better degree.'

'It would look better on paper, but I'd probably feel out of place there. And I doubt if they could teach me any more.'

In view of her capacity for absorbing knowledge, he thought that that might be true. 'I shall miss you,' he said.

'Will you really? I'll miss you too. But we'd miss each other just as much if I went to Cambridge. And Laura Black's going up at the same time, so there'll be somebody there who I know.'

The Wing Commander comforted himself with the thought that at least she was speaking better English at last. Not very much better, but undoubtedly better.

* * *

The summer term ended. Jane's exam results were more than satisfactory and she was

43

offered a university place in Applied Science, which she accepted in a hurry before they could change their minds. She continued to study voraciously, only because she enjoyed doing so and knew no other way of keeping her agile mind occupied. And she worked out regularly at the health club.

She might need transport at university so she fetched her father's car and she and Henry had a lovely time stripping it down and returning it as nearly as possible to new condition. It was only a Maestro and no longer in its first youth, but it was a machine and so it was worthy of attention.

★ ★ ★

Summer, which, as is its habit, had begun so slowly, suddenly rushed away and it was time for the university term. There was a great packing of books and other possessions into the Maestro, Jane went round saying *au revoir* to her favourite people and places and especially to the two cars and then set off on her longest solo drive yet, carefully following the route which Henry had written for her and which she had reprinted in large letters by means of the single, compact, amazingly powerful computer for which she had traded the other two.

Laura Black had been booked into the same hall of residence and the two girls, confronting life among a horde of strangers, clung together during the first days of initiation. They explored the students' union and the other university buildings and looked at the town, which they had thought they knew well, through fresh eyes.

They made a point of reading every notice on the students' union noticeboard and found that they were spoiled for choice of leisure activities. One in particular caught Jane's eye and they joined the University Car Club. They entered several minor rallies and treasure hunts in the Maestro and actually won a prize — thanks to Laura's map-reading rather than Jane's driving. A trip was organised to a karting centre, but Jane was not impressed. It was too easy, had no practical application and after the first few minutes the lack of real speed was evident. But it was better than nothing and she attended now and again, winning as often as not.

As their studies gathered momentum, Jane found that she had already covered much of the material; and whatever was new to her she found no more than logical and easily absorbed. The lectures served the purpose of providing a framework tying together all the miscellaneous parts which she had already accumulated. When Laura found herself struggling it was to her friend that she turned rather than her tutor (who was an impatient man inclined to talk far over his students' heads), and soon several other intimates were following suit.

An outing was organised by the University Car Club to the last race meeting of the season at a nearby circuit. They were in time for the last session of practice. And then the racing proper began. She watched, dumbstruck. She could hardly have named one of the competing cars although she probably knew more about the theories than any of the spectators and most of the competitors. The noise, the spectacle, the danger almost passed her by. What she saw was the beauty of machines designed, built, maintained and operated for a single purpose, to move as quickly as possible within given parameters. This seemed to her to be a perfectly reasonable motivation. The question of which combination of car and driver should arrive first at the end of each race seemed irrelevant.

The club secretary knew somebody. After the last race, they were able to visit the paddock where the cars were being loaded onto trailers or into purpose-built transporters. The saloons and sports cars were interesting enough but it was the single-seaters, dedicated to performance without compromise, that fascinated Jane. She would have liked to approach some of the drivers with technical questions, but these had become heroic figures far beyond her reach.

★ ★ ★

There were other distractions. Early in the term, the two girls agreed to attend a 'hop' in the students' union. Jane's objection, that the art of dancing had not yet figured among her studies, was brushed aside. When the Saturday evening arrived and Jane, bravely dressed in one of the daring party frocks, arrived at Laura's room, the subject was raised and dismissed again. 'They don't really dance any more,' Laura explained. 'Just disco stuff. Stand still and wiggle in time to the music and they'll be round you like flies. I wish I had your figure.'

'You would have, if you took more exercise,' Jane retorted. 'I wish I had your face.'

Laura looked at her in surprise. 'What's wrong with your face?'

'My nose is too long.'

After another and more critical look Laura said, 'Rubbish!' and the subject was dropped.

Laura's advice turned out to be sound. In the crush, nobody could have told the brilliant dancers from the those with two or more left feet. The dress picked out by the Wing Commander's friend was daring enough to ensure a successful evening. Jane left the students' union in the company of a law student, owner of a nearly new Porsche, who took her for a moonlight drive and made a determined assault on her virtue in the almost but not quite impossible confines of the car. He might well have succeeded in his intent if he had offered to allow her to drive the Porsche, but the inducements he was prepared to offer fell short of allowing girls to drive his cherished transport and Jane was not ready to surrender for less.

As the only two girls in the Department of Mechanical Engineering, Jane and Laura received more than their fair share of attention. But Jane was in no hurry to bestow her favours. Of Laura she could not be quite sure. The subject was carefully avoided.

An hour of impassioned foreplay, however, had convinced Jane at last that there might be something in this matter of the birds and the bees after all and, Jane being Jane, she startled the staff in what had become her favourite bookshop by purchasing several volumes which, between them, covered the whole spectrum of eroticism. A few days later she added to her purchases a small carton of condoms. She had no immediate plans but it would not have been in her nature to be caught unprepared.

3

Jane spent another summer with the Wing Commander, lovingly bestowing unnecessary attention on all three cars, attending the health club and chatting with her grandfather. She could have gone to France with Laura but the old man seemed to enjoy her company. She drove him occasionally in the TVR. Keeping the powerful beast taxed and insured was, he admitted, a ridiculous extravagance but he liked to have it available for whenever he wanted to 'cut a dash with the youngsters'.

During the autumn term of her second university year she managed to visit the Wing Commander on several weekends, but in the run-up to terminal exams her time was precious, not so much in pursuing her own studies as in helping Laura and others with theirs. But shortly before Christmas a phone call from Mrs Dodson drove a coach and horses through her carefully organised timetable.

'I think you should come, miss,' Mrs Dodson said. 'The Wingco isn't at all well.'

'He seemed all right, last time I visited,' Jane said.

'He was covering up. He started to slide just after you went back to college. And now he's taken to his bed. He talks about you a lot when his mind's there, but some of the time he's back in the past.'

'What does the doctor say?'

'Not a lot, miss. But he doesn't think the Wingco's got much mileage left, that's what Henry said. Can you come? I'm sure it would do his heart good.'

'I was coming for Christmas anyway.'

Mrs Dodson was doubtful. 'I'm not sure that it can wait that long, miss.'

'I'll come if I can,' Jane promised.

She went to see her tutor who, for once, was helpful. 'Go and do what you can,' he said. 'The old chap was one of the First of the Few, if anyone of your generation knows who they were. We still owe them. The terminal exams don't mean a damn thing in your case. I can give you an assessment based on your work to date.'

'Does that mean that I pass?'

The tutor hid a smile. 'We'll see,' he said.

Jane put a few clothes and some books into a bag and set off in the Maestro for the two-hour run. When she arrived, she thought that the Wing Commander's house looked sad from outside, as though it already knew that the wind of change was blowing cold.

Mrs Dodson came downstairs to meet her in the hall, looking red-eyed and exhausted. 'He's asleep, miss,' she said. 'He was rambling, earlier, but when he's lucid he refuses point-blank to go into hospital and anyway the doctor says that they couldn't do anything for him there that we can't do for him here, except maybe force him to hang on a day or two longer when nature says it's time to go. And he's refusing to have any injections. It's his heart, miss. Worn out, like.'

'And so are you,' Jane said. 'You go and have a rest. I'll sit with him until he wakes up.'

She fetched her books from the car and carried them up to the Wing Commander's bedroom. The old man was sleeping peacefully but she could see that he had lost weight and condition. An oxygen mask and bottle stood by the bed and there was a tray of medicaments on the chest of drawers. She settled beside the window in the only armchair. But for once her mind was not on her textbooks and instead she took out the current issue of a motor sports magazine. She was deep in a highly technical article about tuned exhaust-lengths when she sensed that the sleeper had woken.

'So you came,' he said. 'You're not missing your studies? I wouldn't want that.'

'Nothing important. Did you think I'd stay away when I heard that you were ill?'

'I hoped . . . I don't know what I hoped. I hoped you'd come but I didn't want you to see me like this. God, I wish you could have seen me fifty years ago!'

'So do I. But I can imagine. And I've seen your photographs. You were magnificent.'

'I was, rather. Let me see you properly. Stand up and turn around. You're a sight for sore eyes, girl. Just like your mother, and she was a beauty. I've missed you.' He blinked to clear his eyes. 'You're wearing make-up, aren't you?'

'A little,' she admitted, suddenly feeling bashful. 'One of the cosmetics companies was giving free demonstrations. The lady was good. She explained about colours and counter-shading and so on. Do you mind?'

'Good God, no! It looks good on you. A woman should make the most of her appearance. But you still have a haughty nose.'

She laughed and he managed a wheezy chuckle. 'Look who's talking,' she said. 'You old *thost*!'

He opened his eyes wide for the first time. 'What did you call me?'

She pointed her fingers at him like a pistol. 'Got you, this time! You remember what you

53

told me about swearing? Well, *thost* is a very old word for Number Two. Doo-doos. Excretion.'

'Shit,' he said.

'Older than that. So it should be ruder, shouldn't it? But nobody knows the word, so now I can swear whenever I want to and nobody knows so nobody cares.'

He chuckled wheezily. 'That's the word I was going to tell you when your parachute failed to open.'

'You do tell some whoppers!'

He chuckled again but gently, careful not to let it shake his chest. 'I wish I'd known it years ago,' he said. 'All my life I've been looking for a word like that.' When he smiled he looked younger again. But soon he sobered. 'Listen, child. I only wish I could have made proper provision for you, but I never expected your parents to die like that. I thought that I could afford to be selfish. So I've been living on an annuity. It'll die with me. I've made some provision for the Dodsons by way of an insurance that'll pay them a pension, but — '

'Don't worry about it,' she said quickly. 'I'll be all right. I have Dad's insurance money and at a pinch I can sell the house. Once I get my degree, I thought I might try for a job in the drawing office of one of the more up-market car companies. Aston Martin, perhaps.'

'You'd be good at that. You might be even better on the sales staff — a girl who could pass her test on the very day that she'd old enough to get a provisional licence and in somebody else's TVR.'

'You knew all along that Henry was giving me lessons. Didn't you?'

He chuckled for the last time. 'Henry never could keep anything from me.'

Soon after that, he began rambling. He seemed to be reliving his days in the RAF and the eeriness sent shivers up her back.

He died, quite peacefully, early the following morning.

* * *

Jane stayed on at the house for the cremation and for a meeting with her grandfather's solicitor.

The lawyer, Mr Bastable, looked almost as old as the Wing Commander had been and not much more robust, but his mind was still crisp. She accompanied him from the crematorium to his office. 'Your grandfather left a note with his will,' he said. 'He wished, provided that you have no objection, that his ashes be interred with your parents or

55

scattered on their grave.'

'I think that that's a nice idea,' Jane said. There had been only a little warmth between her grandfather and his son, but she had become genuinely fond of the old man.

'I shall have them delivered to you this afternoon.' (Jane swallowed. She had not expected quite such an intimate involvement.) 'Now to the will,' he said. 'There are one or two minor legacies to RAF charities. And as I think you know, he made provision some years ago for the pensions of Mr and Mrs Dodson. On my advice, these were insurance policies, so there should be no death duties payable on them. You see, as residuary legatee, death duties come out of your portion.'

'Will there be death duties?' Jane asked anxiously. She had felt suddenly vulnerable after the death of her one remaining close relative and more troubles seemed to be looming. 'I thought that they didn't begin until the estate was quite big. Granddad said that he was living on an annuity. It seemed to worry him that he couldn't make what he called 'provision' for me.'

The solicitor sighed for the folly of clients, especially those as old as himself. 'When people have been around for a while,' he said, 'they look on the things that have surrounded them all their lives as being part of the scenery. Your grandfather, as he implied, leaves very little money behind. But have you any idea what a substantial house in that area, with river frontage, is worth today? And did you notice the furniture, much of which has been in the family for generations? And the pictures? Nothing in the Gainsborough class, I'm afraid, but good paintings of what you might call the second rank fetch very nice prices. There are one or two that I would have liked to offer for but I knew that I couldn't afford them. I presume that you do not intend to keep the house?'

Jane's head was beginning to swim but she could still do her arithmetic. 'If I did, I'd have to find the money for death duties?'

'Exactly.'

'I couldn't possibly. If I remove whatever I decide to keep, could you arrange to sell the remainder and the house and settle the death duties?'

'That will present no problem.'

'The Jaguar can be sold. Is the TVR mine now?'

'Strictly speaking, not until we have probate. But if you have been in the habit of driving it, I see no reason for you to stop.' From his desk, he took up a white envelope. 'I have here a letter to Mr and Mrs Dodson.

Perhaps you would care to deliver it? If they have any uncertainties they can write to me or telephone or come and see me, but I think that the insurances are straightforward.'

She took the envelope, rose and shook his hand. 'Thank you,' she said. 'You'll keep me informed? Of course, I'll expect a very full accounting when everything's wound up.'

'Of course,' he said. He wondered how one so young came to be so businesslike. For a moment, when she looked at him, he had felt almost guilty. And he had not done anything wrong. Not yet.

* * *

The Dodsons were still overwhelmed by events and had difficulty taking in any more. 'The Wingco left us this money?' Mrs Dodson said vaguely, looking up from the letter.

'It's a pension,' Henry said patiently. 'It's not a lot, but it would have got bigger and he didn't expect to pop off just yet. We're not at retirement age, not quite. We'll get by.'

Mrs Dodson was not in a mood to be comforted. 'But where are we to go? Who's going to take us on?' she asked. 'At our age?'

'We'll find something. What are your own plans, miss?'

'I can't keep this house on,' Jane said. 'I already have my parents' house. You've seen it, Henry.'

'Nice little property,' Henry said. 'If I might make a suggestion, miss, couldn't we come with you? We wouldn't need wages, or not much, nothing at all until you've finished at university, what with this pension coming in, and perhaps I could get a driving job. We could keep the house and garden for you.'

'Oh, could we, miss?' his wife echoed. 'Please? I don't know that I could face up to starting off again with strangers.'

In a few seconds of furious thought Jane tried to balance the loss of her privacy against her affection for the duo. The deciding factor turned out to be security. There had been a number of break-ins in the vicinity of the family home. She had made up her mind that, if her house would be standing empty for much of every weekday, it would be foolish to take with her some of the Wing Commander's more suitable heirlooms. The presence of regular staff, perhaps with a dog, would make the acquisition of valuables a less rash act.

'I suppose so,' she said at last. 'But don't pack up just yet. I'll have to find out when I can get the tenant out of my house and then try to time the sale of this one. And we'll have to make up our minds which of the Wingco's treasures we take with us and which go to the salesroom.'

'There's some good tools and equipment in the garage, miss,' Henry ventured. Jane guessed that those were, in Henry's view, more valuable than a lot of old antiques.

'We'll certainly take those along.'

Jane spent the remainder of the day on a succession of phone calls to the two solicitors, during which it became evident that the Easter vacation would be the preferred time for the changeover. She stayed with, and was mothered by, the Dodsons over a subdued Christmas and then returned to university. She made the journey driving, very carefully, in the TVR with the small urn containing her grandfather's ashes propped up in the rear window. She would have preferred to have him at the windscreen so that he could see where he was going, but there was no room for the urn to stand. The Wingco would just have to be satisfied with seeing where he was coming from. She left the Maestro for Henry's use and attention. Later that day she visited her parents' grave with the urn, a small trowel and some flowers.

At Easter, Jane and Laura left the hall of residence and moved in. The Dodsons were already installed in the granny-flat, carefully redecorated by Henry, and the house was comfortable. Some of the Wing Commander's furniture had replaced the well-worn and never very expensive possessions of Jane's parents and a few of his pictures and ornaments raised the place far above the usual student lodgings.

* * *

During the summer term, Jane phoned her honorary uncle. 'I'm getting worried,' she told him. 'I keep hearing nothing from my grandfather's executor. Would you represent me and do whatever solicitors do to chivvy each other up?'

'Leave it with me,' Gordon Black said. 'Are you running out of money?'

'I am, a bit. What little money my father left me is invested long-term and this is a rotten time to sell shares. Granddad's house was sold weeks ago. I was counting on his estate being settled by now but so far I haven't seen a penny. I don't want to take out a student loan and be bedevilled for years after I graduate, just when I'll be trying to get by on a salary of about a fiver a year. The way inflation's slowed down, debt isn't a good investment any more.'

'I could probably advance you something

against the estate.'

'Thanks, but no thanks. I've sort of made up my mind, neither a borrower nor a lender to be.'

'*Hamlet*. Your excursions into English Lit. must have born fruit. Your grandfather would have been pleased. But Polonius gave that advice to a son, not a daughter. If it's any help, keep Laura with you through the vacation. She seems to be enjoying it and the family has got rather used to having a room each and a spare bed in the house. You could always sell the TVR.'

'No way!' Jane said. 'If I can't afford to retax it when the disc runs out, I'll lay it up in mothballs for when I'm rich. You can make me an offer for the Maestro, if you like.'

★ ★ ★

The university was particularly strong in the engineering subjects so it was to be expected that a number of overseas students were to be found in the faculty. But the long vacation was a time when halls of residence earned from summer schools the money which would subsidise students' rents and keep them within or close to tolerable bounds for the next academic year.

For several months, therefore, students

were not encouraged to linger. The overseas students, and those Brits who had found vacation jobs locally, had to look for other accommodation. Jane was approached again and again. She consulted Mrs Dodson, who had been aware that all was not well without quite appreciating the magnitude of the problem. Mrs Dodson, after years of catering to the needs of one elderly gentleman, had come to enjoy the vivacity and appetites of students and was happy to have the household enlarged for the summer, or longer if need be.

It was natural that Jane should prefer students from her own faculty. With only two large bedrooms available for letting, it seemed that sharing would be the order of the day, but a singularly well-off Colombian student, Ramon Felidas, paid an inflated rent to have one of the rooms to himself. It was generally believed that Ramon was prevented from going home for the summer because his father was a drugs baron temporarily on the run, but his inability to produce the occasional substance to enliven a party (disappointing to some but a relief to Jane) lent colour to his own explanation that he simply preferred the summer climate of Britain and the company of his girlfriend, a blonde barmaid in the premier local hotel.

Ramon was distinguished among his fellow students by his possession of the barmaid and also of a very pretty sports car which he raced on occasions. Between race meetings he went karting and stood well in the championships. It was understood that he aspired to even more exciting drives.

The other room was shared by a brace of Scots, Bruce McLean and Alexander ('Sandy') Durnin. Each was from the vicinity of Glasgow, they were good friends and yet they could hardly have been more different. Sandy, as if to accord with his nickname, was of the thickset, sandy-haired breed of lowland Scots, while Bruce was a dark and brooding Highlander. They had both found well-paid vacation jobs with a local manufacturer of agricultural equipment.

Vacation jobs were more difficult for the girls. Laura, being funded by her father, was pleased rather than worried by the prospect of a summer of leisure. Jane rebelled at the idea of an office or a shop, but the best that she could find was as cashier and pump attendant at the local garage for evenings and weekends. That work was poorly paid, but there were considerable tips and other side-benefits. Her friend Gunge, who turned out to be the son of the proprietor, insisted on filling the tank of the TVR with free fuel, a practice which both pleased and horrified her; and many a motorist, turning off the motorway to seek help with some mechanical problem, was delighted to discover an attractive attendant who could always diagnose and usually remedy the trouble. She could charge what she liked for such services without any need to share her earnings with the management or the various tax inspectors; and because the help came from such an unlikely quarter she usually received a generous tip as well.

She had leisure and just enough money to return to the local health club, where a new instructor was giving lessons in the martial arts. One or two over-eager approaches by drunken students had suggested that one day she might be the victim of a serious attack. She enrolled immediately, adding the study of karate to her other subjects.

With a mixture of young men and women in the house, there was potential for trouble but in fact there was none. Each was committed to outside partners. Early in the summer, Jane had put petrol into an old but well-kept MG and its driver, much taken with the pretty pump attendant, had invited her to lunch. The two had seen each other over a period of several weeks and eventually she had agreed to his shy approaches.

The event, for which he had suggested an outdoor venue, had taken place in her own home and bed. (It had been an early agreement with the Dodsons that any overnight visitors or extra faces at the breakfast table were invisible and never to be the subject of comment. Mrs Dodson had pursed her lips at first but buried in her ample bosom was a heart both romantic and even slightly Rabelaisian.)

The young man, a medical student, had been slightly more experienced than Jane but thanks to her study of the manuals she was considerably more knowledgeable; and on their advice she had made sure that her first experience would not be physically painful. It had in fact proved unexpectedly enjoyable, yet was an experimental affair rather than one of the heart. When, after no more than six or seven further encounters, they had decided to go their separate ways, it had been by mutual agreement with few tears shed, and those only on his part.

★ ★ ★

Early in October, with the new academic year almost on them, Gordon Black phoned Jane. 'Mr Bastable has died,' he told her.

'I'm sorry,' she said automatically.

'So am I, but not for the same reason. I put off telling you until I could get a little more of the picture. He had been giving me what I can only call the runaround. It now seems that he had been speculating for years, not very cleverly, and using the firm's money. There isn't anything like enough left to satisfy their obligations to the clients. There's a considerable area of doubt as to whether the sums he — um — appropriated were clients' money or the firm's and I'm afraid that his surviving partners are moving heaven and earth to avoid making good the losses.'

'You mean, I don't get anything?'

'I wouldn't necessarily go so far as to say that. There has been a hint that if you accept a comparatively small sum in full and final settlement you could receive immediate cash. But you should have been a comparatively wealthy young woman. So I am phoning to receive your instructions. We can start proceedings against the firm. It might take months or years to come to court — skilled litigants can always find another and another delaying tactic — and you might even end up as the loser and out of pocket in the end. I'm ashamed to say that legal costs can often escalate beyond the amount in dispute. On the other hand, it might induce them to come up with a better offer.'

They talked figures for several minutes and disconnected. Jane called him back a few minutes later. 'I can't stomach the idea of one partner ripping me off and the others trying to shrug off all responsibility,' she said. 'Go ahead and sue. Start quickly before I chicken out.'

* * *

The three male students were delighted to remain as lodgers in a house which was much more comfortable than a hall of residence or a student flat, and the Dodsons were as good as their word in asking no wages. Even so, Jane found that supporting a household of seven, of which only four were paying their way, was heavy going. Her student grant paid for little more than her books and fees. But the stock market was making a slight recovery and she realised part of the legacy from her parents. Reluctantly, she gave up her membership of the health club and instead made use of the university running track and the exercise machines in the basement of the students' union.

Happily, she managed to hold on to her beloved TVR. The tax disc ran until November but her youth, her status as a student and the nature of the car meant that insurance would be almost impossibly expensive. She resigned herself to laying up the car for the winter and using the Maestro. Meanwhile, she was able to enjoy driving the TVR, with occasional help from Gunge at the pumps — help which Mr Fadden, Gunge's father, who was turning a blind eye to what was going on, wrote off as evaporation or spillage and therefore a tax loss.

(Gunge was turning into a respectable young mechanic of good appearance and usually quite clean. He hated his given name of Herbert, after an uncle, but liked the sobriquet Gunge little better. But despite asking all his acquaintances to call him Ginger, Gunge he remained. He secretly adored Jane. He had no real aspirations to win her, considering her far above his touch, but she would have been amazed and perhaps even rather shocked if she had known how she figured in his nightly fantasies. Whenever he was favourably regarded by one of the young ladies of his acquaintance, it was Jane's image in his mind's eye even if quite a different body was quivering coyly against his.)

These last fun-runs with the TVR were nearly her undoing. On almost the last day before the tax ran out, she drove gently past the speed cameras on the motorway and on into the countryside. She had found a circuit of country roads where the police were never seen and where, because of the unhampered visibility, she could hustle the car around in what she considered to be perfect safety. The circuit ended with a long, empty straight and there she let the car go. Halfway along the straight, a car was parked on the verge, but any significance which it might have had was lost on her.

As she slowed right down for the next bend, a policeman with a radio in his hand stepped out and waved her down. She pulled onto the verge and parked, her exhilaration rapidly cooling.

Ramon had been stopped for speeding not long before and from the subsequent mealtime discussions she knew how to behave. She got out of the car and walked to meet the officer, her posture as subservient as she could make it. (And in this, her femininity gave her a major advantage.)

The young constable held himself up a little straighter. They met beside the front of the car. 'Do you know how fast you were travelling, miss?' he enquired. Her posture, almost bowing before the dominant male, may have softened his attitude, because his voice was avuncular rather than stern.

She shook her head and tried to look

appealing. 'I didn't want to take my eyes off the road,' she said. 'I don't usually drive fast, but I'll be laying the car up for the winter soon and I've just given it a last tune-up. I wanted to see how it was running.'

The constable was a motor enthusiast too. 'Not much doubt about that,' he said. 'Given a tail-wind you might have made history in the magistrate's court by having been clocked doing three times the legal limit.'

'Does it have to go that far?' she asked. 'Can't you give me an on-the-spot fine or something?'

He shook his head. 'Not applicable.' He frowned. Not only was he an enthusiast; he was also a young man. 'But tell me this. Do you mean that you tune this car yourself?'

'Yes.'

He looked at her searchingly. 'Tell me . . . how does the ignition advance work?'

It seemed a strange question but at least it was a question that she could answer honestly. She described the advance mechanism, adding a few statistics on the relationship between ignition advance, engine speed and fuel octane.

After several minutes, he stopped her. At least she was not some young flibbertigibbet, blasting around in Daddy's car and putting everybody at risk. He read her a lecture and warned her that a summons would follow. She drove slowly and carefully until she was out of sight. The constable watched her go. *A pretty girl*, he thought. *Nice eyes and a figure to dream about. Pity about her nose.* As he spoke into his radio and called the unmarked car to pick him up, he made up his mind to go as easy on her as his partner would let him.

Ten days later, Jane received the summons for three weeks ahead. She was charged with driving at 88 m.p.h. where the limit was 60. She was surprised and even perversely disappointed, because she had been sure that she was well into three figures, but she did not tell Gordon Black that.

Gordon insisted on representing her in court. She pleaded guilty but he made what he considered to be one of his best pleas for leniency. He repeated her tale about trying out the car after tuning it herself, pointed out that there had been no criticism of her driving other than that of exceeding a somewhat notional speed limit in a car which was generally recognised to be exceptionally safe for such a purpose and he produced a carefully chosen photograph which made that stretch of road look even wider, straighter and emptier than ever. He drew attention to his client's youth and managed to suggest that without her driving licence her ability to continue attending university might be seriously imperilled. He added that the TVR had already, for financial reasons, been laid up and his client would have to plod around in a Maestro — possibly, he implied, causing obstructions by the very slowness of the vehicle and of her driving.

The magistrate had heard it all before, but he was a man and Jane had taken care with her clothes and make-up. She presented him with the picture of a penitent young lady of modest demeanour — if he overlooked the apparently accidental glimpse of a nylon thigh. The magistrate read her a lecture almost word for word the same as that of the constable and imposed a fine and penalty points. He added the words which were to have a thousand times more effect on her life than his lecture. 'There is a place for that sort of driving, young lady,' he said, 'and it is not the public road. It is the race-track.'

Jane thanked Gordon Black prettily for his representation, insisted on a bill (which she never received) and headed, in thoughtful mood, towards where she had parked the Maestro. She had never before seriously considered herself a candidate for racing honours, but when she came to think of it there was more than a little attraction in the idea of being let loose to speed as much as she liked. The possible presence of a large audience of admiring men and envious women was, she thought, not a factor worth considering.

She sought out the secretary of the local motor club. The secretary furnished her with an application form for a competition licence. He also knew a senior official concerned with the TVR Tuscan Challenge series and promised to let her know when Mr Andress was in the vicinity again.

4

Third Year at university was more demanding. They were advancing beyond the areas which Jane had reached in her private, compulsive reading. But she still found the science subjects logical and therefore easy to understand and remember. Certain constants and formulae had to be memorised, but she continued to dictate them onto her cassettes and listen to them while her body was busy. She also discovered a knack for lateral thinking, so that the design problems over which the other students agonised held few terrors for her.

Laura, on the other hand, even with Jane's coaching, had found Applied Science to be heavy going and she had switched to Business Management in the nearby Commercial College. The two girls still met at home and went out together of an evening, but Jane was now the only girl in Engineering and one of only three in her year in the whole faculty, the other two being unattractive, uninterested in men and suspected of lesbian tendencies. Jane, therefore, could have had a different escort for every evening of the term had she so wished but, after a brief, romantic and largely arms-length affair with a law student, she contented herself with attending the student dances, sometimes agreeing to be escorted home and thereafter allowing limited but delicious familiarities proportionate to the manners, prospects and looks of her companion.

In between her studies, her continuing fitness campaign and a sporadic social life, Jane found little time to think about the motor races. But in the late spring she received a call from the club secretary. Mr Andress would be in the club that evening if she cared to meet him.

Mr Andress turned out to be a balding man with thin and ascetic features but a kindly manner. He bought Jane a drink and settled down for a chat in front of the clubroom fireplace. He soon elicited Jane's almost total lack of experience.

'The usual thing,' he said gently, 'would be to start with a few local club events.'

'I thought of that. But they only have sprints. I went to watch, once or twice. You're just getting going when it's all over.'

He hid a smile. 'What you should do,' he said, 'is attend one of our Performance Technique Days, at which you'd receive instruction along with a chance to gain experience. But I'm afraid you've just missed one and there won't be another until later in the year.'

'I suppose I can wait,' she said.

'The problem is that I'm not sure yet that it will go ahead. It's not always easy to get the people and book the circuit all for the same day. On the other hand, I'm not going to throw a young girl to the wolves.' He thought for a moment. Jane held her breath. 'I have a suggestion,' he said at last. 'We have a Tuscan Series race coming up at Silverstone next week. First practice is on the Wednesday. If you care to meet me there at crack of dawn, you could take me round for a few laps while we have the place to ourselves.'

'And then I could race?'

'And then we would see if you're good enough to race or if you have to wait for one of our Performance Technique Days. If you're really good, I could get you an entry for two weeks later.'

'I have exams around that time. Could we make it four weeks?'

Mr Andress raised his eyebrows and said that he supposed so.

'You don't think I'll reach your standard, do you?' Jane said.

He smiled. 'I'm ready to be pleased and surprised.'

Jane's friend Gunge, being the youngest of four brothers all in the business, was often surplus to requirements. His father, an ambitious and far-seeing man, filled the potentially vacant time and idle hands by sending Gunge on courses. Jane had to wait a day for Gunge to return from one such course before she could seek his advice.

He took a seat in Jane's Maestro on the garage's forecourt. 'So what's the problem?' he asked.

Jane repeated what Mr Andress had said, more or less word for word. 'I want to do this,' she said. 'I have a chance to take the TVR, fast, round Silverstone. I'll just die if I miss it.'

'So what's holding you back?'

'I can't get there. I'd have to tax the car. And do you know what they want for insurance? A female student and a car that can do nought to a hundred in under ten seconds? Gunge, could you write me a cover note and then lose the copy?'

Gunge made a noise like a cat being trodden on. 'No, I bloody couldn't,' he said when he had his breath back. 'I'll do most things for you, but not porridge.'

'Not what?'

'Jail. Anyway, we don't need to break the law. I'll borrow the recovery vehicle and trailer from the garage and take you over.'

'Won't they miss it?'

'Nah.' Gunge was enjoying his role as the solver of problems for damsels in distress. 'If somebody breaks down they can take the Land Rover with what they call the 'ambulance' and tow them in that way.'

'Fabulous!' Jane said. 'It means a start in the small hours. All right?'

'For you,' Gunge said gallantly, 'OK. But you'll need all the racing mods. Wheels and tyres. A roll-cage. Harness.'

'Not just to tootle Mr Andress round Silverstone. Anyway, I've got the wheels. They came with the car. No tyres, though.'

'Let's have them and I'll see if I can find a set of racing tyres to fit. I have a pal who knows a lot of people around the circuits and he may be able to find a set of tyres off a wreck.'

★ ★ ★

They reached Silverstone as dawn was breaking. Mr Andress had furnished a sketch map and they found their way into the paddock and thence to the back of the buildings. Jane still had half an hour to the appointed time. She jogged round the circuit, looking for bumps and hollows, kerbs and blind crests. The morning was damp, but she reminded herself that she had passed her driving test on just such a morning.

When she got back to the vehicles, Gunge had taken the TVR off the trailer and warmed the engine. Mr Andress arrived a few minutes later, carrying a crash helmet. 'You'll need a helmet and flame-retardant overalls to race,' he said. 'And the proper shoes.'

'I'll get some,' she said, 'just as soon as you tell me I can race.'

He nodded. He took the passenger seat, strapped himself in. 'Off we go,' he said. 'Have you ever been round Silverstone before?'

'Only on foot. Just now.'

If he was impressed, he hid it. 'Do a few slow laps,' he said. 'Speed up when you feel you know your way round.'

For the first time, Jane found herself free to use the whole width of the road. As a result, she set off too slowly. But she soon worked out the racing lines for herself, swooping in wide, brushing the apex and coming out wide again. From time to time, Mr Andress uttered a few words of what she found to be very sound advice, but mostly he sat and watched, apparently relaxed. Jane never noticed the whiteness of his knuckles. As she figured out the braking distances for each bend she became faster, much faster than she had ever driven before. In theory the car had a top speed of 160 m.p.h. and she was sure that she was nearing that figure but was afraid to take her eyes off the roadway surging towards her. She took no risk of late braking, treating each bend with a steadily lessening degree of respect. Even so, the car was slithering on the bends, but remembering Henry's teaching she stayed in control. The car had a formidable power-to-weight ratio, but Jane had been used to the feel of it. In effect, nobody had ever told her that it was difficult.

After more than twenty laps, Mr Andress directed her back to the paddock. Cars and transporters were already arriving.

Jane had achieved her ambition. She had driven round Silverstone flat out, ticking off one from the long list of life's challenges. Now she could go back to her studies, content in the knowledge that she could do it if she wanted to.

'All right,' Mr Andress said cheerfully. 'You won't come to any harm if you watch your mirrors and let faster cars through. There's been a cancellation for four weeks' time. I can slip you in if you give me your entry money here and now.'

Jane had a lot of nerve, but not enough to admit that she had brought him out at what Gunge had called 'sparrow-fart' and now had no intention of racing. Weakly, she wrote out a cheque for what seemed an uncomfortably large sum of money.

★ ★ ★

Jane had sneaked away to Silverstone without letting anyone but Gunge know where she was going. Now, however, there was no way to keep her plans secret. In general she was given encouragement. Only at home was the contrary expressed.

Ramon was first. 'Even if they let you enter, you will not win anything,' he pointed out. 'Your car is one of the original Tuscans. They were prototypes for the whole marque. But you will be against GPs and later Tuscans with another hundred b.h.p. and there will be professional teams also. You will probably have the lowest power-to-weight ratio of anything there.'

'I don't mind,' Jane said. 'I've never been interested in anything more than what I myself can do. If somebody else can do better, good luck to him. Or her,' she added. 'I just want to drive a good car as fast as I like, somewhere that nobody can say 'Boo!' to me and haul me up in court. Anyway, I've paid my entry fee now so I may as well go. I can always back out if it all seems too much.'

'You'll need a frame in case you overturn.'

'A roll-cage? Ginger's going to let me use the welding plant at the service station. I can weld something up. And his pal got me a set of straps off a Lotus that got badly bent last month.'

★ ★ ★

Mrs Dodson, who believed that driving a car at all was a man's job, threw up her hands in horror at the idea of any young lady actually competing on the race-track.

Henry, on the other hand, objected strongly to the TVR, for years his ewe lamb, being subjected to the stresses and, worse, the dangers of the track. Jane dismissed the danger in a few words. 'That's nonsense,' she said stoutly. 'All the cars are going in the same direction, there's a scrutineer to make sure that they're all safe, there are escape roads and gravel traps and grass for if you run out of track and there are marshals with flags to warn you of any dangers ahead. One man at the club told me that he only goes racing because he feels safer there than driving on the road.'

83

'You're trying to convince yourself, miss,' Henry said, but once he saw that Jane's mind was made up he threw himself into the project with energy if no great enthusiasm.

In the next few weeks, the TVR was prepared with the meticulous attention usually given to a Formula One car. Jane, assisted by Henry and Gunge, embarked on the work, but Sandy Durnin and Bruce McLean were soon drawn in and other students from the department took to spending the occasional weekend hour or two lending a hand, partly as an escape from the confines of student life into the fringe of a wider and more exciting world, sometimes in the vain hope of being rewarded by Jane with a few hours of safe but blissful sex, but mostly because Jane's tapes of their studies, now enlarged by recordings made of lectures, were constantly playing in the background and Jane was always willing to pause and give an impromptu seminar when the more abstruse concepts proved baffling to those present.

The arrival of the sessional exams drove most of the helpers back to more protracted studying, but by then everything that could be polished or balanced was polished or balanced, the engine was in better tune than it had been at any time since it left the factory and the bodywork had been invested with a quite unnecessary shine.

★   ★   ★

Jane found herself in temporary possession of a borrowed set of fire-retardant overalls and a helmet, both of which Gunge had borrowed from his friend, whose stock car had been irretrievably destroyed. The friend, it transpired, had been about Jane's size but not too careful in his personal habits. Jane sent the overalls for dry cleaning and disinfected the helmet. The shoes she had to buy for herself.

The first period of practice was to be in the afternoon and early evening of the Wednesday before the races. Happily the meeting was at a circuit not far from home. Jane arrived in good time. In the vehicle with her were Gunge and Laura, on her mechanic's passes.

They had been allocated a racing number and they found their allocated space in the paddock. The adjacent space was already occupied by a Range Rover coupled to a trailer from which two men were unloading another TVR. The better spoken and dressed of the two, a personable man in what she thought was probably his late mid-forties, was obviously the driver. In appearance he was almost inconspicuous — medium everything,

Jane thought — yet he had about him a confidence which Jane should have resented as male arrogance but didn't.

When the car was down and the mechanic was checking it over, the driver gave Jane a smile which rang a sudden bell in her memory. 'It's Mr . . . Mr Berkeley, isn't it?' she said. He looked momentarily puzzled. 'Jane Faraday,' she added. 'We met at my grandfather's house.'

He smiled again, more easily. 'Lord, yes,' he said. 'You lectured me. But it was a long time ago and you've matured since then so you'll forgive me for not recognising you straight away. Is this your grandfather's TVR? It was our common affection for the marque that threw us together.'

While Mr Berkeley's mechanic led Gunge through the mysteries of taping the headlamps and using the same masking tape to apply the car's racing number to the maroon bodywork, Mr Berkeley put Jane at her ease and, to relieve her inevitable nerves, told her a series of anecdotes in between fragments of advice which, she was to realise later, were both accurate and valuable.

Competitors were arriving in droves but she was able to present herself to the scrutineers after only a short wait. The scrutineer gave Jane a second look which she interpreted as being suspicion of her youth and gender but was more probably male enjoyment of a pretty girl. He even expressed admiration for the ingenious fitting of the new roll-cage. After a few minutes, he seemed about to pronounce himself satisfied with the car when he checked. 'Your tax disc's expired,' he said.

'I brought it on a trailer,' Jane explained.

'The race rules specify road condition.' The scrutineer consulted another official. 'We'll let it go,' he said. Jane was about to heave a sigh of relief when the official added, 'Fined a hundred pounds.'

Jane could have argued. She could have withdrawn from the race. She could have gone away and taxed the car, though at a total cost of more than the fine. But there were other competitors waiting and she would have been ashamed to quibble over what, to them, she was sure was less than pocket money. Her bag was on the passenger seat. Again, she wrote out a cheque on the spot. Well, she had been told that motor racing was expensive.

★   ★   ★

A race may be short but it takes longer for a driver to learn his way round and longer still in the more advanced formulae to adjust the set-up and gearing to suit the circuit. For that reason, different groups had practices on different days with, normally, general practice and qualifying on the Saturday and racing on the Sunday. Not a minute was to be wasted.

Mr Berkeley had patiently explained the drill. As the practice time for the TVR Tuscan Series race approached, Jane managed to be near the front of the queue. As soon as she pulled out onto the circuit, she felt a sense of release. She was almost the first driver out, setting off behind two faster cars, so that for the moment she had the whole track to herself. After feeling her way round for two or three laps she found herself at home as she had at Silverstone. To use the whole width between the kerbs, touching the apex of the corners and straightening out the bends, was no more than an exercise in elementary geometry. She was becoming ever more familiar with the handling of the car and she had an intuitive appreciation of the coefficient of friction between the tyres and the tarmac. She was soon finding her perfect racing line and following it with her tyres just beginning to sing.

She was running the car as light as possible. She went into the pits for Gunge to refuel from a large jerrican and make a small adjustment to the tyre pressures. She snatched a sip of thermos tea for her dry mouth and went out again. There were more cars out now. She watched her mirrors and kept out of the way of faster traffic. One or two slower cars came out, or perhaps she was going faster as she attuned. It gave her a mild satisfaction to pass them on the straight or, benefiting from her fast increasing experience, slip past an equivalent car by braking later and taking a different line.

Practice for the TVRs finished. She returned to the paddock to take aboard Laura and Gunge along with the tools and materials which had been unloaded to save weight.

Jane stripped off the overalls. Experimenting in the privacy of her bedroom, she had found that the overalls were hot and uncomfortable over trousers but that she could slip them down to her waist, don a skirt over the top and then remove the overalls altogether without any loss of modesty. It was rather like dressing on the beach, she thought. When she took off the helmet, she only had to run her fingers through her hair for the old style to come back and she blessed the Wing Commander for his advice. She was feeling satiated, as if after sex. For a moment she wondered whether to return at all at the weekend. She had had her fun. The memories would linger. It would be a pity to cheapen them by repetition. But then she knew that she would be back.

Gunge examined the tyres. 'They'll do for the race,' he said. 'After that, you'll need new.'

'How much will that cost?' she asked. When he told her, she was horrified.

Laura arrived carrying a stopwatch, breathless from hurrying. 'You were doing great,' she said.

Already the euphoria was fading. 'I don't know,' Jane said. 'I seemed to get passed a lot.'

'So some cars are faster than others. Surprise, surprise! You were going a little bit faster every lap. Another week the same and your lap times would have become minus quantities. And I'll tell you something else. In the timekeepers' bus, I heard one man say to another that you had the makings of a damn good driver.'

'I'll second that,' Gunge said bravely from the driver's seat.

'Bless you both!' In the aftermath of the adrenaline rush, Jane felt emotions more strongly than ever before. She was ready to laugh, but for a moment she wanted to cry.

When they reached home, Henry went round and round the car until he had assured himself that she had not collected any dents or scratches. But Mrs Dodson just put a belated meal on the table, and sniffed disapprovingly.

★ ★ ★

At the circuit, on the Saturday morning, the scene had changed. The trickle of drivers able to attend practice on the Wednesday had become a flood. The paddock was thronged with cars and with spectators who had managed to intrude before the crowd control had taken hold. There was a queue for the scrutineer. Practice for the separate formulae had to be so brief that Jane felt that it had been hardly worth the journey.

Then, before she was ready for it, it was Sunday. Race day.

They were still relieving the car of the weight of tools, reserve fuel and several spare wheels borrowed from the service station by Gunge, when a couple appeared beside them. The man glanced at the racing number and consulted a list. 'Race Six?' he said.

Jane had not even looked at a programme. 'TVR Tuscan Challenge,' she said airily.

'That's right. Race Six.' He chose one of the boxes on the woman's tray. 'Take a card, any card,' he said, after the manner of a conjurer.

Mystified, Jane chose a card. It bore only a large number Ten. She half expected to be asked to replace the card anywhere in the pack, but the man made a note and the couple walked off.

Julian Berkeley was nearby. 'What was that about?' she asked him.

'That's your position on the starting grid,' he said.

'I thought the fastest cars started at the front.'

'That's the usual way of doing it, but with so many races on the programme it becomes an impossible burden on the timekeepers. With production cars, it's quite common to draw lots for position.'

'But doesn't ten mean that I'll be near the front? I was counting on being tucked away at the back where I couldn't get in anybody's way.'

He smiled reassuringly. 'Ten would usually be considered a very lucky draw, but I see your problem. Your car won't be one of the fastest and you're rather short of experience. What I'd do in your shoes would be to hold close to my side of the track, let the pack go by and take up position as a tailender. By the time the leaders start to lap you, you'll have settled in. Just watch your mirror and make it easy for them to go by. You'll be all right.'

'Thank you,' she said humbly.

'Not at all. Just go out and have fun.'

That had been her exact intention but it was soon clear that this would be more easily said than done. The TVRs were allocated a short period of practice in the morning. Jane managed to get out early again and enjoyed a couple of laps in comparative isolation, but as other entrants followed on she found that she was sharing the circuit with faster cars, some of them much faster. By watching her mirrors and holding the less favourable side of the track she managed to steer clear of trouble, but it could no longer be classed as having fun and before the end of the session she pulled into the pit lane and back to the paddock.

Mr Berkeley returned a few minutes later. He settled to enjoy a light snack. He beckoned to Jane. There were two canvas chairs and a small folding table beside his trailer. His mechanic was checking over the TVR. Leaving Gunge to do the same to her car, she took the other chair.

'I was watching you,' Berkeley said. 'You drive with precision and you don't waste an inch. Have a sandwich. They're smoked salmon.'

'I couldn't eat,' Jane said.

'Don't force yourself. Eating can be a mistake before a long race in hard conditions, but I found that a short race in a saloon car is neither here nor there. The sandwiches will still be here if you change your mind. How about coffee?'

Jane said that she would love a coffee. They sat in silence for a minute. Jane made up her mind. She had had her fun. She had discovered what she could do. If the others could do better, well, that's how it went. Money would always talk. She would plead a mechanical problem and scratch from the actual race. That decision made, she began to feel more cheerful. She unwound and helped herself to a sandwich.

The other drivers from her practice session were returning. A yellow car stopped beside them. It had been one of the faster cars in practice. It was almost completely covered with decals advertising products, few of which she had ever heard of.

The driver got out. He seemed to be three times as tall as the car. His looks were spoiled by a prognatheous jaw but in her newly relaxed mood Jane was prepared to forgive him for a feature which he could hardly have chosen for himself. She prepared a smile.

'You were cluttering up the track,' he said. He had an accent that might have been American. 'That car isn't for racing, it's for taking an old lady shopping. You'd better get your pretty butt out of the way quicker than that or it'll get trodden on.'

Jane felt her temper rising but she held it in check. She searched her mind for a riposte. 'What grid number did you draw?'

'Eight,' he said.

'I drew Ten,' she said. 'I'll be right behind you. Better get your finger out or I'll drive right over the top of you.'

He gave a rude snort of laughter. 'I believe you,' he said. 'Women drivers!' He dropped into his car and blasted away.

'You'll have to put up with that sort of boorishness from time to time,' Julian Berkeley said. 'You're a girl in a man's world. Don't let it get to you.'

'Who was that?'

'His name's Lansdowne. Carl Lansdowne. He's a Canadian.'

'Not a very couth one,' Jane said. The university had been swept by a vogue for coining new words or reviving old ones by omitting negative prefixes.

Mr Berkeley caught on at once. 'Definitely uncouth,' he said. 'Lansdowne lost his seat in Formula Three Thousand this year, so he may be forgiven if he's somewhat touchy.'

'Not by me.' But Jane spoke absently. 'Right, you bastard!' she was saying silently.

Jane brought the TVR to a halt on the painted line and above the number 10. Her mood had completed its swing from exhilaration to grim determination. She was not, she told herself, a feminist and never would be. She was a girl, and quite happy with that. On the other hand, if one man looked on her as an intrusive female with no business among skilled drivers, perhaps they all looked on her that way, disdainfully, although to condemn her driving ability unseen because of her gender was brutally unfair. Beyond the generous run-offs the circuit was now outlined with faces. Were they all making allowances for her? Well, if her grandfather's TVR could put up a performance, then she'd show them. And as for that arrogant . . . what? . . . She recalled the word which had amused the Wing Commander. If that thost did not get out of the way damn quick she really would ram him up the . . . the bum. She glared at the back of the yellow car and dared him to stall.

The lights flicked out.

Jane got away as fast as she possibly could, but, handicapped by an engine less responsive than most of the others, she saw cars slipping by to her right. But the car in front of Carl

Lansdowne had stalled and Lansdowne had had to brake rather than collide with it. Jane swerved around him before she had time to remember her threat. One car ahead had spun and taken another out; and cars were weaving around the obstructions. Then, it seemed in an instant, the first bend was ahead. The trickle of overtaking cars dried. She snatched a quick look at her mirrors. There were cars behind. But they must be waiting for . . . for her! She twitched the wheel, crossed the track and claimed her place on the racing line. A car, blue over black with a red decal on the side, actually slowed slightly to give her room. Her confidence returned. She was accepted as one of them. She tackled the bend as fast as she ever had in practice, just brushing the inner verge and returning, following the perfect line. The gap to the car in front began to widen when they were clear of the bend and her lack of power made itself felt. Two more cars overtook her but others, expecting the race to be red-flagged, slowed down.

Then she was on her own again. The car in front was a hundred yards ahead. She looked in the mirror and there were several cars behind her and they were not catching up. She settled to enjoy the drive. Her heart was soaring.

She completed the first lap. The damaged cars had limped clear. The first corner again and she saw cars coming up fast in the mirror, the hated yellow car in the lead.

For anyone else she would have slowed and held wide around the next bend and let him through. But Mr Berkeley had explained to her that she was under no obligation to give up the racing line. Carl Lansdowne had made her angrier than she had been since her childhood. The next marshal was showing a blue flag, but she could get away with ignoring blue flags once or even twice — a third offence would mean disqualification.

Lansdowne was just as angry, but mostly with himself. He had been caught out while the tart scraped by. Perhaps the girl was a witch and put a spell on him. The fact that she was attractive somehow made it worse. Well, she could get her broomstick out of his bloody way, there was a *man* coming through.

Jane was just shifting her foot to the brake when the yellow car went by, very fast and near so that she rocked in the slipstream, the driver lifting a contemptuous finger to her as he cut close across her front. Perhaps he had underestimated her speed or overestimated his own talent. Whatever the reason, the yellow car's tyres smoked as he tried to slow in a hurry. Then he was into the bend, the car's rear braking away. He tried to correct, but too late. The car had gone beyond the point of no return. It span.

Jane, firmly established on the correct racing line, saw her way ahead blocked. Suddenly speed, from being a friendly protagonist, turned into a monster, racing to swallow the car and her with it. She might have tried to haul round more tightly, but that was the direction in which the yellow car was sliding, wheels locked. The Canadian saw her coming, closed his eyes and waited for the crunch. She braked, straightened her line, knocked a marker aside and, still braking, took to the grass. A photographer had to jump for his life.

It was Jane's misfortune that field drains had been laid not long before. This had resulted in a long hump, hardly more than an undulation, along which settlement had formed a central furrow. Jane hit this obliquely, still braking but still at speed. The rhythm was exactly wrong. The car flipped. It skated on its roof. Jane had time to kill the ignition. Stones had floated to the surface while the soil was soft. They hammered and tore at the bodywork but Jane was past caring.

★　★　★

99

The first-aiders wanted to lay Jane on a stretcher but she refused. They were concerned at the blood dribbling out of the helmet and thought that she was being brave, but she knew that her nose was broken and if she lay on her back she might drown in her own blood. Her visor had been up and at some point in the car's antics she had managed to punch herself in the face. She got up, supported by one of the men, and walked to the first-aid tent.

The medic in charge made sure, first, that no more serious bones were broken, then that she was not suffering from concussion. He gently removed her helmet, anaesthetised her nose and inserted cotton plugs laced with something that stopped the bleeding. But the broken and displaced cartilage in her nose was more than he cared to tackle in the field. He taped her nose and decided to send her into hospital, using the ambulance which was standing by.

Jane became even less happy. 'I'd be miles and miles from home,' she said thickly, 'and leaving the car here.' Her blocked nose made the pronunciation of *miles* particularly difficult.

Laura had appeared, white-faced but keeping her head. 'You can't possibly travel in the recovery vehicle. Shall I see if I can find somebody going our way who'd drop you at Accident and Emergency?'

'Perhaps I can help,' said Julian Berkeley from the door of the tent. 'I came to see how you feel.'

Jane wanted to ask him how the hell he thought she would feel. She also wanted to say that it depended who was feeling her. But it had been kind of him to come and enquire and even kinder to offer to help. She thought that he must have dropped out of the race to have arrived so promptly. 'I may survive,' she said.

'I hope so. I'll take you to the hospital nearest your home.'

'Can you and Gunge look after the car?' Jane asked Laura.

'I suppose so. If you really want to keep the bits.'

Tears came into Jane's eyes. The others thought that they were tears of pain.

Under Mr Berkeley's direction, his mechanic went off to help Gunge to right the TVR and get it home. Jane, averting her eyes from her mangled car, was settled carefully into the front of the Range Rover. Laura hopped into the back. Mr Berkeley drove very gently — whether for her sake or because of the weight of his own TVR on the trailer Jane could not decide.

Outside the tent, three first-aiders were still arguing. 'Surely there couldn't have been ice on the track,' said one. 'When we got her out of the car, the first thing she said was 'Frost'.'

'She was thirsty,' said another. 'She said 'Thirst'.'

'No,' said the third. 'I don't know what it means but she said 'Thost!' That's what she said. 'Thost! Thost! Thost!' '

5

Laura wanted to accompany Jane into the Accident and Emergency Department, but Jane sent her to show Mr Berkeley where to collect his mechanic while she made her own way inside. The anaesthetic was wearing off and her nose hurt. She delivered a note from the doctor at the races and then went and huddled miserably in a corner of the waiting room.

She had a long wait. It was a time of the week for drunks and joyriders. A party of teenagers had crashed a stolen car, so there were two policemen attending. One of these thought that Jane must have been a passenger in the stolen car, but Jane spotted the other as having been the constable who had first charged her with speeding and later had modified the alleged speed. After studying her from several angles he recognised her. This, for some reason, was accepted as satisfactory proof of her innocence.

The constable settled down for a chat. Despite the pain in her nose, Jane wanted to talk to somebody. In a thick voice but in words made forceful by emotion she described the smash and the events leading up to it. 'So next time you see that magistrate — whatever his name was — you can tell him what came of his advice.'

The constable was amused by the notion that he could tick off a magistrate for handing out unsound advice from the bench, but he was saddened by the news of the car. 'It's a shame,' he said. 'And, of course, your insurers won't want to know about it. Is the car a write-off?'

'I don't know. It was quite gentle, really, but they tell me that I've managed to put at least a major rip into every glass-fibre panel, just with sliding along on the roof and rolling onto one side and then the other. That doesn't sound as if it would be economic to repair, does it?'

The constable shook his head unhappily. 'No, it doesn't. And the car-breakers would only give you peanuts for it. If it's as you say and the works are still good, it might pay you to break it yourself. Advertise the parts for spares. Or you might find somebody wanting to build a sports car who'd make you an offer for the whole gubbins.'

Two minutes later, the staff finished patching up the joy-riders and Jane's friend had to go. Soon after that, Jane was taken into a cubicle where a young doctor tried to set her nose under a second local anaesthetic. His efforts were unsuccessful and they hurt.

'You'll have to stay in overnight,' he said at last. 'This needs surgery.'

He renewed the taping. Jane was removed to a surgical ward. She was too late for the evening meal. After going through the day on half a smoked-salmon sandwich and a cup of coffee her appetite returned with a vengeance, but the staff pointed out that such a comparatively minor procedure would certainly be taken in the morning, but only if she had an empty stomach. A kind-hearted nurse, just before going off duty, made her a cup of tea and with that Jane had to be contented.

Discomfort and anxiety combined to make sleep doubtful, but a long day and two injections of anaesthetic had the opposite effect. She fell asleep at last, only to turn over in the bed and awake in agony during the small hours. She had displaced her broken nose again and restarted the bleeding. The night staff did what they could but Jane had to wait, in some pain only slightly relieved by a couple of aspirins, until morning. She was whisked in and out of X-ray and then had to wait again until the surgeon, already gowned, came round in the morning, accompanied by the usual retinue of helpers and students.

The surgeon studied the X-rays and the

nose itself and then consulted a list. 'This shouldn't be left,' he said. 'It's not a long job. Slip her in here.' He tapped the list with a pencil.

'Please,' Jane said. 'There's one thing . . . '

'Yes?' The surgeon seemed unused to being addressed by mere patients.

'If you're going to be doing things to the inside of my nose,' Jane said, 'could you perhaps make it a little bit shorter than it was?'

There was a ripple of shocked amusement among the hangers-on.

'We don't usually do cosmetic surgery on the National Health,' said the surgeon. 'And I don't know how long your nose was before you broke it.'

'Not *very* long,' Jane said bravely. 'But I never liked it.' She looked around and spotted her friend of the night before. She pointed. 'That's the sort of nose I'd like,' she said.

'You're sure?'

'Certain,' Jane said. 'I think it's a beautiful nose.'

The friendly nurse blushed and tried to melt into the crowd. The surgeon regarded her critically. 'It has its points,' he said. (One of the nurses snorted in amusement.) 'We'll see what we can do while we're in there. But cosmetic work usually has to wait until the swelling has gone. So I make no promises. You'll all bear witness that I never promised the young lady anything beautiful?'

Most of the hangers-on simpered and said that they would. The surgeon moved on.

Surgery began. After an hour, Jane was removed to the threshold of the operating theatre where a chatty anaesthetist knocked her out cold. She came to back in her chilly bed in the ward. Her nose was on fire. She thought that the flames were invisible only because of the padding and tapes. But at last she could breathe through her nose. This was due, apparently, to a fine tube up each of her nostrils. It was not a comfortable arrangement but at least her mouth and throat did not dry out.

The surgeon, when he came round again, was not very reassuring. 'The underlying structure's repaired,' he said. 'I removed a detached fragment, which should have a shortening effect, but we'll have to see what you look like when the swelling goes down. We can always do a little more work if we're not satisfied with the appearance.'

'But I won't have any scars?'

'That much I can promise you. You can go home tomorrow. Come back in ten days. We'll take a look at you and have a good laugh.'

Jane ate her lunch. Her nose might hurt

but her mouth still worked. She had the healthy appetite of youth and this was her second day on half a sandwich, one cup of coffee and a cup of tea. The lady in the next bed had lost her appetite, so Jane ate hers as well. When Laura and Gunge arrived together at visiting time, they found her in comparatively cheerful mood.

'I'm fine,' she said in answer to their polite queries.

'You don't look very fine,' Laura said. 'The bruising looks awful, what we can see of it around the bandages.'

'Bruises fade, they keep telling me. I don't think I'll be able to get around the university for a while. Ask one of the boys to tape the lectures for me. But never mind that. What did Henry say when he saw the car?'

'He went away rather quickly,' Gunge said. 'I think he was crying. Mrs Dodson said that it was no more than she expected.'

'Henry needs something to keep him occupied,' said Jane. 'How are the working parts of the TVR?'

'One front suspension's a little bit bent,' said Gunge. 'Otherwise they seem OK. We'll have to check the engine over if it was still running upside down. But you've got most of the works, all right. It's a car you don't have.'

'If you want, literally, to save something

from the wreck,' Laura said, 'Mr Berkeley said that what caused the confusion at the start of the race was that somebody had a major mechanical failure. He wrecked his engine and gearbox and most of the other bits are suspect. And Mr Berkeley said that it wouldn't be worth spending huge sums rebuilding the working parts because the bodywork also needed some attention. He'd end up with a second-hand car that had cost him as much as a new one. But you've got all the bits and pieces . . .'

'You mean, I could buy that car and make a good one out of the two?'

'If you want. Mr Berkeley knew who the man was and he gave me the name of his firm.'

Gunge, who had privately been bemoaning the fact that his relationship with Jane would be at an end, would have welcomed any excuse to prolong it. 'Great idea!' he said. 'We can have you racing again.'

Jane had made up her mind never to race again, but she saw a chance to get her money out of the TVR. 'Would you give him a phone and find out how much he wants for his car?'

'If you like.'

'Of course,' Jane said, 'it might make just as much sense for him to buy our car and use the working parts to rebuild his own one. You

109

can suggest that and find out how much he would offer. Better do it quick before he decides to scrap his car and it goes into the cruncher.'

'No problem,' said Laura. 'Leave it with me. Jane, did you realise who that was, your Mr Berkeley? There was a profile of him in *Business Today*. He owns the whole of Alex Beauty Products and has large holdings in a dozen other companies. He's a widower. He's on the list of the ten richest men in Britain and lives in a showplace. I think I'm falling in love.'

'Again?' Jane said.

'Yes, again. There's no law says that I can't fall in love with every millionaire in Britain. Is there, Gunge?'

★ ★ ★

Next day, Henry arrived in the Maestro to bring her home. He helped her tenderly into the car and said not a word of reproof. She might have felt better if he had ranted at her, but it seemed that Laura, supported by Gunge and Mr Berkeley, had described the circumstances of Jane's downfall. Henry's ire was directed entirely at Carl Lansdowne as the guilty party.

At home, she noticed that Ramon's sports

car, usually carefully cosseted in half the garage, had been banished to stand on the gravel beside the Maestro's usual stance. There was no sign of the TVR and Jane was still too heartsick about the whole subject to enquire. She was slightly cheered to find an expensive bunch of flowers from Mr Berkeley together with a note wishing her an early recovery.

She was still very uncomfortable as well as being self-conscious about her appearance She spent several days at home, concentrating on her studies between being scolded by Mrs Dodson. Her lodgers were universally sympathetic, as were her fellow students when she did eventually venture back among them.

One of her first outings, after the dressings had been removed, was to the clubroom of the local motor club, in a building shared with the RAC and a large insurance company. There were a few members present, enjoying a leisurely drink or catching up with the motoring magazines. Among them was David de Vine, the medical student who had been her first and only lover. They had decided amicably that no long-term relationship between them would work, but they were still on good, not to say affectionate, terms. He was a classically beautiful young man, which probably assured him of a future in Harley

Street. He bought her a half-pint of shandy and they settled down at a table.

'How's Agnes?' she asked. Agnes had been her successor in his affections.

'Long gone. I saw what happened to you, by the way, from among the massed ranks of the spectators. He thought you were going to back off for him.'

'Then he was out of his tiny mind,' Jane said with some heat. 'He rubbed me up the wrong way in the paddock, making sexist remarks, and I told him to steer clear or I'd drive right over him.'

'You'd've had a lot of general sympathy if you'd done it. He's an arrogant bugger and he's made himself thoroughly unloved. But you didn't drive over the top of him. Why not?'

Jane laughed. 'No. I was tempted, but when push came to shove I felt I couldn't bash into anything so beautiful. And I thought the grass was a softer bet for myself. I was wrong there,' she added ruefully.

'Shame about the car. When you say 'beautiful', you mean the Yellow Peril?'

'Certainly I do. If you look at the real lines and ignore the colour and all those disfiguring decals, yes. The lines are good. They're aerodynamic, functional and sculptural, all at the same time, which is how

112

machines should be. Hardly peccable at all.'

'And for the sake of that, you got your face and your car bashed in and left him unscathed? I always knew that you were a nutcase. You still look like hell. Who fixed you up, by the way?'

'It said Pendleberry on his badge.'

He mimed shock. 'Good God! You didn't let Old Fumble-fingers get his hands on your hooter? Well, at least he seems to have got it the right way up this time. Does it still hurt?'

'Only when I laugh. And I'm not laughing a lot just now.'

'I don't suppose you are.' He waggled his eyebrows evilly at her and ran his hand up her leg. 'Come with me into the cash bar and we'll see if I can't kiss it better.'

Jane was in need of some reassurance. 'That sounds like one of your better ideas!' she said.

'It's one of the first tricks they teach us aspiring docs. Come on, then. Your place or mine?'

'You'll be gentle with my nose?'

'That's one of the second tricks they teach us — how to make love to a patient without aggravating their condition.'

★ ★ ★

The man whose TVR had suffered mechanical failure told Laura that nothing would induce him to undertake a major rebuild and, anyway, he was already in negotiation with Lotus. What he wanted most out of life was to be rid of the damaged car. Gunge went to look at it and reported that large parts of the engine and gearbox and their associated components seemed to be missing altogether but that the car itself was definitely in better shape than Jane's. The price asked was reasonable.

Jane closed the deal over the phone.

From her grandfather's house, Jane had brought away a selection of pictures, chosen because she liked them or because they had been favourites of the Wing Commander. She had grown rather tired of a gruesome Victorian oil painting of *Judith with the Head of Holofernes* (usually greeted by visitors with 'Ah! John the Baptist!') and so she consulted a dealer recommended by Gordon Black as being more honest than many of his kind.

The dealer proved to be not only honest but scrupulous. He identified the painting as being by an artist she had never heard of, not one of the first rank but well placed in the second, and he sold it for her, on commission, for a surprisingly useful sum.

Jane was able to pay off her overdraft, send off a cheque in settlement for the other car and even pay her Council Tax.

Two weeks after her release from hospital, Jane was invited into her own garage. Bracing herself, she accepted the invitation. She could have spared her hesitation. Henry, with occasional help from Gunge and others, had dismantled the battered TVR and the stripped shell had been removed. The engine, wheels, suspensions, all the usable components had been cleaned and methodically arranged on the bench or hung on the walls. The replacement car, already stripped of the damaged components, stood nearby.

At her first sight of it, Jane was depressed. The car, which was a bilious green colour, had been scratched and dented by more than a year's use in hard competition. It was not the same model of TVR as her own vanished Tuscan but a Cerbera. Jane tried to ignore the colour and see the lines. The car was even racier than her Tuscan. It had a take-down top.

Her companions seemed to be waiting for something. 'Thank you,' she said hoarsely.

Gunge had furnished a colour chart of cellulose paints. The colours ringed were those of which useful quantities left over from previous jobs were going begging at the service station. The colour chart went round the table at dinner that night. 'I like the blue,' Laura said.

'Blue pigments tend to fade,' said Jane. 'Red cars always remind me of Post Office vans. White looks like an ice-cream mobile shop and black's old-fashioned and rather sinister.'

'There is yellow,' Ramon said. 'The colour of sunshine.'

'It was a yellow car that got me into this pickle,' Jane said. 'I'm rather off yellow cars for the moment. I think I'll go for the lilac.'

'With your hair?' Laura protested. 'You'd never wear that colour.'

'Nobody'll ever see the two together,' Jane said. 'The way they soak a student for insurance of a large-engined sports car, I'm unlikely to run it on the road before my hair turns grey.'

★ ★ ★

The bruising faded and died away but the swelling remained. Then, it seemed overnight, the last of it was gone. Jane had for so long had an inferiority complex about her looks that, after her accident, a habit of avoiding mirrors had easily become established. She had given up make-up altogether while her

116

face was so tender and was quite used to brushing her hair into its casual style by touch alone. She knew only that her face was more comfortable until, at the breakfast table, Laura said, 'Hey, you look better.'

'I feel better.'

'No, I mean that your new nose looks sort of different.'

Jane had been busy, wondering how to go about uniting the bits of two cars to make one good one and what she would have to sell to meet unexpected costs. 'Does it?' she said vaguely.

'Lord, yes. Miles better than the old one. I hope they gave you a good trade-in. Is the last of the swelling gone now?'

Jane felt her nose, gently and then more firmly. 'I think we're down to bedrock at last.'

'Well, it looks jolly good. Didn't you think so, Sandy?'

Sandy Durnin was the third and last person at the breakfast table. He was more interested in bacon, egg and a sausage. 'Didn't look,' he said ungallantly. He raised his eyes to Jane's face. 'Turn your head . . . Yes, by God! You look quite ravishable. Watch it or you'll get yourself jumped on.' He returned his attention to his breakfast.

Jane bolted her cereal and carried her cup of tea up to her bedroom. She studied her new face in the mirror. With the aid of a second mirror she saw her face in profile. It seemed that 'Old Fumble-fingers' had not only managed to keep her nose the right way up but his scalpel had for a few moments been touched with luck or genius. Her nose was certainly shorter — not by much, but if the amount was small the effect was magical — and although it was perfectly symmetrical, it departed just enough from being absolutely straight to have pertness, charm, all the characteristics that Jane, in the privacy of her own mind, felt that she herself lacked. She made up with some of her old care and went to the university, where most of her classmates looked and wondered what was different about her.

★ ★ ★

She threw herself first into a concentrated effort to recover the physical fitness that enforced idleness had brought. It was left to Henry, aided by Gunge whenever he could be spared from the service station, to make a start to installing the suspensions from the now defunct car.

The university had wound down for the long vacation. Staff turned to research or writing. The students resigned themselves to waiting for their results and, when necessary, studying for resits. As Jane recovered her strength she gave attention to the new car. She would have given all her time to it except that, for purely financial reasons, she had taken a post for the summer with a computer consultancy firm to which she had been recommended by her professor. The work consisted almost entirely of solving the problems which clients encountered with their computer systems and it had to continue without interruption during the holidays of the permanent staff as computers crashed or were contaminated by viruses or new programs turned out to be plagued by serious flaws.

Jane found the work demanding. It was interesting, but not so much so as to distract her altogether from the new car. She spent most of her evenings and weekends at work on it and was not afraid of dirtying her arms to the elbows or breaking her fingernails. Once again some of her fellow students came to help, but she gave short shrift to any who distracted the others or thought to get by with slipshod workmanship.

Her social life was less neglected than ever before. Her changed appearance made her seem less haughty and more approachable, so she found herself more in demand. If those who slipped into her life hoped to go beyond an exchange of petting and slip also into her bed, they were unsuccessful. Jane had no intention of becoming a slut. But she was a kind-hearted girl. She hated to send anyone away disappointed. She would extend the hand of friendship to the occasional young man who was clean, nice looking, fun to be with and who bought her a good dinner.

In mid-September she was working, alone for once, in her garage on a Sunday afternoon. The others had gone to attend the last motor race of the season, and they had taken Henry along with them, largely because Henry was now driving, when required, for a firm specialising in weddings and funerals and could borrow a limousine from his employers. Jane had opted out. Everybody knew that one driver could go faster than another but, if neither of them could be herself, she cared not which. She was not a spectator by nature.

At the sound of a footstep she glanced up expecting to see Mrs Dodson, come to call her to one meal or another — she was too caught up to keep track of time. She was surprised to see the friendly young policeman who she had last encountered at the hospital. In tweed jacket and flannels he looked older and yet slightly gauche.

'Well,' he said, 'you look a thousand per cent better than when I last saw you. Somebody told me that a young lady was building a special here and I thought that it might be you. So I came to see. Do you mind?'

'Help yourself. Spy out the nakedness of the land.'

'It certainly isn't that. You're further on than I expected. It's going to be a handsome beast.'

They stood back and looked at the car. Most of the mechanical work was done but the glass-fibre bodywork and the interior still required a great deal of attention. The new paintwork had been tried out on one small panel.

'But why the lavender colour?' the constable asked.

'It's not lavender, it's lilac,' she said absently. 'It was the only colour we could get for nothing that I didn't hate. I can always spray over it when I'm rich. It's about ready to drive if we jury-rig some wiring. I'd like to have a test run before finalising things. Otherwise it'll get scratched up again. Perhaps I can borrow a set of trade-plates . . . ?'

The constable tutted severely. 'Bad idea,' he said. 'I'd have to prosecute you again. Do you have a trailer or any way to transport the beast?'

'I can find something.'

'Aim to be ready two weeks from today. Give me your number and I'll confirm if it's on.'

★   ★   ★

The constable, whose name, he told her, was Bryant, phoned during the week. On the Sunday morning she was ready with Gunge and with the car on a trailer behind her old friend the recovery vehicle belonging to Gunge's father. She also had two ten-pound notes with her.

They followed Constable Bryant for an hour. He led them to the Road Research Laboratory, where he seemed to be on friendly terms with the gate-keeper. The two tenners changed hands and Jane was free to use the test track for the day. At first, the car felt different and yet the same as its predecessor, like meeting an acquaintance who has gained or lost a lot of weight. But she soon settled down and worked up from a crawl to a canter to a tyre-smoking hurtle which lasted only for a few minutes until she remembered that she had gained a good set of tyres with the Tuscan but might not be so lucky again. Before starting for home she allowed Gunge and Constable Bryant each to do a few laps while she bit her lip in white-knuckled anxiety.

Gunge's mother took a rigid view of mealtimes and her time for the evening meal was past before they returned home, so Jane swept him inside to dine with her household. They barely had time to clean themselves up.

Over the meal, discussion about the car was inevitable. Jane had had time to think on the journey home. 'It felt good,' she said. 'Driveable right on the edge. You could go sideways and still catch it. The centre of gravity needs to come forward a touch — we'll start by moving the battery. And the pedal positions need adjusting. It went like stink, but I have a nasty feeling that it's still going to be outclassed all the same.'

'It is,' Gunge said. 'I told you.'

'And I keep telling you that I'm only doing it for fun. All the same, I don't want the car to be outclassed by more than it has to be. I want some weight skimmed off the flywheel and the compression ratio upped by facing off the cylinder head.'

Gunge nodded. 'If we dismantle them during the week I can take them in to the engineering shop with a load of other parts. How much do you want taken off each?'

'I don't know yet,' Jane said 'I'll — '

'Write a computer program,' said the others in unison. The words had become her signature tune.

'Well, I will,' Jane said. She pretended to sulk. If she had been honest she would have admitted that, although she was becoming capable of concocting such a program, her usual starting-point was one of several programs belonging to a racing team based in Surbiton, hacked into by Jane with the help of one of her more experienced colleagues at the office.

★ ★ ★

They were soon immersed once more in the pressures and distractions of the academic year. The stresses were the greater for this being, for most of them, the final year of the degree course, with yet more advanced subjects and the threat of degree exams. Work went forward on the car, but in fits and starts. Yet there was time for fun. Jane had planned to spend Christmas Day working alone or with Henry in the garage. But friends dropped in, fugitives from too much jollity at home or too little in digs, some with small presents, not for Jane but for the car — a car compass, a pair of wing mirrors, a set

124

of woolly dice for the non-existent back window. Constable Bryant arrived. He had turned out to be the only visitor who combined the skill and patience needed to make sense of the TVR's hugely involved wiring diagram, and had turned his hand to reinstating the wiring of the car. Mrs Dodson produced, apparently out of thin air, a series of seasonal snacks which were wolfed as fast as they arrived despite the fumes of polyester resin as the scratches and rips were filled or patched.

A huge punchbowl was set up on the workbench and kept filled with a fruit punch so mild that, by Constable Bryant's calculation, anyone could have drained the whole bowl twice and still passed the breathalyser test. But when the mood is right, the merest suggestion of alcohol is enough. As the day progressed and old jokes were taken out and dusted off, amusement became hilarity. Jane amazed herself by remembering, word perfect, and reciting without a single mistake several humorous monologues. Bruce McLean turned out to have a huge fund of limericks but which entailed so much Glasgow dialect as to be about as comprehensible as the wiring diagram — which, to judge from the few fragments that Jane could understand, was just as well.

A surprising volume of work had been accomplished, but when somebody produced a large aerosol and wanted to spray the car pink, Jane had to call a halt. At the start of term, the culprit approached her with an apology. 'But it was the best Christmas party ever,' he said, 'and not a trace of a hangover. Can we do it again next year?'

'Next year,' Jane said, 'you build a car and we'll all join in.'

'I might just do that.'

After the party, Constable Bryant lingered for a chat. 'Have you made up your mind whether you're going to race this car or sell it?'

'No, I haven't,' Jane said frankly. 'Objectively, I've been thoroughly illogical, which isn't like me. I had all the components on my hands and no prospect of buying a car of quality so I decided to build one. As a result I've spent a lot of money and I can't afford to insure it for the road. It'll have to go. I've accepted that racing is not for me — it's far too expensive for a student to keep up. I'd have liked to race once or twice more, just to show that I really can compete without destroying the car, but I'd have to tax it for the road first. In fact, I've been the victim of just the sort of muddled thinking I'd despise in anyone else. I'm busily painting myself into a corner.'

'There's one possible way round your main problem,' Bryant said. 'Get a cover note, buy a tax disc and cancel the insurance the same day.'

'Is that legal?'

'As long as you don't run it on the road. Your insurance wouldn't have any effect while you were racing anyway.'

'You're a pal,' Jane said. There was a sprig of mistletoe hanging in the garage. She kissed him under it and sent him on his way. After she got into the house she found that her lips were still tingling.

★ ★ ★

Jane was determined that the car should be finished to a worthy standard down to the last inch of leather trim. It was spring again by the time she considered the car truly finished. In addition, she had, in a rare mood of optimism and extravagance, acquired her own flame-resistant overalls and full-face helmet. As a consequence, she was running desperately short of money again and had to make another raid on her slender investments.

It was at that time, when she might easily have abandoned hope and sold the car for what it would fetch, that Mr Andress paid another visit to the local motor club. He spotted Jane as soon as she entered and carried her off to a corner table.

'You had all my sympathy at the time of your accident,' he said. 'I was told that your face was damaged though I must say you show no sign of it. And your car, too. But I'm afraid that those are some of the hazards you have to accept if you want to go racing.'

'I'm not grumbling,' Jane said. 'Even though I didn't do anything wrong.'

'I'm sure you didn't. But it has been suggested that a certain lack of physical strength might have contributed to the accident.'

'What idiot suggested that?' Jane demanded. 'Carl Lansdowne, I suppose. It was his performing a spin in front of me that made me take to the grass. He's just being defensive. If you have any doubts about my strength, would you care to arm-wrestle?'

Mr Andress laughed until he nearly spilled his whisky and soda. 'Good God, no! I'm much too old for that sort of caper. I'm told that you've done a total rebuild of the car.'

'I've put the working parts from my car into the body of the Tuscan AJP that had the huge blow-up,' Jane said.

'Do you intend to race again?'

Jane had been asking herself the same question. 'Probably,' she said. 'Just once or twice, if I can afford it. And after that I'll learn a little sense and sell the car.'

'The reason I ask,' said Mr Andress, 'indeed, the reason I sought you out, is that we're having an event in June. Not one of the Tuscan Series. There's been some political infighting and a group of races were withdrawn from the circuit where you had your mishap. We were asked to provide a curtain-raiser to plug the gap, and we thought we'd resurrect a formula from the past. Something to give the novices an equal chance with the experts. So we're running a reversed-grid race. A handicap, in fact. The cars are sent off at intervals calculated to bring them to the finish together. Exceed your qualifying speed by more than ten per cent and you're disqualified.'

'That seems fair enough,' Jane said. 'What made you think of me?'

'If you're still on the same engine, you're handicapping yourself. This would even things up a bit.'

'As long as the dates fall clear of exams,' Jane said, 'count me in.'

★ ★ ★

Studying and revision kept them occupied. There was also the car to check over and tune. The pursuit of absolute fitness took up more of Jane's time. The arrival of race week brought a sense of relief, of *reculant pour mieux sauler*. Jane had one exam still to come and Laura two.

Laura declined to attend the Tuesday practice, pleading the demands of studying, so Jane and Gunge were alone in the recovery vehicle. In return for the loan, several advertisements for the service station were carefully attached to the car — with wallpaper paste, to permit easy removal from the immaculate finish.

'Doesn't your father mind you taking so much time off?' Jane asked as they approached the course.

Gunge shook his head without taking his eyes off the road. 'My brothers take care of most of the real work. Dad says I'm learning more with you than servicing a lot of tin boxes in the workshop.'

'Golly!'

Jane had no problem with the scrutineer, who inspected the car with interest rather than suspicion. 'You built this with the bits of the TVR you rolled last year?' he asked.

'That's right.'

'You built it yourself?'

Jane bristled. 'Why not?'

'No reason. You won't win much, but I take my hat off to you all the same.'

Jane felt her hackles subside. 'I got by with a little help from my friends,' she said.

She practised. The scrutineer, along with everybody else, was right. Other cars, with the advantages of lesser weight, larger capacity engines and racing modifications, pulled away from her on the straights. Carl Lansdowne, in the Yellow Peril, seemed to take a particular pleasure in blasting past her, dangerously close. She had to put up with a little ribbing, mostly good-natured, in the paddock.

At home, she found Laura deep in her books. At first, Laura was reluctant to take the Saturday away from her studies.

'Are you going to help me?' Jane asked finally. 'Or do I find myself another best friend?'

Laura threw up her hands in despair. 'But, Jane, this comes in the middle of the exams.'

'If I can get ready for the exams in a couple of days, you can do the same,' Jane suggested. 'They don't hold exams at weekends. I'll help you revise.'

Laura could have pointed out that she did not have Jane's capacity for instant absorption of learning, but that might only have led to a lecture on Positive Thinking and Mental

Concentration. 'Oh, all right,' she said weakly. 'What do you want me to do?'

'Look at it this way,' Jane said. 'Mathematically, the race is bound to be won by the fastest car to exceed its practice speed by nine point nine recurring per cent.'

'I see that, I think. So where does little me come in?'

'I'm trying to tell you, if you'll only shut up for a minute. You know that white jacket of yours?'

'You want to borrow it?' Laura asked, puzzled.

'I want you to wear it over my red jumper.'

★　★　★

On the Saturday, when Jane went out to the first practice session, Laura followed her instructions to the letter. Armed with stopwatch and notebook, she walked out to a point on the circuit diametrically opposite to the start-and-finish line and the timekeepers' window. When the car had warmed up, Jane alternated deliberately slow laps with others taken flat out.

To the timekeepers, Jane's times would have been modest. But over a sandwich and a cup of coffee it was easy, from Laura's notebook, to arrive at an accurate estimate of what Jane's best time would be. From that, it was a simple calculation to determine what lap-time she should permit the timekeepers to record.

The TVRs were allowed one more short practice period. Jane placed Laura just short of the timekeepers. Laura was wearing the white jacket over the red jumper. As Jane circulated at progressively increasing speeds, Laura checked her times. When Jane put in a lap-time which came very close to the figure which they had calculated, Laura opened her jacket. Next lap, Jane saw the bright red jumper appear and she slowed before crossing the line.

All was set. There was to be one more practice session on the Sunday morning but Jane decided to miss it. The track would be more crowded and there would be unnecessary strain on the car and wear on the new tyres. Also, she might accidentally put in too fast a time.

She took a walk up the paddock. She exchanged a few words with Mr Beverley and then excused herself. She was admiring the single-seater cars but her mind was elsewhere. Conscience was beginning to trouble her. If she was only out for the pleasure of the drive, why was she applying her mathematics to improving her chances? Was it unethical?

Should she put in a fast lap in the morning and take her proper place in the start? What was Conscience really trying to say?

Gunge was also on the prowl, picking the brains of the racing mechanics.

On her return to her car, Jane did not at first notice the act of petty vandalism. When she did, her first thought was that this could not be spur-of-the-moment malice because it must have been prepared in advance. She began to seethe. To the laboriously polished leather of the fascia had been glued a white plastic notice, apparently purloined out of a taxi. It said FASTEN YOUR SEAT BELT, but the word 'seat' had been milled out and 'suspender' inserted, not quite straight.

Quickly, Jane looked round. But she did not catch any obvious smiles. Carl Lansdowne was visible, talking to a mechanic, but he did not seem to be looking her way.

'Right, you buggers,' she said aloud. 'Watch out! That's all. Just watch out!'

* * *

'For God's sake,' said Laura when they got home, 'you joined in, uninvited, to play with their toys. You committed the unforgivable sin of being better than at least some of them. You must expect a little needling. If you want

134

to win, that's OK by me. But anger isn't a sound basis for competitive driving.'

'It'll do for me,' Jane said between clenched teeth. 'In point of fact, I drove rather well. I was really flying but I was always under control — I just didn't let anybody bully me any more. If I had the line on a corner, I stuck to it. And this wasn't a little needling, it was rampant sexism.'

'I thought it was rather funny.'

Jane's voice went up an octave. 'I don't give a thost for your thoughts, I never wore a suspender belt in my life.'

Laura spluttered with laughter. 'What will you use when your sex-life needs spicing up?' she asked. 'Bondage?'

★ ★ ★

They were only a mile or two along the way to the Sunday races when Gunge lifted his foot. 'Look at this,' he said.

'This' was a large Japanese ATV with a trailer at the back supporting a small racing car, all parked in a lay-by. The bonnet of the tow-car was up and the driver was standing back in despondent contemplation of a cloud of steam. Gunge pulled in and they all walked back.

'Radiator hose has split,' the driver said.

135

'You wouldn't have a spare?'

'Not that size,' Gunge said.

'Looks like I'm going to miss out.'

'Not necessarily,' Jane said. She felt a sudden surge of desire for a racing car just like that one, and her desire almost transferred itself to the driver. 'Switch your racing car to our trailer and I'll drive mine to the track. Then . . . you have a mobile phone?' The other driver — Jeremy Francis, she discovered later — produced a slim phone from his vehicle. 'Give it to my mechanic. He can phone for someone to come and fix your hose.'

Twenty minutes later, as Jane was driving the TVR towards the circuit, she arrived at a major road junction. Here, traffic heading for the same destination was conflicting with others trying to get to two other sporting events. Tailbacks were developing and a policeman was directing traffic. With a sudden stab of guilt she recognised Constable Bryant and remembered that he was the one person sure to know that her car was carrying no insurance.

The traffic in Jane's lane moved forward a dozen paces and halted again with Jane near the head. A colleague took over from Bryant, who headed in Jane's direction. She tried very hard to look like somebody else, somebody whose pockets bulged with the legally necessary insurance policies.

That effort, it seemed, was vain. Bryant headed straight for her. He leaned over. 'You are a very naughty girl,' he said. Jane swallowed. She seemed to have lost her voice. The line of traffic was moving again. 'Drive very, very carefully,' Bryant said. 'I'll come and have a serious word with you one of these days.'

He stepped back. Jane pulled out onto the main road. She felt as if she was gasping for breath. She had been within a whisker of losing her driving licence. There was little accounting for Constable Bryant's forbearance, but perhaps that kiss had had something to do with it.

6

The paddock on race day was little different from the way it had been during practice. There were the same trailers and transporters, the same brightly coloured cars and the same drivers — the extroverts talking too loudly and the introverts trying to avoid them. But on race day there was something extra in the atmosphere that made Jane prick up her ears, like a warhorse at the sound of a trumpet or a gun dog at the smell of gun-oil.

While she waited for Gunge and Laura to arrive, Jane went for a jog up the paddock for no better reason than that time was precious and it was her habit to exercise whenever nothing else was demanding her attention. The noise of engines and the smell of burnt fuel and hot metal only stimulated her. Near the far end, she met Julian Berkeley, his racing overalls as immaculate as ever.

Jane tried to hide her pleasure, but she was less preoccupied than usual and was ready to talk. Mr Berkeley reminded her of a much younger version of her grandfather. 'I hope I wasn't rude yesterday,' she said.

'You were full of thoughts,' he said. 'More

people should try thinking now and again. A very pretty job you've made of the new car.'

'I'm still outclassed.'

'But you're serving a valuable apprenticeship. Why did you choose that purple shade?'

'It isn't purple, it's lavender. Lilac, I mean. I don't know. I just disliked it less than I did any of the other colours I could get for nothing.'

'Perhaps it reminded you of something with happy associations.'

'Perhaps,' she said. They were walking on up the paddock together. She stopped at the pit occupied by a stark single-seater. She looked at the rank of polished carburettors and glanced at the suspensions. Then she stood back and absorbed the picture as a whole. 'That's what I should have,' she said suddenly. They walked on. 'I'll tell you something. I've become disenchanted with sports cars,' she said. 'They're a compromise. I can appreciate a saloon car, which is a rational design as road transport — if you accept that steering a rubber-shod vehicle around on a flat surface is rational, which I don't. One sneeze and everybody's dead. Also there's no scope for a serious answer to pollution. But that's another subject.'

'It is indeed,' Mr Berkeley said gravely.

'I'm coming to the point. I admire that

racing car, which is a sound piece of engineering designed with the express purpose of going round a track as quickly as possible and arriving before anybody else. It must be marvellous to drive something like that. What I've gone and built is an unsatisfactory compromise between the two.'

'There is much in what you say,' he said, smiling. 'You have five or six good points there. Some time, you must tell me what you envisage as a solution to the world's transportation problems. But that car is not for you. Not yet. There is a very definite ladder to climb in the world of single-seat racing-cars, and if you try to climb it too quickly your entries simply won't be accepted. You must always gain experience before you move onto the next stage. It is essential. Believe me, I know. In my day, I got as far as Formula Three Thousand, which is one rung below the full Formula One Grand Prix level, but I wasn't good enough to go further and I knew it. And then . . . other factors intruded. My TVR is all that the accountants will let me drive these days. As far as they're concerned, it's my road car and therefore it's safe. But I have to agree with you, it's a compromise. The car you looked at was Formula Three. If you want to enter that world, you must work up to it. First look for something like this.'

They paused beside another single-seater, smaller than the other but not dissimilar. Hearing Berkeley's words, a young man with a bright smile on what Jane thought of as an Irish pug-face jumped up out of a deckchair. 'If the young lady's interested, I'll be putting this one up for sale soon.' Jane's first impression was confirmed by a trace of an Irish brogue. 'Formula Vauxhall Junior. I'm moving up to Formula Vauxhall Two Thousand and if my new car isn't delivered soon I'll be having a tantrum, because I want the rest of this season to shake down. You're driving the puce TVR?'

'It isn't puce,' Jane said absently. 'It's . . . What is it?'

'Lilac,' said Mr Berkeley.

'That's right. Lilac.'

The two men stood by while Jane studied the car. After a few minutes she realised that she was no longer seeing the car itself but the avenues which opened beyond it. 'Give me your name and address,' she said. (The young man produced a card.) 'Write your absolute rock-bottom price on the back of it.'

The young man, whose name from the card was Moran, did as he was told. 'If you're seriously interested,' he said, 'we might be able to arrange for you to have a test drive.'

'I'll know whether I'm interested when I see how you get on,' she said.

He grinned broadly, showing very white teeth. 'Fair enough.'

'You wouldn't care to do a swap?'

The grin faded to a faint smile and he shook his head, regretfully but firmly.

They resumed their walk. She showed Mr Berkeley the figure on the card.

'That's a lot less than a new one would set you back, but it still seems to be on the high side,' he said. 'He might come down if you haggle. It depends a bit what spares are included.'

'Thank you,' she said. 'I'd have forgotten to ask about spares.'

'You might get almost the same figure for your TVR, if you want to sell. You don't mind my pontificating?' he asked almost anxiously.

'Heavens, no! You're the nearest I've got to a mentor.'

'Well, then, if you decide to make the leap, go and take lessons at one of the race-driving schools. You'll benefit, and it will make you more acceptable. And you'll find out whether the difference lies in the car or the driver. You understand me?'

'You mean, I'll find out whether the reason I'm at the back of the field is the car or because I'm a rotten driver?'

Mr Berkeley kept a straight face but there was a smile in his eyes. His old friend should have lived to see how the granddaughter had matured. 'You're certainly not a rotten driver,' he said. 'You drive reliably. You're also fast. You drive with the head as well as the guts. The best drivers are made that way. The question is whether you're one of them.'

'Isn't it just?' she said. She left him and set off back towards her car. It was almost time for the race.

Halfway down the paddock she saw Carl Lansdowne approaching. She would have walked past but he thrust out his big jaw and stopped in front of her. 'Try and keep your car on the track this time,' he said loudly.

Jane's ears went hot. She felt that a hundred faces were grinning at her embarrassment. 'Keep yours in a straight line if you can,' she retorted at the top of her voice. 'Then I won't have to choose between hitting you and taking to the grass . . . again.' She walked on, feeling better. One or two men caught her eye and smiled. One of them mimed applause.

She donned her flame-resistant clothing and helmet, belted herself in, warmed the car and did deep-breathing exercises to exorcise her anger. Laura had already gone down to the track. Ginger took one look at Jane's face and stayed out of the way.

Time, which had been dragging, suddenly slipped away. Cars for the TVR handicap went round to the pit lane. Jane identified her place in the queue. The faster models and more experienced drivers were further back. The queue moved forwards, came under the orders of the starter who, flanked by two time-keepers with clipboards, began sending the slowest cars away according to their handicap times. Jane moved up to the head of the line. The wait seemed endless. Then he dropped his flag. Jane hustled the car off the line.

As soon as she was moving, she forgot her anger in the pleasure of driving fast. She had been too keyed up to notice it in practice, but there was a different feel, a change in sound and smell, racing an open car for the first time. She felt more in touch with the world.

The leading cars were already out of sight beyond the end of the first straight. In her mirror, the next car was still waiting to be released.

She took the first curve and the bend that followed, overtook one car and then another. These were inexperienced drivers, out for the fun of it but nursing their expensive machines. Well, she told herself, she had passed that stage. Nearing the end of the back straight, she glanced across. The fastest cars — expensive, overengined masterpieces — were still waiting to set off. She put them out of her mind, concentrating on the car and the road ahead. When she came round to the start again there was one car still waiting, the yellow car of Carl Lansdowne, but seconds later it blasted past her, still almost a full lap behind.

Picking off slower cars was easy. She found a rhythm, passing on a straight or using acceleration to overtake coming out of a corner. The TVR's suspension, slightly modified after the testing at the Road Research Laboratory, proved ideal and she soon had faith enough in the adhesion and handling, and in her own mastery of the car, to snatch at chances. There was enormous joy, she found, in carving a way forward, leaving others to eat her dust. The track flowed past around her.

So for lap after lap. There were only two cars in front of her when she looked in her mirror and saw one of the fastest cars behind her, a long way back but coming up fast.

She saw Laura but no red sweater, so she was still within her permitted speed. A few moments later, she crossed the start/finish line. The starter held out his flag, motionless, the signal for the last lap.

From some hidden reserve, Jane found fresh determination or courage or folly, call it what you will. She threw away reserve, forgot about safety margins. She left her braking late, attacked her corners more savagely but still coaxed the car through each curve on the perfect line, tyres singing shrilly, an ounce short of a desperate slide. There were three cars in her mirrors now, closer. It was not easy to judge distances by reflected images, but when she turned out of the back straight there was a car, a yellow car, in her mirror only a few seconds later. She attacked the last of the slowest cars and it fell behind.

The last bend before the finish was a fast curve. Jane held slightly out from the apex, leaving what she judged was not quite enough room for the yellow car to pass on the inside. For a moment she thought that he was going to try to bully his way through, expecting her to make way. But he hesitated. She thought that she might be able to beat him to the line, but he used his power advantage to blast past her as soon as they were out of the curve. As he went by, she saw a single finger raised in rude salute. Jane took the flag a few seconds after him. She had believed herself to be without any competitive instinct but, as she completed her slowing-down lap, her rush of emotions included chagrin, disappointment and a return of indignation.

When she turned into the *Parc Fermé* she saw the yellow car already stopped beside the office occupied by the clerk of the course. Lansdowne seemed to be complaining to somebody. If he wanted to lodge an objection to her driving, she would make a complaint about his rude gesture. There had to be a rule about it somewhere, there seemed to be rules about everything else. She parked in the space to which an official was pointing, took off her helmet and ran her fingers through her hair. 'What do I do now?' she asked.

'Hang on,' the marshal said, and hurried off to intercept another car.

She climbed out of the car, pulled her overalls down to her waist and clipped her summer skirt around. Laura had materialised, having slipped past the marshals into the *Parc Fermé*. She hugged Jane. 'You're a marvel,' she crowed. 'I didn't know you had it in you.'

Jane was ready to burst with the mixture of joy and laughter but she managed to keep a grave face. 'When I have it in me,' she whispered, 'you're not *supposed* to know.' Laura clung to her for support while the two girls sobbed with laughter. The men nearby, who had not heard the exchange, grinned sympathetically.

Jane was still struggling out of the bottom

half of her overalls when a large open car pulled up beside her. In the back were two men in racing overalls and baseball caps. The man at the wheel, who she recognised as a club official, leaned out. 'Quickly,' he said. 'Hop in. Didn't you know you had to do a lap of honour?'

'Nobody tells me anything,' she said. She left her overalls and helmet in the car and fluffed out her hair. The back of the car seemed rather full and Mr Andress, grinning broadly, was occupying the front passenger seat. 'Where do I go?' she asked.

'Tradition,' said the driver, 'all of eighteen months old, requires that, as the winner, you stand up in the back.'

'But Carl Lansdowne passed me just before the line.'

'He's been disqualified. He bettered his practice speed by just a little too much. A blatant attempt at sandbagging. We don't have a trophy for this event yet, but you get a bottle of bubbly. You'd better hold that aloft instead.'

A huge grin began somewhere in Jane's cerebral cortex, spread warmly through her whole body and arrived last at her face. She clambered over the feet of the nearer of the two drivers in the back of the car and received the champagne from Mr Andress.

The car started with a slight jerk. She grabbed and held onto the back of the driver's seat.

As they pulled out onto the course she saw Lansdowne, still beside the office. His jaw was thrust even beyond its usual and his scowl was a disfigurement. Just as the car surged forward, she let go of the seat back to return his salute. She would have fallen back but the men on either side of her, perhaps instinctively, put up a hand each to press her forward. They supported her throughout the lap of honour while Jane, her grin still in place, held up her champagne and waved to the crowd with her other hand. She could hear very little for the wind in her ears, but she could see the flutter of waving and handclapping and she felt the warmth of their pleasure.

★ ★ ★

Julian Berkeley, who had managed an honourable sixth-place finish, seemed not to grudge her her triumph. He walked down with Jane to watch the race for the Vauxhall Junior racing-cars. She collected congratulatory smiles all along the way.

Peter Moran, as Berkeley pointed out, had earned himself a place on the third row of the grid and when the flag fell he made a good start. Instead of enjoying the spectacle, Jane forced herself to concentrate, teaching herself a little more of the tactics. In the light of her recent experience, she had eyes now to see now how one driver might hold another back and the other make his own chances to crowd by.

Peter Moran drove well but could only manage fourth. The car sounded healthy. But Jane had reservations. 'I'll tell you what I think happens,' she said seriously. 'A designer gets everything right on the drawing board. But it doesn't happen exactly like that for production reasons. Any engineer will modify a design if it makes it cheaper to build or gets rid of one moving part.'

'And when you're a graduate engineer, you'll do the same?'

'I hope not,' she said seriously. 'That engine could produce a little more power. And the front suspension could stand a little tweaking.'

'You've decided, then?'

'No, certainly not,' Jane said. The idea was madness, but in the euphoria of her triumph she couldn't help toying with the idea.

'Very sensible,' said Julian Berkeley. 'But if you do decide to consider it, a trial run on a recognised circuit will cost you money. There are some private roads at my house. Just give me a phone.'

'That's very kind of you,' Jane said.

'Anything for your grandfather's granddaughter.'

★ ★ ★

That evening, Mrs Dodson put up a late supper for the returning heroes. It was served by Henry, who had again borrowed a limousine and brought a group of cronies to the races along with a case of beer. Raymon, who had been with the limousine party, joined them and at his request Henry visited the local pub to procure two large bottles of wine.

Gunge, who had been invited to join the party, was on a high. Jane, though slightly ashamed at having won the race strategically rather than by brilliant driving, was still smiling.

Laura, as Jane well knew, had two faces. Privately, between the two girls or with a boyfriend, she could be ribald, even Rabelaisian. In public, however, she showed a prim and prudish face. She had come down out of the clouds and was definitely disapproving. 'Have you any idea what you looked like?' she demanded.

'I thought that our hostess looked very beautiful,' Raymon said.

'Well, you would.' Laura gave him a glance expressing contempt for all men and especially Central Americans. 'For God's sake, Jane, what do you think the photographs in the local paper, and probably the nationals as well, will look like?'

'I don't suppose there'll be any.'

'You're out of your skull. There were photographers there, a girl winning a motor race is news and if you think they'd miss the chance of printing a photograph of you being groped by the drivers who came second and third — '

'Oh, come on!' Jane protested. 'I know what a grope feels like, and that wasn't it. All it was was that they were each supporting me with a hand on the back of my thigh.'

'With a hand up your bum,' Laura corrected sternly. 'And not outside your skirt, either. I thought you said you never wore stockings.'

'I said that I never wore a suspender belt,' Jane retorted with dignity. 'I never said I didn't wear hold-ups.'

Laura shook her head warningly. Mention of suspender belts while men were present was taboo. 'The way your skirt was blowing around, everybody knows now.

152

Creet, definitely.' (In the jargon of the students, *indiscreet* was considered to be a double negative.)

'If anybody had asked me, I'd have told them,' Jane said. 'It's no secret. I hate tights. And,' she added with a twinkle, 'that wouldn't have made such a good photograph.'

'Mrs Dodson will be shocked out of her mind.'

Henry had finished serving and joined them for a glass of Raymon's wine. 'Don't you believe it,' he said. 'My missis isn't so easily shocked. And she's very proud of Miss Jane.'

'Not from where I'm sitting,' Jane said. 'She still scolds me for wasting good time and money on fast cars which are properly the men's toys. She thinks I should be sitting by the fireside with my needlework.'

'It's a different story when you're not there,' Henry said. 'One of her chums at the social club said much what you just said, and the missis turned round and bit her head off. She said that when she — the other lady — could build a car as good as you could, and drive it as good as you could, then she could open her big mouth without putting her big foot in it. I wasn't there at the time,' Henry added regretfully, 'but I was told. And that was before you even won the handicap, miss.'

'Then she might not take it too badly if I switched into Formula Vauxhall Junior? I was offered one today, the one that came fourth.'

'Whoops!' said Gunge. 'Here we go!'

'Are you thinking of it?' Laura asked.

Jane had been toying with the thought, but only as a fantasy. Under the influence of Raymon's wine, her tongue was more adventurous. 'It's mad, but I might, if I could sell the TVR.'

'Perhaps I could help you,' Raymon said. 'At the race meeting, I met a young man I know. He is an arrogant puppy and not even from my own country, but we Latinos must stick together. His father has all the money to burn. The boy went to relieve himself when your race was just beginning and his English is not so good. He was most impressed by your win and I think he saw himself standing up in the back of a big car, waving a bottle of champagne to the applauding peasants. He wants to make a start in the racing. I could make an introduction. Of course, he did not realise that it was a handicap race. You could tell him or not, just as you pleased.'

* * *

154

The last examinations went by. For the others they were final degree exams, but Jane had made up her mind to go on for a honours degree and Laura had lost a year through changing courses. The two Scots would be leaving to take up jobs in Glasgow. They celebrated by taking Jane and Laura to dinner and seemed only slightly disappointed not to end up in their beds; but, as Laura had pointed out with more force than tact, after the amount of their native drink which had been taken the beds would only have been useful for their primary purpose.

Raymon would also be leaving to return to his native Colombia, where it was understood that there would be a place in a racing team awaiting him.

Unresolved was the matter of the cars. Jane still knew that the thought was madness, yet in her dreams she saw herself as mistress of a pure single-seat racing-car. Her competitiveness was satisfied and in those dreams there were no other drivers. She was alone on a track with a piece of elegant engineering to drive.

She phoned Laura's father, not for the first time.

'I'm sorry,' Gordon Black said. 'I know it's taking the very devil of a time. The civil law's a lumbering machine at the best of times, but it shows at its worst when one party wants to delay. However, I think we may be getting an offer of an interim settlement shortly. On behalf of you and two other creditors, we pointed out that we would definitely be claiming for business opportunities missed due to lack of working capital. That seemed to put them in the mood to part with their loose change.'

'What do they consider to be loose change?' Laura asked.

Gordon Black mentioned a figure which, to Laura, seemed quite substantial, although not to be compared to what her grandfather's house and effects had sold for. 'There would be the rest to come?' she asked.

'I think so. Eventually. Less whatever my professional brethren help themselves to along the way.'

'Get me what you can for now, please.'

With some kind of assurance of financial stability, Jane felt free to explore a little deeper into this adventurous new world.

She began by cornering Laura in the garden. 'If I go ahead with this,' she said, 'I'll need your help. I need a business manager.'

'I'm supposed to be doing a work project during the summer,' Laura said defensively. 'I thought I might go home and work in Dad's office.'

'He wouldn't pay you any more than you're already getting from him as an allowance,' Jane pointed out. 'This would be a perfect project for you. Business Manager to Faraday Racing Enterprises. Pay yourself a pittance out of the petty cash.'

'Add the word Developments on the end and you could call it FRED as an acronym. What would I have to do?'

'Everything except mechanicking and driving. Register for the championship and get the list of races. Find out what support and parts Vauxhall can provide, cheap if not free. Get us some sponsorship.'

'Sponsorship?'

'All the cars have advertisements on them. And I know that some of them get freebies of things like tyres if the car carries the maker's decal. That must be how they make ends meet if they don't have a rich dad. I'm told that the entry money would hardly be worth running after if it blew out of your hand and there can't be enough prize money to go round. Check with the Vauxhall dealers. Even free fuel . . .'

'I'll think about it,' Laura said.

'Well, while you're thinking, phone Mr Berkeley and ask if we can try Peter Moran's car next weekend at his house and let Raymon's pal have a test-drive in the TVR.'

'But we can't — '

'He *told me* we could,' Jane said sleepily. The deckchairs were surprisingly comfortable and she was lulled by a breeze in the trees and the sound of golfers' voices.

The story in the local paper, or perhaps the photograph of Jane with her skirt blowing in the wind, brought her to the attention of the local media. A woman's magazine sought an interview, a local radio station invited her to join a panel and she was asked to judge the *concours d'élégance* at a motor rally. 'You'll have to speak to my business manager,' was her unvarying response.

★　★　★

Jane had resumed her vacation employment with the computer consultants. Too often, a computer system could only be taken out of service and reprogrammed outside normal office hours, so Jane, with racing in mind, had made the sole proviso that her weekends would be free when she so wished, in return for which she would, whenever other engagements permitted, do any overnight or weekend duty required of her.

That weekend, the firm was engaged to disinfect the computer system of a large industrial complex, which system had been contaminated by several different computer viruses introduced by disaffected ex-employees with the appropriate skills. Jane promised to attend on the Sunday if still needed but, Mr Berkeley having expressed willingness, Jane and Gunge set off on the Saturday, complete with recovery vehicle, trailer and TVR.

Grey Gables, Mr Berkeley's house, was a well-known showplace and so was easily found. According to the glossier magazines, the present owner had caused two huge and hideous Victorian extensions to be demolished, returning the house to its original more modest eighteenth-century elegance. The house had originally been surrounded by spacious parkland which was now largely given over to farming.

'But,' Mr Berkeley explained after greeting them, 'there are plenty of roadways and drives. They're narrow but manageable and the stock's well accustomed to vehicles tearing around.' He drove them in his Range Rover round a circuit of estate roads extending to more than a mile. 'This is a circular tour that I — and one or two favoured friends — use for testing. Everybody on the estate has been warned to keep clear of it today between eleven and one. Go as you like on the tarmac but I'll be grateful if you take it easy on the one section of gravel.'

Peter Moran arrived a few minutes later, towing the little racing-car behind a Land Rover. The Formula Vauxhall Junior was unloaded in a yard between the house and a row of stables now apparently used as garages. Jane felt again the pang of pleasure at seeing engineering philosophy taken so near to purity and uncontaminated by mundane practicalities. She was given an exhaustive set of instructions on how to handle the car and solemn warnings about what would happen to her if she bent it. Then the car was readied and she donned her helmet. The car was started, using its own starter but a lead from the Land Rover to save the lightweight racing battery. She was ready to go.

She had expected the car to be different from anything that she had driven before, but not quite as different as it proved. For the first time, she was driving a machine which was fast, not because it had more than four litres of swept volume and nearly 400 b.h.p. but because it had been built down to a featherweight, so that a standard family car engine of 125 b.h.p. gave it an acceleration similar to that of the TVR.

Most of the estate roads were narrow and in places there were trees and other solid obstructions uncomfortably close to the verges. Only in one place was it possible to open up, and for only a few seconds. At the comparatively low speeds attainable the car seemed eager and responsive although she sensed that on an open circuit it might soon seem under-powered. The steering, heavy at first due to the wide tyres and lack of power assistance, became lighter at speed. She found the right-hand gear change with its very narrow gate difficult at first but once she had mastered it she found that she was already becoming attached to the look and feel of the car and the crisp rattle of the exhaust. It was a formula intended to help novice drivers to learn, in comparative safety, about such matters as tuning and set-up and the tactics of race driving, and at what some might consider to be modest cost.

So be it. She would try to strike a bargain, knowing that she would have to content herself with what she knew already to be financial folly, and the first time that she inflicted more than a minor dent on it, she would walk away with no more than a sigh.

But there was another essential step to be taken before she could think of committing herself to such an expenditure.

Rolando Valleja, Raymon's acquaintance, had arrived, later than promised, and was waiting beside a new-looking Audi saloon when she pulled up beside the trailer. He was tapping his foot as though he had been on time and everybody else was late. Jane had only met him for a brief introduction in the motor club. Seeing him in full daylight for the first time, she thought that he looked very young — but Raymon, she decided, had been right. The boy had an arrogance about him that grated on her. He was not quite as tall as she was and yet he somehow managed to look down his nose at her.

'Can you wait a little longer?' she asked Peter Moran. He nodded.

Rolando Valleja disdained any opening pleasantries, or else he did not have enough confidence in his English. 'I do not like the colour,' he said carefully.

It was a statement rather than a question so Jane saw no need to reply. He frowned. 'Very well. Let me try it.'

'All right,' Jane said. 'I'll come with you.'

She found herself looking up his nostrils. 'I do not need a girl to show me how to drive.'

Jane, pricked by conscience, had earlier made up her mind to explain that her win had been on handicap, but conscience and expediency began to take a rear seat. She rarely gave her temper full rein, but she prepared to snap back with an answer which, if only he could understand it, would have sent

162

the young pup back to the jungle with his tail between his legs. But while she was still mentally translating it into English simple enough for a five-year-old or a recently arrived Latin to understand, Julian Berkeley, who had been standing by with an air of interested amusement, broke in.

'It's always wise to have the owner with you,' he said. 'And Miss Faraday knows which of my roads you may take.'

Evidently ownership of such an estate was enough to convey authority. Valleja nodded and dropped into the driver's seat. He frowned again when Jane replaced her helmet. She strapped herself in, but evidently such precautions were beneath his dignity.

Jane had intended to say a few words before setting off, on such matters as the handling of the car and Mr Berkeley's wish that the one stretch of gravel be left undisturbed, but he set off in a burst of wheelspin before she could speak.

It was immediately evident that young Valleja was a capable driver, his reactions were very quick and his judgement good. That, Jane decided within the first few seconds, was just as well and was all that could be said to the good. A wise driver, in a strange car and on strange, narrow roads, would have set off carefully and felt his way, adding speed only gradually. Valleja made no such concessions to caution. He tackled the roads as though they were personal enemies. Jane hardly had time to signal him which turnings to take at the junctions and she had no chance at all to slow him down over the gravel, much of which he scattered over the grass to the later fury of Mr Berkeley's gardener. Jane, who loved speed for its own sake and was usually the most placid of passengers, was frankly terrified. Trees flicked past, seemingly so close that she drew her elbows in while stamping on imaginary brakes.

The episode seemed almost certain to end in tears. But she had one, literal, avenue for escape. As they came round to complete their first lap of the circuit she signalled him to take a driveway which led back to the yard. He pulled up there with a yelp from the tyres.

'I have not finished trying the car,' he said.

Once again, Mr Berkeley intervened quickly before Jane could blow her top and ruin any chance of a deal. 'You've had a fair test,' he said. 'And you know the race result. That should be enough for you. Miss Faraday will not want any more wear and tear on her car, any more than I want more wear and tear on my roads.'

There was a delay while young Valleja

worked out the meaning of the words and then decided on his own reaction. 'Is OK,' he said sullenly at last. 'We talk money?'

Tactfully, Peter Moran drew Gunge aside and she heard them discussing fuel injection. 'I'd like Mr Berkeley to be with me on this, if he doesn't mind,' she told Valleja. 'I may need advice.'

Mr Berkeley raised his eyebrows but said that he would be happy to be of help.

Despite that help, ten minutes later Jane was in despair. Valleja had offered a figure which, Mr Berkeley advised her privately, was low but within an acceptable bracket. Peter Moran, consulted separately, pointed to the volume of spares which he was including with the deal and declined apologetically to come below a figure substantially above Valleja's offer. The difference which she would have had to find would have been more than she could have justified to herself.

'I'm sorry,' she said at last. 'All deals are off.'

'One moment,' Mr Berkeley said. He drew Jane aside. 'If I understand you rightly,' he said to Jane, 'you'd be happy with an exchange, no cash adjustment. Yes?'

'I wouldn't even object to a cash adjustment,' she said. 'I just don't have it available.'

'For any commodity, there's a wide disparity of prices at which it changes hands. Otherwise, dealers could not subsist. Leave me for a moment with these two young men. If we can't do a deal, I'll find you another Vauxhall Junior car, one that's a couple of years old and runs in Class B. This car's almost brand new.'

Hope, which had been definitely defunct, began to twitch again. Jane walked to where Gunge was sitting on the tail-gate of the recovery vehicle, well within earshot. 'What do you think?' she asked vaguely.

Gunge took the question seriously. 'I think we'll have a lot of fun. But I'll be sorry to see the TVR go. We put a lot into that car.'

She looked at Mr Berkeley, who was arguing vehemently first with one and then the other. 'You think he'll be able to arrange something?'

'I'll bet you,' Gunge said slowly, 'that man gets whatever he sets his mind to.'

After another twenty minutes, Gunge was proved right. There were handshakes all round. Valleja gave Moran a cheque. Peter Moran unloaded what seemed to be a mountain of spares, winked at Jane and departed, towing the trailer which he had refused to throw in with the deal. The TVR was loaded onto its trailer and Gunge set off to follow the Audi. 'No need to come back,' Berkeley told him. 'Your acquisition, Jane — I may call you Jane? — will be quite safe in one of my outbuildings for a day or two. You'll see why in a minute. Stay to lunch, hear my proposition and I'll drive you home myself.'

'Is this to do with the sponsorship you mentioned?'

'That's the only proposition that I'm making to you today.'

Jane almost lost the thread of the discussion. She pulled herself together. 'Then I should phone my business manager to join us,' she said.

'Please do,' he said. 'Come into the house.'

★ ★ ★

It would be half an hour's drive at least for Laura in the Maestro. Julian Berkeley allowed Jane to gloat over her acquisition for a few minutes and then swept her into the house to telephone, dispensing the perfect G-and-T and chatting modestly but knowledgeably about the paintings on the walls of the drawing room. Old though it was, the house was in mint condition, but Jane noticed modern radiators and even more modern intruder detectors. Jane had half expected to be the target of a pass which was never made.

167

She wondered later why not and what her response would have been.

Laura's arrival was the occasion for another visit to the stables to display the car.

Lunch was cold chicken and salad with a chilled white wine which Jane, though no connoisseuse, recognised as excellent. There followed strawberries. Jane, after several glasses of the wine, could have floated to the ceiling. Laura, however, contented herself with a sip of the wine, waiting warily for the first mention of business.

It came with the coffee. 'As you probably know,' Mr Berkeley said, 'I'm very much involved with Alex Beauty Products.'

'You own it,' Laura said gruffly.

He shrugged, unsmiling. 'Insofar as anyone owns anything outright these days, yes. It's named after my late wife. I started the business in a small way in my youth, and it's still growing.'

'I use their products all the time,' Jane said. With the sudden perception of the slightly fuddled she added, 'The packaging is almost exactly that lilac colour. Is that why you said that I probably associated it with something pleasant?'

'I'm glad to have my guess confirmed. We have a good share of the market but we have to cling onto it and we're always struggling

168

for more. I've had it in mind for some time that a model stepping out of a car at the end of a race and still managing to look good would put over the message that our products can be trusted to stand up to rough conditions and bad weather. It might even bring in a section of the market that we may have been neglecting, the outdoor woman. We could feature it in our advertising, but more advertising would follow free.'

'But I'm not a model,' Jane objected.

'You're a very attractive girl and you photograph well. And that's not an idle compliment,' Mr Berkeley said, 'but the truth. However, the girl we choose would have to be able to drive well enough at least to qualify for races and you're the first to come along with that combination of looks and driving ability.'

It was all going rather too fast for Jane. 'I love what you're saying,' she said, 'but I don't think that I should listen to any more. It's good for my ego but bad for my swollen head. You two thrash out the details. I'll go outside for a breath of air.'

Her feet carried her, of their own accord, back to the stables. She squatted down to study the suspension. It had seemed to her, while driving the car, that there had been a slight and manageable but unnecessary

169

transmission of vibration to the driver's hands which must have been returned again to the road wheels. Through eyes which were now as critical as they were doting, she assessed the steering geometry. The design theory was sound but she was almost sure that a detailed examination would reveal a tiny discrepancy between theory and execution. The Ackermann angle, also, had been designed for a car with a different wheelbase.

She fetched a rug from the Maestro. It seemed appropriate to lie down on it. She and David de Vine had made love on it, high on a hilltop in summer, but the euphoria then had been no greater than today's. She studied the undertray. She wondered whether the car's makers would lend her a scale model for wind-tunnel testing. When Laura came out of the house, she was sound asleep on the rug with her head in the rear suspension.

In the Maestro, with the car heading for home, Jane asked grumpily, 'Why do we have to leave Junior there?'

Laura, at the wheel, slowed down. She never liked to drive and talk at the same time. 'It's all part of the deal we worked out. Mr Berkeley has interests all over the place. There's an engineering and painting department. I think it's where they look after the transport for Alex Beauty Products. He'll have the car moved there, resprayed lilac — '

Jane made a sound denoting distress. 'I thought we'd seen the last of that colour. You were right, it doesn't go with my hair. Couldn't they leave the car red and change the colour of their packaging?'

'Don't be silly,' Laura said sternly. 'How much did you have to drink before I got there? They'll paint the car lilac and put the Alex trademark on it. We're free to put other decals on, but no beauty products without prior agreement. I had to agree that you'd be paid on a per race basis — otherwise you could have taken the money and never shown the flag.'

'What sort of money are we talking about?' And when Laura told her, Jane commented, 'It's not a lot, is it?'

'We can get others, if we're lucky. And that's only a starter for ten. You get the same again if you get in the points, more for a podium place and more again for a picture in the press, still more for a radio interview if you manage to mention the product, a jolly good fee if you appear on television and double if you can get the car into the picture.'

'But I can't do any of those things,' Jane protested.

'Not on your own. But he's going to tell somebody from their PR department to liaise

171

with us. With your luck it'll be a good-looking bloke. With mine, he'll be gay.'

'That sounds all right, all except the gay bit. What's the downside?'

'I don't think there is one. Except that you're expected to be glamorous at all times when in the public eye and to make it clear to the media that you owe it all to Alex Beauty Products.'

'I can manage that,' Jane said. 'It's probably true.'

'Rubbish!'

A few more miles went by in contented silence.

'If Junior can't be raced for the next fortnight — '

'It'll take that long or longer to get entries accepted,' Laura pointed out.

'Don't interrupt. We may as well give the engine a little tuning. Could you ask Mr Berkeley to have it taken out and delivered to the heat engines lab at the university for me? The car can be mantled again at the service station.'

After a moment's thought, Laura identified *mantled* as the reverse of *dismantled*. 'I can try. You do realise that it's a sealed engine?'

'It can still be improved. And would you phone the racing drivers' school at Brands Hatch? I think it's called the Nigel Mansell

Racing School or something like that. See if they can fit me in for a lesson.'

'Steady on!' said Laura. 'You don't have to win anything, just as long as you qualify to enter.'

'And hang around looking pretty? Bugger that!' Jane said flatly. 'If I'm going to play with the big boys, I want to keep my end up.'

'But which end?'

Jane laughed without opening her eyes. 'That didn't sound quite right, did it? But you know what I mean. I don't want to be tolerated just because I'm nice-looking and forgiven because I'm only a token woman driver.'

'Point taken,' Laura said. 'But couldn't *you* phone them? I'm supposed to get what we agreed down on paper and sent to Mr Berkeley as soon as possible, for signing.'

'Do that later.'

'We don't touch any money until it's signed.'

'Good point,' Jane said. 'I'll do the phoning as soon as we get home. I'll have to go in and help the office tomorrow.'

'Ask if they'll sponsor you,' said Laura. 'And, Jane, don't waste your time setting your cap at Mr Berkeley. I know he's remarkably kempt, but there was a dyed blonde turned up just before I came away. A horsy type,

173

dripping money out of every orifice. Just when I was going to make him the sort of offer that nobody's ever refused yet.'

★ ★ ★

During the ensuing week, Jane saw very little of Laura. The employees made redundant during the streamlining of the client's business had excelled themselves in messing up the ungrateful employer's computer system. The reprogramming and protecting of that system finished late on the Tuesday evening. Jane claimed a day off in lieu and spent the Wednesday in the university's Heat Engines Laboratory with her friend Mr Yates, the chief technician. Mr Yates, who anyway had a soft spot for Jane, was happy to be kept occupied at the quietest time of the year. They coupled Junior's engine to the big dynamometer, Mr Yates produced some very sophisticated timing devices and they brought the machinery to a pitch of tune not even dreamed of by Messrs Vauxhall.

The racing school at Brands Hatch had had a cancellation and was pleased to book Jane in for a day for the Super Trial on the Saturday.

Without any boarders in the house, money was dribbling away as fast as Jane could earn it and she had a real fear that her cheque to the racing school might bounce. She sold two of her grandfather's pictures and his silver porringer and gave Gunge and the Dodsons each something on account of the wages for which they had never asked. (The Dodsons protested almost angrily; Henry was now under-manager as well as senior driver for the car-hire firm and the Dodsons had more money than ever before in their lives and nothing to spend it on.) Jane told them not to be silly. She put most of the balance into Laura's hands and went off to Brands Hatch.

The Initial Trial and the Super Trial, she knew, were different grades of instruction and test which, in theory, would either lead to longer and more intense courses or provide evidence of the competence of those wishing to enter more advanced stages of racing, but it was soon clear to Jane that more than half of the group attending that day had come for the fun of it and had no intention of setting even a toe on the ladder of the racing hierarchy.

The day began with a safety briefing and a lecture on the theory of high-speed driving which covered such matters as racing lines and techniques for cornering and braking. Most of it Jane had already discovered or figured out for herself by a mixture of

175

mathematics and common sense.

Outside again, a heavily built man introduced himself to her as her instructor. Jane's reading of the motoring journals was mainly devoted to the technical articles but she recognised the name of Jerry Foulds as belonging to a successful saloon and rally driver. He put her into the driver's seat of a BMW 318 and sat impassively as she felt the car out and gained enough confidence to put in a couple of fast laps. Then he took the wheel. Without pausing in a lucid explanation of how to get the most out of the car and how its handling would differ from a single-seat racing-car proper, he whipped the car round the circuit at the very limit of adhesion. His command of the car was absolute. Jane forgot to be nervous and did not once tread on imaginary brakes; she was much too taken up with filing away in her mind the technical explanations and, with even more care, the finest subtleties of noise and G-forces to which she was being exposed.

Next, she was introduced to a small single-seat racing-car. 'I want to know one thing,' Gerry said. 'You seem to have paid out good money on your helmet and overalls. Are you one of the joyriders who come for a thrill and something to talk about over the dinner table? Or are you going to be a serious driver?'

'I have just bought a car, almost the twin of this one,' Jane said with dignity.

'Good for you! Now, go out and show us what you can do. You're not allowed to go over three and a half thousand revs. And don't look at me as though I've stolen your lollipop. It'll take you to about eighty-five, which is quite fast enough for novices until we know what you can manage, and if you take Paddock Hill Bend at that speed on the adverse camber and probably a foot off the ground, it's like falling off the edge of the world on a tea tray.'

Jane went out again, alone this time. In the wide-open spaces of Brands Hatch, the car was subtly different from anything she had driven before, except that Junior would have had similar responsiveness if the driveways at Grey Gables had permitted. Armed with all that she had been told and shown, she attuned herself to the car and the track and soon the old joy of speed in a refined machine took over.

All too soon, Jerry flagged her to come back into the pits. She took off her helmet to hear what he was saying. He gave her a cup of tea and some words of advice and then turned aside.

One of the other pupils, a thin boy whose nose could have benefited from the attention of Old Fumble-fingers, smiled at her. 'Are you having fun?' he asked her.

She considered the question. 'I suppose I am,' she said. 'But that isn't what I came for.'

'What did you come for, then?'

'To learn, of course.'

'So that you can impress the boyfriend?'

Jane held onto her temper. 'So that I can be a driver on my own account,' she said firmly.

The thin boy sneered. 'Come off it! Girls don't get anywhere in this game, it doesn't come naturally to them and they don't have the physique or the judgement. Anyway, you'll only get yourself pregnant and have to give it all up.'

'Well, if I do,' Jane said grittily, 'it won't be bloody well yours.'

The other instructor tapped the thin boy on the shoulder. He nodded and picked up his helmet, but after turning away to his allocated car he delivered a Parthian shot over his shoulder. 'I'll tell the world it won't,' he said with feeling.

Jerry sent Jane out again. She left in a cloud of burnt rubber.

The two instructors watched. 'That girl,' Jerry Foulds said, 'will be good some day. She's very precise, very controlled, very

178

scientific, her reactions are fast and her judgement's good. She just needs a little real motivation. If she could release a little of that pent-up aggression . . . '

'She's releasing it now,' said the other instructor as the two cars went by. Jane was snapping at the heels of the thin boy. 'I hope she's safe.'

'She's still in control. Driving a car comes as naturally to her as farting. She's just too controlled. Most of the pupils we get here need to learn a little discipline. She needs to unlearn some of hers. I needed to work on her feminist temper. Did you see that red hair?'

'I'd have called it auburn.'

'Same difference. I put one of the lads up to making some sexist cracks, and now look at her go! But I'll bet you she still doesn't put a wheel over the line.'

The two cars came round again. Jane was in the lead and pulling away. He gave her the signal to come in on the next lap. She obeyed and stopped beside him. The Director's figure was approaching angrily. Jerry bent down as if giving Jane some advice, while resetting the telltale on the rev counter to a bland 3,650 — just enough over the permitted revs to be believable.

When the time came for debriefing and

evaluation, somebody had to go and look for Jane. They found her in the workshop behind the pits, arguing with one of the mechanics about the finer points of setting-up and tuning.

7

On her return from Brands Hatch, Jane was surprised to see a rather seedy camper-van parked in the garden. She supposed that it signified a visitor and ignored it. Mrs Dodson had gone out, perhaps with the visitor, but she had left a cold supper for Jane which she carried out into the garden. A warm day had become a beautiful evening. She found Laura reclining in the corner of the garden, enjoying the shade of the copper beech that stood just beyond the fence and in the grounds of the golf course.

Jane dropped into the second deckchair. 'Wow!' she said. 'Some day!'

'All right for some,' said Laura. 'If I've got to be the business manager, the firm should provide me with transport. When you take off with the Maestro, I'm stuck.'

Jane immediately felt both guilty and defensive. 'We can't afford to buy you a car yet,' she said. 'Wouldn't your father — ?'

'I couldn't possibly ask him for a car. Not just yet. He's been too good already, what with keeping up my allowance and letting me stay on here when it would be cheaper at

181

home. But I'm only winding you up for gallivanting off and leaving me with everything to do,' she said in more kindly tones. 'Now, before I forget, you'd better give me your receipts for today. It's a legitimate business expense and we may want to set it off against tax later on. In fact, I want all your expenses including last year's little fiasco. We have to build up an accumulated loss.'

Jane had managed to eat some of her meal during this speech. She swallowed quickly. 'But we're not earning anything worth taxing,' she protested.

'One of these days we may be glad of a loss to set against income. We've been having lectures about it at the College. And if you go along with what I've been doing it may be sooner rather than later. And, by the way, I really was pulling your leg about the car. We've both got transport.'

Jane wanted to know what Laura had been up to but, even more, she wanted to satisfy her hunger and tell Laura all about Brands Hatch. There was no possibility of indulging all three appetites simultaneously. But there was something that she wanted above all else. 'When do I get Junior fetched here?' she asked.

'You don't,' Laura said.

Jane breathed in a fragment of lettuce and

choked. When the paroxysm was over and she had wiped her eyes and blown her nose, she said, 'What the *hell*?'

'Now will you shut up and let me explain? You won't be racing until a fortnight tomorrow. The car stays at Alex Beauty Products until then because Mr Berkeley told Mr Waterton, his liaison man with us, that he preferred his paint shop to have control over what happens to the appearance of the car. Your other sponsors agreed that it would be better that way. It doesn't cost us anything,' she added hastily. 'I'm afraid none of them are paying very much money in the first instance, but we have the same sort of deal as with Mr Berkeley, with bonuses for successes or for interviews. I'm getting quite good at driving that sort of bargain.'

'What other sponsors?' Jane demanded.

'I tried Dad, but he didn't think the Law Society would approve of him advertising on a racing car. Then I phoned your boss — '

'Laura, you didn't!'

'Of course I did and he was very pleased because, after all, there are plenty of computers used in and around the racing cars.'

'But — ' Jane began.

'I'm trying to *tell* you. Then I had a few words with Mr Fadden, Gunge's dad. He wouldn't put up any money — as he said, we've been getting free use of his vehicle and trailer and a whole lot of petrol. He wants us to carry an ad for the garage and service station and also leave the car with him for his showroom window when it isn't being either raced or worked on.'

'But — ' Jane began again.

'Let me *finish*. In return we can have the trailer, because he wants a new one anyway. So the old trailer's gone over to Alex Beauty Products to be sprayed along with the car. Gunge can go on helping us. And, Jane, did you think we could sleep in hotels when we're too far away to get back here overnight? Do you know what that *costs*?'

'I haven't had much time to think about it,' Jane admitted. 'My mind's been too full of cars and things. I suppose I thought you'd enter me for races within reach of here. But that's not really practical.'

'No, not by a mile. Several hundred miles. So, for the other part of the deal, Mr Fadden gave us a camper that somebody traded in for a top-bracket used car. He said that it didn't owe him anything. I think he's hoping to get a Vauxhall dealership and thinks that Junior may catch the eye and impress the agents. The camper was a bit rusty and the inside's been converted by a not too clever DIY

184

enthusiast, but it's a sound goer and it has a towbar. Gunge wanted to know if there was a bunk for him in it, but I said definitely not, so he's going to bring his tent.'

Jane was horrified at the thought of juxtaposing her lovely racing car with the tired-looking camper. 'But if you're talking about the camper that's sitting in our driveway and making the house look tatty, it's *hideous*! I'm sorry, Laura, when you've done so well, but honestly it is.'

'I know. It does look rather tinguished at the moment. I tried to get either Mr Berkeley or Mr Fadden to have it sprayed for us, but neither of them was that daft. But I got Mr Fadden to go over the rusty bits with a sander and I'll pick up some paint and brushes on Monday. That'll be my first expenditure, other than phone calls, because I got Hugh to drive me around.'

It was all a bit much for a mind tired by a day of novel experiences to absorb, but Jane felt that she must seize on the introduction of an unfamiliar name. 'Hugh?'

'Sorry. Hugh Waterton, Mr Berkeley's go-between. He's rather dishy. And he can't do enough for us. He says he'll come over and help with the painting. And he'll come to most of the meetings where you're driving, if he's free.'

'He sounds like a gem. We'll have to breed from him.' The implication in her words brought another thought to Jane's mind. 'I don't have to sleep with him, do I?'

'No, of course not,' Laura said indignantly. 'That's my job.'

'Don't be silly,' Jane said. 'I meant, he doesn't have to share the camper with us, does he?'

Laura lowered her voice. 'In fact, I wasn't being silly. Because, between you and me and the bedpost, I've already done it.'

Jane sat up straight. Laura was inclined to let her tongue rather than her passions have a free rein. She carried with her and sometimes exploited an aura of sexuality, but Jane suspected that her actual experience might be less than she claimed. 'Laura, have you really?'

'Ssh!' Laura pointed to the hedge, beyond which the sound of golfers' voices could be heard. 'I shouldn't have said that. Anyway, it just sort of happened, the way it does. We clicked, and we were both carried away by all the new happenings.'

'So you christened the new camper?'

'Certainly not.' Laura sounded shocked. 'We went to a motel.'

It was some little time before the talk returned to business.

The camper was hastily hand-painted a lilac colour close to that of the Alex BP packaging and immediately looked more nearly respectable.

Hugh Waterton was a man in his early thirties though a prematurely receding hairline added a few years to his apparent age. He had the tough and slightly battered look of the rugby player and Jane, without herself being tempted, could quite understand why Laura seemed ready to melt in his presence. He and Laura did most of the work between them. When it was finished they stood back to admire their handiwork, but while the paint was still sticky a puff of breeze carried grit from the drive onto it. It still passed muster from a few yards away and, as Laura said to Jane, 'It looks no worse than if it had done a few miles since it was last washed.'

'When we're rich,' Jane said, 'we'll buy a better one. Or at least have this one decently sprayed.'

'We might even get a proper transporter,' Laura said.

'Don't get carried away.'

The interior, though habitable, lacked facilities. Laura visited the nearest caravan

187

shop and was indignant when the proprietor would not accept an advertisement on the side of the camper, or even the racing car, as part payment of his account for a small cooker, gas cylinders and a Portapotti.

The racing car and trailer were brought to the service station by Hugh Waterton. Jane, Laura, Gunge and his father and Hugh stood in the forecourt, admiring them. The lilac colour looked more appropriate than it ever had on the sports TVR and the logos stood out crisp and clear. The Alex Beauty Products insignia in particular had been executed in gold leaf and looked as smart as a Guardsman's badges.

'Well,' Laura said, 'I must say that they've done a lovely job. Jane, if you damage it I'll scratch your eyes out.'

'That's nothing to what I'll do,' Hugh said.

But Mr Fadden Senior leaped immediately to Jane's defence. 'Don't make the girl nervous,' he said. 'Her job is to win. Damage is a risk she has to take. If it happens, it happens, and she'll have to mend the car any way she can. We can help.'

'Point taken,' said Hugh. 'We'll just have to do the painting over again.'

Jane had been checking to make sure that the reinstallation of the engine had been properly carried out, but she became aware of the direction the talk had taken. 'If I damage the car badly,' she said, 'I've had my fun. That's it over. I've no more money. So I walk away.' She walked away.

Mr Fadden looked at Hugh. 'We could work something out,' he said.

★ ★ ★

Half the season remained. There began what Jane came to think of later as a halcyon period in her life. She had still not received even an interim settlement of her grandfather's estate. Money was going to be tight but the girls — they still thought of themselves as girls — made up their minds to enjoy life. Penury might come later.

Mr Fadden was willing for Gunge to continue dancing attendance on them. The garage and service station had been promised its dealership and Mr Fadden, rightly or wrongly, attributed this to the presence of Junior in the showroom and the fact that the men from the manufacturers had been shown that it was powered by one of their own engines. Beside Junior had been exhibited a huge enlargement of a photograph of Jane on her lap of honour, exhibiting her bottle of champagne and a lot of leg. The foundations were now in for the prefabricated extension to the showroom.

One important point was for immediate negotiation. 'Will you please call me something else? Ginger would do. Smartarse if you insist. Anything. But not Gunge.'

'But Ger ... Ginger,' Laura said, 'we didn't know you minded. You should have said.'

'I didn't mind, exactly,' said the rechristened Ginger. 'But we're going in among professionals now, some of them. They may look down their noses at me. Well, I'm big enough to take it. But there's no point asking to be laughed at and giving them a starting point.'

So Ginger he was from then on.

Jane was abashed to see that Ginger had feelings. She was ashamed to realise that she had been looking on him almost as an automaton. 'Does it bother you if I refer to you as 'my mechanic'?' she asked him. 'It has a good sound to it when I'm among the wealthy boys.'

'That's OK,' Ginger said. 'It's what I am.'

'I'll say you're my friend, if you like,' Jane offered. 'That's what you are.'

'There's no need to go overboard,' Ginger said austerely.

Backed by a glowing report from Brands Hatch, Laura had registered Jane for the championship and had had entries accepted for seven races, one almost every alternate weekend — which, Jane agreed, was quite enough of a programme for a beginner. They felt, at first, like new girls at school. They were met with a variety of attitudes, and although some were suspicious of Jane's lack of experience very few were hostile. Most were friendly, some were flirtatious or even lecherous, one or two were patronising, but, as soon as it was seen that Jane was competent and neither a threat nor a danger, she was accepted.

There were other outfits on shoestring budgets and a camaraderie developed among them. They pretended an inverted snobbery, looking down on the teams with money to burn, the avenues of entertainment pavilions, the townships of luxurious transporters.

Their routine began to become established. Jane could not always get away for midweek practice but, by working through the intervening weekend, managed it more often than not. They aimed to arrive early. While Ginger shifted tools and wheels into the driver's area of the camper, Laura readied the living area and began preparations for a meal or took a walk through the village of marquees to see what free hospitality was on offer. Often they managed to subsist by crashing some reception and making a meal from the hors d'oeuvres, thus making valuable savings on food and gas.

Jane, who was still determined to keep an edge on her physical fitness, would run or jog round the circuit while taking note of bumps, hollows, kerbs and any other features worth her notice. In the light of her observations, she and Ginger might adjust the set-up of Junior. She made a point of getting out as early as possible for each practice session and putting in a few furious laps while the track was uncrowded. She also went out early at qualifying sessions but was careful not to put up a time which would have brought her far from the back of the grid. She was becoming absolutely familiar with Junior, whatever the set-up, but lack of experience made her feel very vulnerable in the middle of a jostling pack; and with her finances at such a low ebb a single shunt might put her out of racing for ever. So she would set off near the back and spent most of each race picking off less able drivers or those whose cars were less well prepared. She enjoyed herself immensely and often finished halfway up the field. She made a point of getting out of her overalls and into a skirt as soon as she was out of the car.

The Formula Vauxhall Junior race would only take up a small fraction of a weekend.

Far more was devoted to ancillary events in which the drivers were expected to confront either the media or the public. As one of the very few female drivers — and the only one at that time with any claim to beauty — Jane had more than her due share of media attention, which, as Laura pointed out whenever Jane objected to being put on display, all helped to postpone the day when the kitty would be completely empty. That day seldom arrived, usually seeming to be a week or so ahead, but there were times when Jane closed her eyes to the uncomfortable certainty that the Dodsons were settling the grocery bills.

Her fifth race-meeting with Junior proved a turning point. As soon as the qualifying session opened, she went out and put up several fast laps — faster than she had intended, because the circuit was very much to her liking. As the other cars began to occupy the track she pulled off; and at that moment, out of a cloudy but bright sky, came the rain. It was unexpected and dead against the forecast. It fell in a steady downpour, rattling on the roof of the camper as they ate and bouncing off Junior's tarpaulin cover, only letting up as racing began.

There was some grumbling among the majority of competitors who had left their qualifying laps too late, but most shrugged. It was the luck of the draw and only a few had benefited by getting in their timed laps before the deluge. To her great trepidation, Jane realised that she had qualified third, earning a place in the second row of the grid. The snarling pack — of wolves, she just checked herself from thinking — would be starting behind her this time. For a few minutes she considered faking some mechanical fault and withdrawing. But no. Ginger was giving up his time for her, paid irregularly if at all. Laura was working for her and Laura's father, her own solicitor, was continuing Laura's allowance when he could have insisted that she take a properly paid summer job. Her sponsors had put up good money to help her keep going. And there were the Dodsons . . . She could not let them all down. She would have to stay out in front until the pack thinned out.

Ginger joined them for lunch in the camper. Jane, never much of an eater on race day, could hardly swallow a crumb. In her mind was a vision of arriving at the first corner with a dozen cars, driven by crazy drivers, all around her and determined to pass at any cost . . .

'Know who's here?' Ginger said suddenly. 'That Valleja guy. There's Tuscan Challenge on the programme and he's running the TVR. He's sprayed it silver. Looks good. He's put a lot of the racing mods on but he's still outclassed. Do you know what he's telling people?' Ginger failed to see a sudden agonised warning look from Laura. 'He's putting it about that he only agreed to buy the car so that you'd sleep with him.'

The silence in the camper made the drumming of the rain seem all the louder.

'He's only trying to explain how he came to buy a car that can't keep up,' Laura said nervously. 'He's a louse and far from gusting. Put him out of your tiny mind.'

Jane thought of spreading the true story around. Surely that would make Valleja look enough of a fool. But no. She knew where Latin pride was centred.

'I am not very gruntled. You get out there,' she told Ginger. 'Spread the word. Tell them that the story's true. But tell them that when it came to the point he couldn't get it up. Say that I was laughing about it next morning.'

Laura chortled but Ginger had to be persuaded. He knew how deadly was the slur.

Jane was still irritated as she approached Junior, ready to go out onto the rapidly drying track and make her way down to the start. The driver in the adjacent pit, one Harry Appleby, who had qualified in pole

195

position, pushed up his visor. 'How come you've got all the advertising?' It was true that several more decals had arrived on Junior, among them one for a smoking-cure preparation. It had occurred to Laura that, if much of motor racing was funded by tobacco advertising, the converse might also be acceptable. 'I suppose it's because you're prettier than I am.'

Jane was amused but in no mood to take the remark as a compliment. 'I see it the other way round,' she said. 'It's because I'm not as ugly as you are.'

'What's bugging you? Is it the wrong time of the month?'

Jane stiffened. She was blessed with very light periods and had never experienced a change of mood. It never occurred to her that he might be as nervous as she was, as perturbed at finding himself on the front row and as worried about sponsorship money. As they went round on the warming-up lap she focused her annoyance on the back of the leader's helmet, and when the lights changed, while Appleby lost time with excess wheelspin, she made the perfect start. The second-place starter should have been able to tuck between them before the first corner, but she left him no room and he fell back.

Jane was in full control of the car and her

temper, but she was determined to show the chauvinist pig that she could drive. Appleby found himself pursued by a demon. At every corner he felt that he was being attacked from one side or the other, sometimes both. Inevitably, he made a mistake at last, braking too late and leaving a gap on the inside of a corner. Instantly, as it seemed, the lilac car was into the gap. Appleby could not afford a contact any more than Jane could. He gave way.

Now established in the lead, Jane paid more attention to her mirrors. The pack was still bunched terrifyingly not far behind her. But even if the cars had been strung out, she would not have slowed. Her frustration had blown away, but now she was on top of her own little world. She held the lead to the end.

Appleby, who had fallen back to a humbler fifth place, arrived in the *parc fermé* when Jane was already out of her overalls. She had almost forgotten the reason for her irritation; indeed she was feeling almost contrite at her treatment of him, but she could not pass up the chance to have the last word.

'What was the matter with you?' she asked him. 'The male menopause?' She went on her way and forgot the incident, never realising the resentment that she left behind. In her view, it had been no more than tit for tat.

When Jane had had her moment on the podium, the prizes had been presented and the interviewers had had their pound of flesh, Jane returned to the camper. Laura and Ginger and Hugh Waterton were waiting for her. She was roundly kissed. Somebody (unidentified) pinched her bottom. The champagne was opened.

Jane thought at first that Laura's ecstasy over her win was solely out of pride in her victory or possibly feminist triumph, until Laura explained. 'I'm pleased,' she said, 'because of the money I can claim off your sponsors. They thought that they were getting the best of the bargain, but now they have to cough up. Solvency may even rear its head.'

Jane had almost forgotten that there was a financial side to her success, but it was soon forced on her attention. The event had been attended by television cameras on behalf of satellite television, but Jane's win and subsequent presence on the podium, conspicuously girlish compared to the overalled and baseball-capped men on the lower steps, turned their footage from Feature into News. Jane's win was not unique. Other ladies had won races. But Jane was photogenic. She featured on the TV news. Photographs of her being sprayed with champagne appeared in papers and magazines. (Her own bottle of champagne she had brought away unopened. It seemed a shame to waste it when her small team deserved a taste of her success.)

She was interviewed several times on radio and once on an off-peak television chat-show. She insisted on leaning against Junior while the TV interviews were conducted or photographs were taken. The empty bank account of Faraday Racing Enterprises began to look almost healthy again. Debts were settled and further sums were distributed in lieu of proper wages.

From then on, Jane's confidence never deserted her again. She had a proper respect for the dangers entailed in racing — she witnessed enough accidents to make sure of that — but she never again threw away an advantage out of caution. Whenever she felt that the aggression she needed to drive her onward was deserting her, she had only to think of the very occasional sneers which she had received and then to imagine that all her male competitors were similarly resenting the presence of a mere girl in their august ranks. But her anger was never hot and it was focused on whipping the car round each circuit without wasting a fraction of a second, in order to demonstrate that she was there on merit, not on sufferance.

She had been entered for two more races that season. They went to the first with high hopes, but other cars were as good as hers and the drivers were more experienced. She qualified well, for the third row of the grid, but inexperience and the need to stay out of trouble told against her and she finished seventh, just outside the points.

The next meeting would be the last of the season. It would also be a major occasion at which the championship for that year would be decided. There were still four drivers in possible contention. Competition would certainly be fast and furious. But Jane was determined to do her utmost. There was a long winter ahead. If Junior suffered less than total damage, there would be time to carry out repairs at home.

The circuit was new to Jane. She set off, soon after arrival, on her usual jog round the track. Several other drivers were walking round and one was being carried along the straights in a chauffeur-driven Daimler, only dismounting to explore each bend on foot. But to her surprise there was one other jogger. He overtook her as she paused to study the apex of the second bend.

'You're Jane Faraday, aren't you?' he said.

'I've seen you around.'

'In your mirrors, probably,' Jane said. 'You're Peter Fasque. Right?' She recognised the lanky figure and tight-knit brown curls of one of the four drivers in contention for the title.

His smile relieved the harshness of a lean face. 'I've seen you in my mirrors, yes. But I've seen the back of your head too. I was chasing you for all I was worth, that time that you won, and I couldn't make any impression. What on earth have you done to that car?'

She was tempted to say 'Driven it,' but Fasque was not patronising her and she sensed that it would be the wrong answer. 'Took it to pieces and put it together properly,' she said.

They finished their examination of the verges. 'Let's move on. No, seriously,' he said. 'I gained slightly on you at the corners but you were pulling away from me on the straights. Where did you find the extra power?'

'I'll tell you, if you tell me where you got the extra grip.'

They jogged round companionably together. Neither got short of wind. At the curves and hairpins they exchanged comments, but on the straights they had time to converse. He was ungrudging in advice which, she found, was mostly specific to Formula Vauxhall Junior and so took her a step beyond what she had learned at Brands Hatch. At first, for her part, she was hesitant, because she was not quite sure that all of her adjustments to Junior were quite within the spirit of what was supposed to be a one-design formula, but his questions were directed towards what she considered to be tuning rather than modification. She answered frankly and when he thanked her he sounded sincere. She thanked him in return. He said that they should form a mutual admiration society. She asked where she should pay her subscription.

The morning practice was less satisfactory. Junior ran well and she put up a fast qualifying time but on what was intended to be her fastest lap she suddenly saw yellow flags. She slowed immediately. At the chicane, a badly damaged car was being removed from the trackside but she was relieved to see that the driver, still shrouded in his helmet, was on his feet. She thought that she recognised Peter Fasque's car.

Sure enough, Fasque returned to the pits on foot half an hour later, after practice was finished. His way took him past where Jane and Ginger were giving Junior a last check-over. He paused beside them.

'What happened?' Jane asked him.

'Sudden and total brake failure. Result, expensive disaster.'

'What did you hit?' Ginger asked him.

'Everything,' he said simply.

'Much damage to the car?' Jane asked.

'It's repairable,' he said, 'but not today. So bang, quite literally, go my chances of the championship. Which is a real pain in the backside, because my father said that he'd pay for me to move up to Formula Vauxhall if I won it. I think he thought that his money was safe, and now it seems that he's right.'

'Would I like your father?' she asked.

He grinned reluctantly. 'I doubt it.'

'Then drive my car.' As soon as the words were out, she wanted to call them back. She had a vision of Junior lying crumpled beside the other car, endless arguments about money and an end to her own racing career. 'That's if you can fit your big bum into it,' she added. He was about the same height as she was.

His face lit up. 'You mean it?' Before she could deny any such intention, he had slid into the cockpit and settled himself.

'Do you have clearance for your knees?' Ginger asked him.

Peter fitted the steering-wheel into place

and ran his fingers round the rim. He transferred his foot from clutch to brake and back again. 'It feels pretty much like my own car,' he said. 'Which, of course, it should.' He removed the wheel again and climbed out. 'I'll be back. I have to make it all right with the clerk of the course.' He cantered away along the pit lane.

Jane looked round. Laura, Hugh and Ginger were gaping at her. 'Did I do something stupid again?' she asked the three of them.

'Probably not,' Hugh said. 'But if he wrecks the car . . . '

'I know,' Jane said. 'Do you think I don't know that?' Hugh nodded and slipped away. Jane later realised that he had gone to alert the media. 'He's already bashed up one car. It'll be at least an hour and a half before he's ready to bash up another one. I know, I've been there. If he did, I think he'd make good,' she finished unhappily.

'But you're not sure,' said Laura. 'Jane, I never thought I'd live to see you give up a chance to drive, let alone put everything at risk.' She lowered her voice, a sure sign that she was also about to lower the tone. 'What got into you? Is it his blue eyes or his sweet talk? I saw you come back together from inspecting the track. What did you get up to, out in the boondocks? Whatever boondocks may happen to be.'

'Absolutely nothing,' Jane insisted. 'I just didn't think it was fair that he should lose his shot at the championship out of pure bad luck.'

'It may not have been bad luck,' Ginger pointed out. 'Brake failure sounds to me more like sloppy maintenance, in which case it was his own damn silly fault.'

'I'll remember that any time my brakes let me down,' Jane retorted. 'Anyway, maybe he won't be allowed to switch cars.'

But even before Peter Fasque came loping back to them, the PA system had announced the change of race numbers and Jane's retirement. Ginger helped him with several minor adjustments to make the controls a better fit, but Jane, now that she was committed, was too nervous to watch. Her car and her future were on the line.

She climbed into the camper and tried very hard to listen to a radio talk about Gregorian chant. Then she walked along the avenue of marquees until she found a champagne reception that she could crash. But when the time for the race came round, she was watching from the wall of the pit lane. If there had been a *concours d'élégance*, she thought, Junior would certainly have won. The little car shone. She could see little of the track beyond the start and finish straight and could only hear the commentary in the moments when no cars were passing, but she could imagine the cut and thrust, the bluff and counter-bluff, even the game of Big Boys' Dodgems that might be going on in what Laura had called the boondocks. She found herself wondering what a boondock might be. Did it have a mother? Did it just sit there looking stupid? Did it, by any chance, wonder what *she* was?

Jane pulled herself together. This was a mere mixture of champagne and mental escapism. Peter Fasque was driving well. After losing a place or two at the start, possibly because of the unfamiliar feel of Junior's clutch, he seemed to be recovering a place almost every lap. But by the time of the last lap the leaders were mixed with the tail-enders and she was not quite sure . . . Then, as the noise died, she heard the commentary. Peter Fasque had come second.

'Thost!' she cried at the top of her voice.

Laura had joined her. 'I don't know what that word means, but you never use it when you're gruntled.'

'I'm not gruntled now. He only got second. After I gave up my drive for him!'

'Second's pretty good. It may be enough.

And at least he doesn't seem to have dented the car.'

'Thank goodness for small mercies.' Jane had not followed the championship scoring and Laura's meaning was only just becoming clear. 'You mean he may still have won the championship?'

'Yes, of course,' Laura said impatiently. 'The winner of the race wasn't still in contention. As long as the wrong person didn't come third or fourth, your dreamboat's home and dry.'

Before Jane had time to ask who was the wrong person, Hugh Waterton arrived, panting. 'Fix your make-up and come along,' he said. 'Press conference.'

'Did he win the championship?'

'Yes, of course. Surely a mathematician could work that out?'

Jane was bustled along the pit lane to the interview room where Peter Fasque was waiting. He smelled of wine but, along with two trophies, he was nursing an unopened bottle of champagne. If he had had a tail, he would have been wagging it. 'I remembered your habit of saving your bubbly for your team,' he said. 'Somebody said that champagne is only white wine that a frog farted in, but I thought you had a sound idea. But this time, your team has more claim to it than mine. We'll crack it later.' The driver who had won the race, beaming from ear to ear and right up over his receding hairline, handed her an opened bottle and a glass and they toasted each other politely.

The few journalists present, and later the commentator who interviewed them leaning proudly over Junior, were less interested in the race than in the loan of the car from one driver, and a female one at that, to a man and presumably a rival. Jane tried to point out that she had not been a rival for the championship, but nobody seemed to be listening.

They continued not listening as she and Peter denied any suggestion of a romance between them. Then the television commentator asked Peter if he didn't owe Jane a debt of gratitude.

'Of course I do,' Peter said. 'I'm more grateful than I can tell you.'

'Deeds speak louder than words,' said a woman reporter. 'Give her a kiss.'

Jane and Peter Fasque faced each other, ready to laugh. But the laughs faded into a smile and they touched lips. Neither tasted of anything but champagne. Peter was still in an exalted state over his championship while Jane was happy that Junior had carried him to victory, been given a share of the glory and returned undamaged. Neither felt like breaking off what was proving to be a rather pleasant experience. He took her round the waist and without any conscious intention on her part her arms went up and her glass emptied down his neck. She was feeling the effect of what had been rather a lot of champagne.

Jane was jerked back to reality by the realisation that Peter was developing an erection. She withdrew her tongue and broke off the kiss.

'For God's sake don't move,' Peter whispered. Jane put a decorous inch between them.

'Now ask her to marry you,' said the woman reporter. She had an American accent, Jane noticed.

They both laughed, but Peter added a wink and, for the benefit of the cameras and the listening microphones, said, 'Will you marry me?'

'No, I bloody well won't,' Jane said. 'I want a husband who can be trusted to go home in one piece while I'm away racing.' Everybody laughed. 'That's it,' she added. 'Interviews over.' She could feel Peter's erection beginning to subside. She turned her back to him, still hiding his mid-section from the cameras. She caught the eye of the American reporter.

'Tell me,' she said, 'what is a boondock?'

'Military slang,' said the reporter. 'Literally a mountain, but it's applied to anywhere in the backwoods. It comes from some Indonesian language.'

'Thank you,' Jane said. 'I've been wondering.' She felt gently with her bottom, but Peter's erection had quite gone. Cameras were being stowed. It was safe to move away from him.

'I've something to tell you,' Peter said. 'I'll come back to your camper with you.'

'It's not confidential, is it?'

'Not from your team.' As they walked he said softly, too low for Hugh Waterton to hear, 'I hope you weren't embarrassed by that. Any of it.'

She was both amused and touched by his consideration. Her knees still felt slightly uncertain. 'I took it as a great compliment,' she said. 'All of it.' He said nothing but when she glanced at him she saw that the smile was there again.

Ginger must have collected Junior from the *parc fermé* because the car was back on its trailer. Jane was conscious of a pang. It was as if her beautiful car had been unfaithful to her, carrying somebody else to a podium position. She hurried with Peter into the camper where Laura had already put out cold snacks and tea. Glasses were produced. The champagne made a satisfactory report but Jane cocked her head and said, 'Timing's a bit too far advanced.'

Only Ginger laughed.

Jane found that she was ravenous. Laura and Hugh would have to drive and so contented themselves with a single glass of champagne apiece, but Peter's elation had already infected Jane and now spread to Ginger.

Peter held up his glass. 'I ought to make a speech and drink a toast out of your trainer, but I'll limit myself to saying that I'm eternally in your debt and if I can ever return a favour you'll only have to ask. Anything. Anything at all.'

Jane wanted to shout, *Yes! Sweep me off my feet. Carry me off to some mountain-top where you can ravish me slowly and beautifully, paying no heed to my screams.* 'Was that what you wanted to tell me?' she asked.

'No. What I wanted to tell you' — Peter paused, thought back and remembered — 'was that somebody made me an offer for your car. A damn good offer. He didn't want me to tell you who he was, but I owe you and I don't owe him a damn thing so I don't see why I should be secretive about it.'

'So who was he, then?' asked Laura.

'Didn't I say? Young chap, sort of Spanish-spoken. Valleja's his name. Very taken with your car but he seems to think that if you knew who was after it you'd rip him off. Again, is what he said.'

'Hold everything,' Hugh said. 'Before you decide anything, I want to speak to Mr Berkeley. He'll know what's best. Where's my mobile? In my car,' he said, answering himself. He stepped down out of the camper and they saw him rush to his car and hunt among the coats on the back seat for the phone.

'How come that guy Berkeley knows all about racing?' Ginger wanted to know. 'All right, so he worked up to Formula Three Thousand, once upon a time. Well, big deal! Does that make him an expert?'

'No,' Laura said. 'What makes him an expert is this. When he was re-equipping and modernising the factories at Alex Beauty Products, he put a lot of work to . . . Just a minute.' She paused and wrinkled her forehead. 'It was all in that profile I told you about, Jane. Yes. KB Tools. He liked the firm but decided that there was room for streamlining and better quality control, so when he became chairman of Alex, with his Alex BP hat on he bought a whole lot of their shares and got voted onto the board. He's vice-chairman now and due to be chairman next year. And KB Tools owns Leopold, lock, stock and barrel.'

'Leopold Engines?' Jane said, sitting up. 'I didn't know that. Racing engines? Fire pump engines? Generator engines?'

'To cut a long story short,' Laura said, 'yes. Every kind of damn engine. And Leopold run a successful Formula Three team to develop and test and promote their engines. That's why I've been straining every sinew to keep in with him. He could help you a lot.'

'Wow!' Jane said absently. 'You should have told me.'

'And have you offer him your little pink body in exchange for a drive? That's my job. Don't listen to us,' Laura added quickly in Peter's direction. 'We're only joking.'

'I guessed that,' Ginger said. He took a gulp of his champagne. 'Are you going to sell Junior?' he asked.

Jane was wondering the same thing. 'Let's see what Hugh comes back with,' she said. 'Is there anything left in the bottle?'

Hugh was back in five minutes. He consulted a page of notes in his little book. 'Mr Berkeley says that it's entirely up to you. Well, he always says that. He's confident that you're ready for the next stage. We both are.'

'Well, thank you for that,' said Jane.

'Not at all. And Mr Berkeley's been very pleased with the exposure so far. He went on to say that he's about to offer another driver a place in Formula Three, so there will be a good Formula Ford car on the market. That's a step between, in case you didn't know. He can secure it for you if you want it. If you go ahead, he'll offer better terms on the publicity deal and we'll look after the paintwork and decals as before.'

'We've a load of spares,' Jane said. 'We've been Vauxhall Junior up to now. They'll be no use to us.'

'I could take a list along and bump him up a bit,' Peter said. 'He's coming to meet me after the last race.'

'Which is about now,' Laura said.

Jane had been thinking furiously. 'Would my entries be accepted if I climb up another step?' she asked.

Hugh looked down at his notes. 'Mr Berkeley covered that point. He said your results in the Junior series qualify you. And entries have fallen since they switched to the Zetec engine.'

Jane made up her mind. She had half hidden from herself the thought, germinating two weeks earlier, that Junior had begun to seem rather underpowered. She would relish a car which could go as fast as she could drive it. 'We keep the trailer. Are you sober enough to handle a deal?' she asked Peter.

'I'll go along with him and see fair play,' said Hugh.

'Then go ahead,' said Jane. 'But one thing. He does not get his hands on Junior until we have the money in our hands. And I don't mean a cheque which could be stopped.'

'Leave it to us,' Peter said. 'If the deal comes off, I'll arrange delivery. Now I must rush. He'll be looking for me. And my girlfriend will be wondering what's happened to me.'

Laura looked in a file and produced a sheet of paper. 'You'll want this,' she said. 'I keep a stocklist of our spares.'

Peter and Hugh set off in a hurry.

'He has a girlfriend,' said Laura.

'Don't they all?' Jane said.

8

Jane's racing season would have been finished even if she had still had a car. The last race of the season was over and the autumn term was almost on them. This would be Jane's Honours and Laura's final year.

But first, provision had to be made for the next season. Jane was still of a mind to continue racing. When the money finally ran out, she would retire.

Jane and Ginger went off in the Maestro, which was now definitely feeling its considerable age, to inspect the Formula Ford car. The Maestro complained but it managed the hundred-mile round trip without actually breaking down. The racing-car was also in far from pristine condition. It was only a few months old but looked many times its real age. The owner had been more concerned with getting to the head of the field and staying there than with such refinements as sparing the car or systematic maintenance. He admitted that the engine had already earned an honourable retirement. Jane and Ginger poked and prodded and crawled over and as far as possible under, deciding that many of the moving parts were due for replacement. But the parts were relatively inexpensive, the design was basically sound and after a little haggling the price was lowered to match the condition of the car.

Jane handed over a cheque which represented a large part of what she had been paid for Junior. Ginger went back next day with the camper and the trailer to collect the car, which they had agreed would be called Henry Two, after the ingenious Mr Ford but to distinguish it from Henry Dodson, who was allowed to believe that it had been named in his honour.

For once, time was singing in tune with Jane. The interim settlement of her grandfather's estate had been paid at last. (A brisk attempt had been made to have her endorse it as 'full and final', but Jane and her honorary uncle had warded it off. There should be a substantial sum still to come, but Gordon Black warned her that unless they could reach a settlement before the case reached the civil courts, she might see very little of the money.)

Even the finances of Faraday Racing Enterprises, now at their healthiest ever, were sadly diminished by the expenditure that followed. It seemed only sensible to carry out the necessary replacement of parts, along with the subtle alterations to suspension and steering geometry that Jane deemed necessary, before handing Henry over for beautification; but the number and cost of the parts to be replaced rose steadily, in contrast to the bank balance.

'I might almost as well have bought a new car,' Jane grumbled to Laura, looking without much favour at Henry Two. They were checking over the car and filing receipts in the garage at home. Mr Fadden was not interested in having the car in his window while it was grubby and half dismantled.

'So far, about two-thirds of almost,' Laura said. (Jane knew exactly what she meant.) 'But if you'd bought a new car you wouldn't have had all these for spares.' She pointed at the bench, where the old gearbox dominated an array of smaller components. 'Flutter your eyelashes at Ginger and he'll recondition them all for you.'

'I'm busy,' Jane said. 'Flutter yours. It's all part of the job. Ginger doesn't give a damn who it is, as long as it's female.'

Laura had watched Ginger watching Jane, but she knew better than to say anything that might provoke a breakdown in a valuable economic relationship.

One more engagement had to be fitted in before term began. The recent publicity had spread through the media because of human rather than technical interest. This brought an invitation for Jane to appear on a premier television chat-show and — wonder of wonders! — to be paid a substantial fee for it plus travelling expenses. This, taken together with the bargaining power that Laura would gain over the various advertising sponsors, was too good to miss.

Junior was gone and Henry Two was not ready for public display, but at Laura's insistence the interview was conducted against a projected background showing a large blow-up of Junior. Jane, nervous at first, was put at ease by a preliminary run-through with the friendly interviewer and early in the interview she explained, calmly and clearly, the attraction that driving held for her despite her respect for the dangers entailed; and she denied any suggestion of a romance with Peter Fasque or, indeed, anyone else.

'Then why,' asked the interviewer, 'did you give up your own drive and lend an expensive and uninsured car to a comparative stranger, with a strong possibility that it could be seriously damaged?'

'I've wondered the same thing myself,' Jane replied. 'It was an impulse. I must have been mad. But I knew how much his chance at the championship meant to him.'

The interviewer suddenly departed from the run-through. 'Or was it all an advertising gimmick?'

'I beg your pardon?' Jane said stonily.

'What I'm suggesting is that your presence at these events is an advertising trick — a publicity stunt. Do you, in fact, always use the products of Alex Ltd.?'

Jane told herself to stay calm. 'Almost invariably,' she said.

The interviewer prepared to pounce. 'Almost?'

'Ninety-five per cent of the time. They stand up to the conditions very well. But if things are going to be very wet, or sweaty, I use the base by Miladyship. It's even more dependable but, of course, it's three times the price.'

The interviewer frowned. He was a portly man but with so much charisma that even his frown had charm. 'I accept that women do figure in motor racing as drivers,' he said, 'but they never make it to the top. They seem to lack either the physique or the competitiveness. Would you agree?'

'I suppose it's as true as any other generalisation. And like any other generalisation, there are exceptions.' The cameras made the most of her sudden grin. 'Would you care to arm-wrestle? Now?'

The interviewer had heard about Jane's physical regime. 'Some other time,' he suggested. 'I return to my original point. Would you accept that your presence is an advertising stunt?'

'No more than anybody else's. Did you think that motor racing was still a sport?'

'It's always referred to among sporting events, but I suppose not.'

'Or entertainment? Show business?'

'Not quite that.'

'Of course not,' Jane said reasonably. 'Sometimes it's a business. But mostly, it's advertising. Alex Beauty Products happen to think that their image is enhanced by a woman managing to step out of a car after a race still looking glamorous, and I can see their point. Now look at the big teams in Formula One. Some manufacturers are in it to advertise their cars. Engines are supplied for similar reasons. Other firms may run a team to advertise some other product. Some are financed by tobacco or other sponsorship. I'm racing, at a much more lowly level, because I enjoy it, but I couldn't possibly afford it without the support of — ' and, on a mischievous impulse, she rattled off a quick list of her sponsors.

The interview concluded a few seconds later. When the cameras were off, she said, 'I suppose you'll edit that last bit out?'

'Unless a majority of your sponsors pay an advertising fee,' the interviewer said quite seriously.

'You showed yourself up as a sexist pig.'

The interviewer smiled the smile that usually set several million female hearts fluttering. It did nothing for Jane. 'That's the bit that they'll edit out.'

When the programme went out, it included Jane's list of her sponsors but not the original reference to female lack of physique and competitiveness. A more innocuous comment had been dubbed in by the interviewer over a shot of Jane's face. Mention of arm-wrestling had also been expunged.

'Will Mr Berkeley mind what I said about Miladyship?' Jane asked Laura.

'I'll find out.' Laura went to the phone. When she came back she was laughing. 'He was delighted. ABP's on the point of buying Miladyship, to add to their range.'

'That's all right, then.' Jane switched off the television. Only then did the impact of Laura's words strike her. 'Laura, when a firm's taken over, the shares shoot up, don't they?'

'Usually,' Laura said. 'But for God's sake, Jane, you can't use that. It was told to me in confidence. It would be insider trading or something.'

'Then you shouldn't have told me. I call that thoroughly creet of you. What sort of business manager are you if you can't be trusted to keep a secret? How much money do I have in the bank? And how much can we expect for the TV appearance? And how much do our sponsors have to cough up because of the TV thing?'

* * *

Jane spent more than she could really afford on the purchase of a reconditioned engine for Henry Two, appropriating the worn-out engine for her own purposes. Henry Two, overhauled and slightly modified, was road-tested at the Road Research Laboratory and then consigned to Alex Beauty Products for the full cosmetic treatment.

The approach of the new academic year brought enquiries from more students in search of lodgings. Jane totted up the rents to be expected along with the money in the bank. She added the small but useful profit made by speculation in Miladyship shares and the fees and sponsorship due after her appearance on the chat-show. The total seemed almost healthy and she still had one or two of her grandfather's pictures available to sell, so the Maestro was at last sent for

223

scrap and replaced by a Ford hatchback no more than three years old. Ginger's father was pleased to make a special price on the car.

It was by now the last day of the long vacation. Already, first-year students were wandering helplessly around the corridors of the wrong university buildings, which had been signposted on the assumption that the visitor already knew where he wanted to go and how to get there. Mrs Dodson was on a flying visit to a niece in Edinburgh. As a last small extravagance before the pressure and penury of the new term and to celebrate the acquisition of suitable transport, Jane and Laura decided to bypass the students' union and meet at the motor club for a meal.

Jane was first to arrive. There was no sign of the steward and at first she thought that the big room was empty. She waited at the bar, intending to treat herself to a dry white wine whenever the steward appeared.

A figure rose from a half-secluded alcove in the corner and approached unsteadily. Jane was irritated rather than perturbed to recognise Rolando Valleja. 'So!' he said. 'It is you!' He did not seem pleased at the discovery. Jane guessed that, in addition to carrying a grudge, he had been drinking.

She decided that a soft answer rather than

a sardonic one might turn away wrath. 'Have you seen the steward?' she asked politely.

The question was ignored. His nostrils were elevated and flared. 'What for you let your mechanic tell people I am eunuch?'

'I don't think that we said quite that,' she said gently. 'But how come you told everybody that I'd slept with you?'

He waved a hand. 'Was only joke to pay you back. You sold me a crash rebuild.'

'That I did not,' Jane said stoutly. 'The car I sold you had never been crashed. But I'd replaced many of the moving parts from the car I'd rolled over.'

'And you never said race you won was handicap and not part of series.'

Jane's patience began to go. 'You could have looked in the programme. Anyway, I was going to tell you but you started behaving like the arrogant little prat that you are,' she said.

He seethed for a few seconds, but decided that grievance outweighed insult. 'I have been at disadvantage. But no more. It was I who bought your Vauxhall Junior car.'

'I know that,' Jane said. 'I wish you the best of luck. I'm moving up into a more senior class.'

The idea that a mere girl should be outranking him as a driver came close to being the last straw. But Valleja was still spluttering, trying to formulate a suitable riposte for which his English was inadequate, when a second and larger figure emerged from the same alcove and revealed itself as Carl Lansdowne. Jane quickly decided that this was definitely not her day. Her two least favourite people in the world had evidently been drinking together. She must have done something really wicked, if Somebody up there was so determined to punish her.

'Well, well!' Lansdowne said thickly. 'Little Miss . . . what was the name?'

'Faraday,' Jane said.

'I knew it was something reminded me of Fellatio. Learned to drive yet?'

Jane knew that she should have turned and walked out. Instead, she said, 'Look who's talking!'

Lansdowne sneered. 'Who wrote off Daddy's TVR, then?'

'Who span in front of me and made me leave the track rather than hit him? And who lost his seat in Formula Three Thousand?'

It seemed that she had touched a nerve. 'I'm being taken on again next season,' he snapped.

Jane knew that Formula Three and Formula Three Thousand were the hinterland between the smaller classes, where owner-drivers might scrape by with their own money and such sponsorship as they could gather, and Formula One in which drivers were paid, usually very well paid, employees of highly organised teams. In those formulae, money might pass in either direction, a professional team paying its chosen drivers a fee while other, richer drivers, anxious to climb the ladder, might give a team financial support in return for a season's driving.

'How much are you going to have to pay them?' she asked.

It was the ultimate insult. She saw his eyes bulge. 'You . . . little . . . bitch!' he growled.

Valleja seemed to have abandoned the effort to translate his condemnation into English. He uttered several words in Spanish, of which the only one that Jane recognised was *puta*, which she thought meant 'whore'.

Lansdowne went further. 'I ought to spank your butt,' he said.

'Good idea,' Valleja said. 'You hold her. I spank.'

'Yeah!'

They meant it. They moved forward together.

It was too late to run. They were between her and the door.

Quite definitely, nobody was going to get away with spanking Jane. She threw her mind back to the karate lessons at the health club.

Lesson One had been disguised with a fancy title, but it had boiled down to the optimum technique for delivering an old-fashioned kick to the crotch. It had been stressed that karate was only to be used in self-defence, but what else was this? Lansdowne was probably the more dangerous of the pair but she thought that Valleja would be more sensitive about the state of his testicles. So as the two men closed in she kicked him, exactly as she had been taught.

Lansdowne grabbed her by the wrists but her strength surprised him. Rolling together Lessons Two through Seven, she broke his holds with a quick twist against the thumbs, at the same moment stamping on his foot and attempting a head-butt, all the while trying to keep her own remodelled nose from harm. The result was satisfactory. Her forehead caught him on the mouth with a heavy thud and as he stepped back she finished with a backhand slash to the side of his neck. The straight fingers aimed at his solar plexus were wasted effort, because he had already recoiled out of reach.

At some point the steward had entered the room. He thrust himself between them. 'That's enough of that,' he said. His intervention was unnecessary. Valleja was curled in a foetal position on the floor.

Lansdowne had collapsed into a chair. He spat out a tooth and groaned.

Jane found that she was shaking. 'They . . . ' she began. 'They . . . '

'It's all right, miss. I heard them.'

'So did I,' said Laura from the doorway. 'Jane, are you all right?'

'I . . . I think so,' Jane said. Her hand was bruised but she was pleased to discover that her forehead hardly hurt at all. The need for a good cry would soon go away.

The steward shot her a glance but decided that there were others more demanding of his attention. He satisfied himself that neither of the men required hospitalisation, then helped them to their feet. 'You're leaving, gentlemen,' he said. 'Reciprocal agreement or no, please save us embarrassment by not coming back. And don't try to drive. There's a taxi office on the corner. Your car will be safe where it is for a day or two.'

He saw them to the door and returned. Jane was seated, with her head down on her knees. He looked down and smiled. The two men had given him an unpleasant afternoon. 'You could do with a small brandy,' he told Jane. 'On the house.'

'Thank you,' Jane said faintly.

'Not at all. And in future, miss, please

don't bully the male members or their guests. They're just not up to your weight.'

Jane looked up quickly. His face was bland again but his voice had been warm. She decided that her leg was being pulled.

★　★　★

The academic year got into its swing and Jane found herself busier than ever. In addition to her studies and her physical fitness regime, her appearance on TV had brought her to the attention of the producers. They saw a 'personality' who combined the advantages of being an attractive girl, a woman in a man's world, adventurous and a clear and quick-witted speaker.

On Jane's behalf, Laura turned down several invitations to participate in panel games, pleading that pressure of studying would have first claim on her time until the following summer. But as Jane's bank balance once again became depleted by the need to live, support the household and amass a reserve of spares, she found herself committed to a minor but well-paid role in several motoring programmes. She even found herself on the other side of the microphone, interviewing a successful lady rally-driver. The two had found so much in

230

common that they had quite forgotten the presence of the cameras and microphones and happily discussed the differences in technique between race and rally-driving. The result, instead of a three-minute slot, was skilfully edited and turned by an opportunist producer into a half-hour programme in its own right, illustrated with extensive library footage. The programme was hailed as a great success and was repeated regularly.

Another remunerative spin-off, to bear fruit in the coming season, was a contract to carry a tiny television camera in all her races for the next year.

'Pointing forward?' Jane asked.

Laura looked at the letter of confirmation. 'It doesn't say,' she said. 'But probably.'

'I expect so. That'll be because they expect me to be at the back. Somebody told me that you've really arrived when they mount the camera looking backwards. You can buy one or two videos of a few circuits but, I wonder, would there be a market among wannabe racers for videos giving a driver's-eye-view of the complete set of circuits? After all, there's only about a dozen RAC-registered circuits in Britain.'

'I'll find out.' Laura made a note.

Through all this activity, Jane still managed

to find time for one procedure which she considered essential. Henry Two had been delivered to Fadden's Garage and Service Station, very prettily tidied up, sprayed and emblazoned and looking, Laura said, 'like a scaled-up perfume bottle'. The engine had then been very carefully removed and smuggled into the Heat Engines Laboratory along with the old engine, now fitted with new shells and piston rings. The latter was the subject of lengthy research by Jane, who spent many Sundays in the lab, with the connivance of her friend Mr Yates, on an apparently endless series of experiments on the combined effects on power output of such factors as exhaust length, ignition advance, compression ratio, valve overlap and fuel mixture at various engine speeds. At first she was covering old ground, but her intention was to produce an all-embracing computer program aimed at identifying the optimum range of r.p.m. and adjusting all the other variables to suit.

By Christmas, the program was advanced to the point at which she could begin to apply it to the racing engine, but staying within the permitted modifications. The engine was polished within and without and was assembled with a care usually devoted to brain surgery. Jane intended to spend

Christmas Day at work in the lab. She expected to be alone but she had mentioned her intent to one or two fellow students. Word had gone round, as had descriptions of the Christmas party the previous year.

Quite by chance Professor Barnes, the Professor of Mechanical Engineering, had occasion to visit the building on Christmas Day in search of his favourite pipe. He found this irreplaceable comfort, as expected, on his desk and was passing through the foyer on his way out of the building when he heard an engine running somewhere among the laboratories. The sound stopped but, impelled by no more than curiosity, he decided to take a look into the Heat Engines Lab. As he approached, he heard a voice expounding the calculations determining the optimum length of an exhaust system.

Jane, greasy to the elbows and with her hair flying, was in front of the large chalkboard, which was becoming covered with symbols and calculations. A dozen students were clustered around, seated on whatever they could find. Cans of beer and a few bottles of wine were to be seen but were largely being ignored. The Professor smiled to himself. Jane's unofficial activity was supposed to be a closely guarded secret, although most of the staff were in the know and turning a very blind eye. The more the students could teach themselves and each other, the more time would be left for research and writing.

Jane was saying, 'I hope to have other spin-offs. The next steps are refining the program for choosing the perfect set-up and gear ratios for a given circuit.'

There was an immediate chorus of questions. Jane turned back to the chalkboard. The Professor smiled again, listened for a few minutes and then walked softly away.

That episode was in his mind on a wet and blustery day in March when he was closeted with the Vice-Chancellor. Sir Thomas Melville, the Vice-Chancellor, was frowning. 'It's most unusual,' he said, unconsciously echoing the words of a popular song.

'But not unknown. You know as well as I do, Tommy,' — the Vice-Chancellor's secretary had left the room and the two men had been friends and colleagues for many years — 'that we've made appointments of fresh graduates before now. And I will have a vacancy on establishment when Oates retires.'

'Couldn't you get a part-timer on agency contract? That seems to be the in thing these days.'

'Good God, no!' said the Professor. He had

deliberately chosen the afternoon after a meeting of the University Court for the discussion. Sir Thomas was inclined to do himself rather well at the subsequent lunch and would usually sign anything put before him in the afternoon. The Professor was not to have known that his doctor had put Sir Thomas on a strict diet with no alcohol permitted, or he would have known to broach the subject on any other day of the month. All that he knew was that he was going to have to justify what would usually have gone through on the nod. 'I want this particular girl,' he said.

'She hasn't even sat her finals yet.'

'There is as much chance of her failing her finals as of the Earth colliding with Mars. And I want to make sure of her now. Otherwise she'll go down the brain drain, as have so many others. She's intelligent, she can put her subject over clearly — and she's developing a following among the students, which means that they'll listen to her.'

'She'd hardly ever be here. She'd be away riding her motorbikes or whatever it is that she does.'

'Driving cars,' the Professor said patiently. 'What you don't appreciate, Tommy, being the classical scholar that you are, is that what she learns from her racing activities and the research that she puts into them are perfectly to the point so far as my department's concerned. She may be away a lot, but that would be mostly in summer when we're quiet or virtually shut down. And the time she'd put in on developing her cars and her computer programs would be original research, far from wasted from my stand-point. The girl's a human dynamo. She can make up any amount of lost time. And we can work around her absences.'

'In that case, a part-time post might suit her very well,' said Sir Thomas. There was a gleam in his eye. Nothing pleased him so much as having bested a colleague in argument. 'Give her plenty of time for her motoring.'

'And the university gets a whole job for a half salary?'

'Don't knock it,' said the Vice-Chancellor, descending to the vernacular. 'It would leave you another half-time post vacant, if you could make a case for it. I'll go along with a part-time appointment of this girl as a junior lecturer — if the Senate agrees.'

The Professor sighed but accepted that he had got most of what he came for. 'You know that the Senate eats out of your hand, Tommy,' he said.

'We shall see. They'll probably insist on the

post being advertised.'

'They can advertise all they want as long as Miss Faraday gets the post in the end.'

'Understood. But the appointment doesn't start until October, mind.'

The Professor called him a petty-minded skinflint, but not aloud.

★ ★ ★

The academic year ground on its way. Jane was offered the post of part-time junior lecturer, subject to successful results in her honours degree exams. Pleased at the prospect of earning a salary at last, and without having to give up access to the laboratory, she accepted the post immediately and then almost forgot about it.

Her first season with Formula Ford and Henry Two came rushing at her. It began even before her finals but, Jane being Jane, she fitted in the first two races of the season without interrupting her studies. As was her custom, she entered the examinations with a profound sense of doom, only to be astonished to find that the examiners had set such foolishly simple questions. She then put the whole subject of academe out of her mind until she was mildly gratified at being notified that she had indeed obtained a very good honours degree.

Laura had also successfully completed her course and been rewarded with the gift of a neat little MG sports car from her father, who was only too pleased to see one more of his daughters attain independence. He then, without prompting, offered her a post in his own legal practice, which Laura was pleased to accept. But this entailed either a great deal of commuting or a return home to take over the room vacated by her elder sister, now married to an architect in Bournemouth.

'At least it will give you another room to rent,' she pointed out.

'But will your father let you get away enough to go on acting as my chaperone and business manager?' Jane asked her anxiously. 'You'll still come to the circuits with me?'

'Lord, yes! I'm Practice Manager now — an appointment long overdue, I might add. I make the rules.'

'That's all right, then.'

Laura just nodded. Her romance with Hugh Waterton was still in full flower and neither of them had any intention of missing the chance of weekends in close collaboration. 'I may come back to you if home gets on top of me,' she said. 'Dad has a dog now, Bosco. A damn great golden retriever. He's a dog of charm but frighteningly regular in his habits. Dad leaves home at ten past eight every day and walks Bosco before he leaves. So Bosco's bowels move at seven forty-five. So he starts barking at seven-thirty and if nobody gets up to let him out there's a mess on the carpet.'

'He has the merit of predictability,' Jane said.

Jane was in the middle of a romance of her own. At one of the first meetings of the season, an attractive Frenchman had visited from nearby in the paddock, ostensibly in search of an unusual size of spanner but actually drawn by the presence of two attractive young ladies. His name was Pierre Duclos. Jane found the name Pierre — Peter — propitious, reminding her as it did of Peter Moran and Peter Fasque — and she was predisposed to accept his advances.

These were properly circumspect. Pierre, the son of a major French industrialist based in Britain, was another driver competing in the Formula Ford championship. He soon developed the habit of inviting Jane out to dinner after the races finished. On the first such occasion, the affair did not advance beyond dinner and small talk. On the second, a chaste kiss was exchanged. On their third date there were some delicious intimacies in the rear of his Patrol. Only on their fourth outing together did he make, and she accept, an invitation to a nightcap in his hotel room. Thereafter, whenever Laura was similarly occupied with Hugh, Ginger was given undisputed use of the camper, on the strict understanding that he would have it spick and span in the morning.

Money was again in very short supply. A final settlement had at last been reached over the Wing Commander's estate. As Gordon Black had warned her, the amount was disappointing and Jane suspected that the various lawyers involved had done better out of it than she had. The house needed painting, the boiler had to be renewed and the drive was overdue for resurfacing. But at least the kitty was replenished enough for her to enjoy one more season, provided that they practised every possible economy and Henry Two suffered no major traumas. After the summer, she would be earning money of a sort.

But the peculation of the late Mr Bastaple still rankled. If he had behaved as a good solicitor should, Jane would have been able to pursue a driving career free from financial worries. On one of the weekends when Jane was not racing, she invited Laura to come over for a short weekend. 'And bring Bosco,' she said.

'Why on earth?'

'Because I have a fiendish plan.'

'Then of course I'll come.'

On the Sunday morning the two girls rose before dawn and drove through almost empty streets to a pitiless London graveyard. Laura stayed with the car while Jane walked Bosco among the graves, looking for a certain name. Just after twenty to eight, she was accosted by an indignant verger.

'Get that dog out of here!'

'He's on a lead,' Jane pointed out. 'It only says that dogs must be kept on leads.'

'But he's sniffing at the graves. We can't have . . . *No, get him off there!*'

It was too late. Bosco's bowels, regular as ever, had caused his daily offering to be deposited among the flowers.

'If you've any respect for the dead,' hissed the verger, 'you'll clean that up at once.'

'I do not have respect for this particular dead. That grave belongs to an embezzling solicitor,' Jane said. 'He stole my inheritance. You can pick it up if you like. As far as I'm concerned, it's in the right place.' She made for the gate. Laura swept up in the Ford. Jane and Bosco were out of sight before the verger got there.

The man trailed back to the grave. The task did not attract him. Tidying up the graves was not really his job. And if that grave really did belong to a solicitor who had robbed his clients, maybe he'd asked for it. Let the worms cope if they could.

* * *

Jane tackled Formula Ford with the same cautious dedication that she gave to any fresh challenge. She jogged around each circuit although she already knew most of them. She practised assiduously. As in the smaller formulae, she was content at first to start each race from well back on the grid, picking off the easy targets, waiting for the car to become as familiar as her own footsteps.

There were few familiar faces now and once again she was looked on, and treated, as a seven-day wonder. But as her confidence grew she moved up the ranks. By late summer she was starting in the front half of the grid, picking up points from time to time and even achieving occasional podium places. She was soon recognised as a force to be reckoned with and almost 'one of the boys'. Gradually it became commonplace to pocket male pride and ask her advice when serious scientific-technical problems arose. Jane herself was learning valuable lessons all the time, one of the most valuable being to know the other driver's styles and attitudes and to read the race ahead, ready to take avoiding action if a foreseeable multiple shunt began or to dart into an inadvertently left opening.

Most of the races were attended by a small team of television technicians who set up cameras on the few cars contracted to carry them. Jane became friendly with one of the men, universally known as Tubby, in the inverted manner of nicknames, because he was lean to the point of gauntness. The TV team, as Tubby explained to Jane, belonged to an independent organisation and recorded the action on behalf of satellite television and in the hope of a spin-off in the form of sales to newsrooms and disaster programmes in the event of events sufficiently dramatic.

'You're vultures,' Jane told him.

'Yep. That's us,' said Tubby.

'Just as long as I know who I'm talking to. How would you like to let me have a copy of every inch of tape you record from my car?'

'No problem. You pay for the tape. What do you want it for?'

'There might be a market for videos, each describing a circuit, taking the viewer round and round it with a voice-over describing where to change gear and how to take each corner. Not just for would-be competitors. I can imagine all the enthusiasts who have no hope of ever driving in a race wanting to own copies and learn their way around the circuits.'

Tubby thought about it, whistling tunelessly. 'You could have something there,' he said suddenly. 'I'll talk to the boss.'

'Have him speak to my business manager.'

At the seventh race meeting of the season, Jane noticed that a new decal figured prominently on each side of her car. It was a day to make the heart rejoice, thin white clouds in a dark blue sky and just enough breeze to keep strong heat away. The two girls had taken to a rug on the grass. Last practice was over, the race still an hour away. Jane had won a place on the third row of the grid. Pierre would be immediately in front of her.

'Klinkenhammer?' Jane said idly. 'That wouldn't be the fashion house?'

'Of course it is,' Laura said. 'Alex BP are diversifying. They hope to embrace the whole range, glamour and beauty and . . . and so on, eventually. They've just bought Klinkenhammer.' She waited for the storm to break.

'Well, I like that,' Jane said indignantly. 'I wondered how you were managing to come out with a lot of new clothes that didn't look like C and A. I was sure that they were originals and I couldn't think where the money came from. I was going to have you audited.'

'What I could embezzle from you wouldn't keep me in knickers,' Laura retorted. 'They were quite generous during the negotiation stage. But now that it's signed and sealed — the usual sort of terms — they aren't quite so forthcoming. I suppose it's your turn now.'

'About bloody time,' Jane said.

Race-time approached. Jane fitted herself into her flame-proof overalls and helmet. Ginger plugged in the travelling battery. The engine fired. Jane went down to the pit lane, was allocated her place in the queue and set off on her warming-up lap.

From the moment of the start, she knew that it was her day. Pierre made a good start and she was hard behind him. Two drivers on the other side of the track fluffed their starts and let them through into second and fourth places. Henry Two felt sharp and sounded crisp. In her mirrors, Jane saw the gap behind her stretching out. She was on top of the world.

The driver in front of her was sandwiched closely between herself and Pierre, fending her off but unable to make any impression on the Frenchman. Halfway through the race, Jane thought that Pierre's driving had changed. It took her another lap to realise that he was tempting the other driver, leaving half-chances and then slamming the door. She could only see one reason for such tactics. She pulled up close. At the next bend, Pierre slowed marginally and took the bend on a tighter line than the ideal. He seemed to be leaving the other driver a chance to run round the outside. The driver entered the trap, tried the outside line and found himself cut off while Jane spurted past on the inside line. She tried to take Pierre as well, but the Frenchman was having none of it. He was away and eating into the leader's lead, with Jane using all her skill and nerve to stay with him.

One lap from the end, the leader was harassed enough to fall into error. Attempting to save that last vital hundredth of a second, he misjudged his braking, arrived too fast and skated off into the gravel. Pierre and Jane finished first and second.

Laura had standing instructions to meet Jane at the *parc fermé* with shoes, a skirt and a comb at the end of every race, because there was no telling when a photographer or a TV interviewer might pounce. Jane managed her usual undressing-on-the-beach trick of shrugging out of her overalls while donning the skirt, before hurrying to catch up with the other two. It was a podium finish with champagne provided.

The other driver, who had finished third, took his defeat philosophically — as well he might, because he had been running third before falling into the trap. He was bubbling with laughter. 'You cut me up to let your girlfriend through. Only a Frenchman would think of that. You're a Froggy bastard! What are you?'

'I am a Froggy bastard,' Pierre said amicably. 'Next time, you remember that.'

'I'll remember.' But the other man, good loser though he was, made a point of dousing both of them thoroughly with champagne.

Jane returned to the camper, carrying her own champagne unopened. She was in a dampened mood. Hugh was waiting to carry Laura off. 'I want an introduction to the designer at Klinkenhammer,' she told him.

'I can get you clothes. You don't have to meet the designer.'

'For this I do,' Jane said. 'I'm fed up getting soaked with champagne. It takes about three days to wash the smell out of my hair and I have to change to the skin and sponge myself down before I can go out with Pierre, or else I reek of drink and everybody looks at me sideways. When I'm rich, I'm going to get a caravan with a shower. Meantime, what I want from Klinkenhammer is to have my overalls altered and a new rig designed so that I can get changed quickly and easily without any risk of showing off my underwear. And the new rigout's got to be in champagne-proof material and have a hood that I can whip up over my hair. But it's also got to look smart.'

'And we do not expect to have to pay for it,' Laura added.

Hugh sighed. 'I'll see what I can do,' he said.

9

The season came to an end. Jane finished with a modest but passable eleven points. Pierre, who had scored steadily, was placed third and inclined to crow.

Jane was already launched on her teaching career. She settled quickly into her stride. At first she was only entrusted with those elementary subjects with which the students should already have some degree of familiarity, although they frequently showed signs of hearing of their existence for the first time. The Professor occasionally eavesdropped on the lectures and tutorials, but she was putting the facts over well and, to judge from the questions, the students were taking them in.

Jane was earning a salary at last, but it was only the salary of a part-time junior. And Henry Two, though carefully maintained during the season, was in need of substantial renewal before returning for exhibition in Mr Fadden's show-window. The time had arrived when she was expected to start repaying her student grant. The bank account seemed to be leaking like a burst radiator. But, whether she knew it or not, easier times were just around the corner.

With the syllabus already established, Jane found herself, for the first time in years, with leisure to spare. Putting a voice-over on the first videotapes of racing circuits was soon accomplished. She had ample time to pursue her search for the ideal computer program, aided by dimensioned plans of the various circuits pirated over the telephone lines from the computers of others.

She accepted one or two of the invitations, which Laura brought her from time to time like a puppy retrieving a stick, to appear on TV panel games. The producers knew, apparently by intuition, that she was favourably viewed by the public and she began to find herself in demand as motoring commentator and a pontificator on any scientific subject. She was becoming a Personality and was soon being recognised in the street — much to her embarrassment, because exposure to public attention had not gone to her head. She earned as much from a half-hour's programme as from a week of lecturing.

During the autumn, she was surprised to receive a visit from Pierre and be carried off for an expensive dinner. She supposed at first that he had failed to find a substitute for her overnight companionship and found himself with hormones to spare. Expecting a demand to make up for lost time, she began to settle herself into a mood suitable for the acceptance of his advances. But she soon learned that the reason for his visit was, at least in the first instance, different.

'I had a trial in Formula Three Thousand,' he told her over the sweet course. 'Now I have been offered a seat for next season.'

Jane's immediate reaction was professional. 'European or Japan?' she asked.

'European. So I shall not be driving in Formula Ford next year. They pay me a fee,' he added proudly. 'But not very much.'

Jane hardly heard him. 'You'll enjoy that,' she said. 'It's a big step forward.'

'It is,' he agreed. 'Formula Junior was the infant school, what you call kindergarten — '

'I would say that karting was infant school,' she argued.

'Very well,' he said impatiently. 'Then Formula Junior was what you call primary school, and Formula Ford is secondary school.'

'Formula Three is Technical College?' Jane suggested.

'Yes. But Formula Three Thousand is the university. And Formula One is real life, where one hopes it is all leading. The one leads to the next. But, my darling, it means that we shall not be bumping into each other at the weekends any more.'

At any other time, Jane would have laughed and pointed out that his choice of the words 'bumping into' might be considered unfortunate, but this was hardly the time for levity. Clearly, Pierre was looking for a sentimental parting of the ways, which she was quite prepared to allow him.

'Very sad,' she said politely. 'I shall miss you terribly.'

'It is sad,' he agreed eagerly. 'It is. So this may be our last meeting, our last chance to exchange pledges of our love before we go out of each other's lives for ever.'

Jane gathered that Pierre was looking for rather more than sentimental farewells. Like many women, she was quite uninterested in sex until aroused, usually by soft talk and caresses, but once aroused she had an appetite that Pierre seldom managed to quench. For, despite being French and gifted with a romantic approach, in Jane's limited experience (for he was only her second lover) his performance in bed was disappointing. Only rarely was he willing or able to protract his efforts until she had attained fullest satisfaction. Her few attempts to explain her dissatisfaction had been perceived as deadly insults.

She reached across the table and patted his hand. 'It is better that we part as friends rather than lovers,' she said. 'The pain will be less. And perhaps we might be business associates.' A fresh idea was blossoming in her mind. 'If they're only paying you peanuts — I mean not very much,' she explained in deference to his sometimes incomplete understanding of English idiom, 'how would you like to carry a video camera on the car?'

His face, which had fallen, made a partial recovery. 'This would be for money?'

'Certainly it would. I'll have my business manager get in touch with you.'

The recovery was not sustained. 'If that is the young lady who they are calling Cut-throat Clara — '

'Who does?'

'Everybody. The suppliers. The Avon Tyres gentleman said that he was grateful to be left with the buttons on his jacket.'

Jane made a mental note to congratulate Laura on a good job well done. 'I'll tell her to be nice to you. Not as nice as all that,' she added as he brightened again. 'Tell me, do you have any spares going begging?'

'A mountain,' he said. 'We talk about it at breakfast?'

Lie back and think of England . . . But Jane pulled herself together. She had several TV appearances scheduled. 'We'll talk about it now,' she said firmly.

★   ★   ★

There was no Christmas party that year as such. But the stimulus of Jane's activity and enthusiasm had led more than the usual few students to take an interest in motor sport. Rather than lay herself open to a charge of riding her hobbyhorse, Jane had avoided referring directly in her lectures to engineering aspects of motor racing, but questions on the subject became common, some arising out of lectures and tutorials but others coming very much out of the blue. These she tried to parry, until a small delegation tackled her with the suggestion of an extra lecture devoted to the engineering of racing-cars.

Laughingly, Jane gave what she thought was an evasive answer but which was taken for an affirmative. This soon came to the ears of Professor Barnes, who always knew what was going on in his own department (and, as often as not, outside it).

The paucity of students entering the engineering disciplines was and is of concern to those who wonder where the next generation of industrial expertise is to be found. 'Engineering', conjuring up as it does

254

an image of oily dungarees, may not attract the brightest or even the most. The Ministry of Education was concerned. So were the various engineering professional bodies. Professor Barnes's concern was as great as anyone's and in Jane he had seen a chance to spread a little favourable propaganda. If an attractive young lady could not only enter engineering but make practical application of it with obvious success, surely it would be seen that other bright youngsters could follow.

Jane was not apprised of the Professor's plans until they were far advanced. The modest lecture, which had been scheduled for the last afternoon of the autumn term, was quietly moved to the evening and rerouted to the university's biggest and best lecture theatre, a large auditorium equipped with every known audio-visual aid, and the Professor broadcast invitations to attend. He also instructed Mr Yates to record the entire proceedings on videotape.

The first that Jane knew of her intimate talk to junior students of mechanical engineering having become a major local event was when members of the Motor Club and others of the academic body began assuring her how much they were looking forward to it. Professor Barnes seemed to be avoiding her but eventually she managed to pin him down in the staff club, only to have her worst fears confirmed.

But the Professor was a wise judge of staff. After a brief period of inner panic, logic reasserted itself and Jane began preparing for the fray, demanding clips of video film from the library of her television contacts, preparing or borrowing slides and filling any gaps in her personal experiences by means of an intense inquisition, by phone or electronic mail, of anybody likely to have the information she wanted, whether she had ever met them or not. She would thus be able, on the day, to begin sentences with 'I am assured by . . .' and drop the name of some former or present world champion or the designer of the car currently meriting the Constructor's Championship.

'You and I,' she told Mr Yates firmly, 'are going to have to do some work. I'm damned if I'm going to break off to quote and write up on the board formulae which half the audience won't want or understand. I want to speak steadily and I want formulae, film clips, slides or what-the-hell to appear on the screens at the right moment without my having to stop and ask for them. You dig?'

'Young lady,' Mr Yates retorted, 'I was doing this job before you were born. Tell me what you want, give me a note of your key phrases and then leave it to me.' He spoke without heat. Jane had been one of his favourites among the students and she was far and away his favourite member of staff.

The day arrived far too soon, as such days usually do. Jane faced a crowded lecture theatre. Many among the sea of faces were known to her but she had to think twice to understand why some of them were there. She was nervous. When she prepared to speak, she expected her voice to come out as a squeak but when it came it sounded perfectly normal. She had prepared one or two little jokes in the hope of keeping the audience on her side. The first was answered by a gust of warm, male laughter focused back towards her. Instantly, she was at her ease and rather enjoying herself. She overran her allocated time but nobody seemed to mind. At the end, she received what amounted almost to a standing ovation with a vote of thanks from the Vice-Chancellor.

Professor Barnes had persuaded the university to push the boat out in pursuit of good public relations. The lecture was to be followed by a cocktail party in the Great Hall. Jane had had no intention of going within a mile of the place, but the Professor swept her along with him and she found herself shaking hands and exchanging smiles until her face ached, her only compensation being a succession of champagne cocktails. She smiled into one face and was about to move on before her dazed mind realised that this was one face that she was glad to see.

'Mr Berkeley!' she exclaimed. 'What are you doing here?'

'I've known Professor Barnes for years,' he said. 'When he invited me and I realised that I knew the speaker, nothing would have kept me away.'

Jane was feeling the aftermath of triumph and champagne cocktails, a heady mixture. '*Anything* could have kept *me* away. I've been dragooned, conscripted, conned and black-mailed and now my feet hurt but I have to go on grinning from ear to ear — or possibly even from there to there — and try to make conversation with ten thousand people I hardly know.'

Mr Berkeley was laughing, but he asked, 'Do you want to make your escape?'

'As I've never wanted anything before.'

He glanced around. Nobody of importance was paying them any attention for the moment and they were near a door. He led her out. Escape, she realised, was as simple as that!

'Do you have a coat?'

'It's . . . it's in my car,' she said. 'But I don't think I'd better drive. Could you get me a taxi, please?'

'We can do a little better than that.' He made use of a mobile phone from his pocket. 'When did you last eat?'

She tried to remember. 'Lunchtime, I think. Just tea and a biscuit. I wasn't hungry.'

'We'd better get some solid food into you. Thou shalt not live by champagne cocktails alone.'

They drove to a restaurant reputed to be so expensive that Jane had never dared to enter it, but tonight it seemed to be the right place for her. As she ate, the champagne fumes blew away and the exhilaration faded, leaving behind a quiet contentment and a ravenous appetite. 'I apologise if I'm doing my celebrated imitation of a starving tapeworm,' she said, 'but I hadn't realised how hungry I was.'

'I've enjoyed seeing my food give so much pleasure,' he said. 'Make the most of the appetite of youth. It won't last for ever.'

'Don't sound sad tonight,' she said. 'I feel that I want everyone to be happy.'

'A very proper way to feel.'

'You're laughing at me.'

'No. I'm quite sincere.'

They talked for an hour. She had not

realised how much she had been missing her grandfather's conversation, his worldly wisdom and philosophy honed by experience. Her fellow students had seemed to be callow striplings by comparison. Mr Berkeley was another man of the world, a charming companion, not only witty but capable of bringing out the bubbling humour that was buried deep in Jane and only emerged in the right company. They talked about life and about motor racing. When the restaurant was closing he signed the bill — a staggering bill, she managed to read it upside down — and then she was whisked home in the Range Rover. In the car, she felt his presence strongly. He smelt of aftershave and manhood.

She had had time to gather her courage. 'Walk me to the door?' she asked.

'Of course.'

At the door, in the moon-shadow of the house where he could not see her face, she said, 'You'd be welcome to come in for a brandy or one last cup of coffee.' She was not very experienced but she thought that there would be no doubt that more than a drink was on offer.

He hesitated. 'You're very kind,' he said at last. She could hear the smile in his voice. 'And very tempting. But perhaps it's too late. Or too early.'

'What do you mean?'

'I was a friend of your grandfather, remember? When we first met, you were little more than a third of my age. Now you're about half. Perhaps when the difference becomes even less striking . . .'

'I've made a fool of myself again, haven't I?' she said in a very small voice. 'Are you in what they call a 'steady relationship'?'

'No, I am definitely not. And you're nobody's fool. I have had my affairs. As a well-heeled widower, I could hardly avoid them. But you're beautiful and intelligent and if I was going to have a 'steady relationship', you'd be as close to my ideal as anyone I ever met. But it would not be a good idea, for your sake.'

He put out a hand to find her and touched her breast by accident. Then he kissed her cheek and walked out into the moonlight.

Laura had waited up to hear how the evening had gone but Jane went straight upstairs and slammed the door. That did not seem enough, so she opened it wide and slammed it again.

★ ★ ★

261

Jane had spent the waking hours of the night trying to convince herself that Mr Berkeley's rejection of her invitation had not been because he had assumed that she was pursuing him for his money or, alternatively, that she was a sex-mad nymphomaniac making a pass at the only immediately available male. She was reassured and her mood somewhat restored in the morning by the arrival, by chauffeur, of a dozen roses and a card which read, *Thank you for the charming invitation and a pleasant evening.* The tactful chronology was not lost on her. She asked the chauffeur to wait while she wrote a note in reply. This read, *The invitation was spontaneous, the evening delightful.*

If, in retrospect, the whole occasion seemed to have come out of *Alice in Wonderland*, the aftermath was almost as surprising to her. On a bleak day in February she was summoned to Professor Barnes's retiring room. The Professor was watching a video of her talk. 'Come and join me,' he said. 'Take a seat. This is the result of some serious editing, of course.'

Jane sat down. She saw herself on the screen and heard her own voice. One of the aerodynamic formulae was overlaid on the screen. 'This downforce,' her voice was

262

saying, 'is so great that at speeds above a hundred m.p.h. a car could run upside down along the underside of a flyover. I've never tried it myself and I never will, but calculation insists that it's so.'

The screen showed the packed auditorium and smiling faces, to the accompaniment of male laughter. The camera returned to Jane's figure and her voice resumed. 'This downforce introduces another anomaly. The downforce gives greatly increased adhesion when cornering and more than makes up for the drag effect, but it's at its least when the cars are going slowest, on the corners, when it's most needed. Conversely, of course, it's at its greatest when the cars are travelling fastest and in a straight line, which is when downforce and drag are least needed or wanted. And this introduces a second anomaly. The downforce is greatest when the space between the road and the undertray is least. On straights, therefore, it was quite common before a recent change to the rules' — at this point Jane's face was replaced by film of a handful of Grand Prix cars approaching along a straight with sparks showering from beneath, but her voice went smoothly on — 'for cars to bottom on the straights. Yet the lowest ride-height for the greatest downforce is needed on the bends, the very places where the car tends to ride higher. For that reason, the suspension on a Formula One car is almost rock-hard and after a two-hour race, one former champion told me, he feels as though he has fallen down all the stairs in a tower block.'

As Jane reappeared on the screen, to the sound of more male laughter, the Professor lifted a remote control and stopped the video. 'That's enough for the moment,' he said. 'I wanted you to see how well it turned out after editing.'

Jane frowned. 'I did not know that I was being put on record for posterity,' she said.

'Of course not. You might have become nervous.'

Jane decided to keep her temper. 'Professor, I *was* nervous, thanks to you broadcasting invitations to what was intended to be an informal talk to a few of my students.'

'There was no sign of it. You faced them like an old hand. I was proud of you, Miss Faraday, and grateful. And now, I would like you to sign this.'

Jane skimmed through the document. 'You seriously expect me to give my consent to this tape being used in any way the university wishes, all revenues, fees, royalties and emoluments to belong to the university?'

'Your talk was given by a member of staff

in university premises and university time,' Professor Barnes pointed out complacently.

Jane began to breathe heavily through her nose. 'I beg to differ, Professor. My talk was given in the evening after the term officially finished. And, as a part-time member of staff, my evenings should have been my own. I will not sign your paper.'

It dawned on the Professor that he had not played his cards to best advantage. 'But think, Miss Faraday, think. You come over as a shining example of an engineer in . . . in . . . '

'In her natural environment? I doubt it.'

'I was going to say, on the threshold of a fine career.'

Jane refused to be more than slightly mollified. 'Who do you expect to see this video, anyway?'

The Professor sighed. His ace was being finessed, quite unwittingly. 'You are already a television personality.'

He had reminded Jane of something that she had been trying to ignore. She had submitted to the demands of the media in order to finance her racing. If television money was about to be earned from her talk, fair was going to be fair or else. 'If it ever appears on the flickering box,' she said, 'you can have your PR for what it's worth. But before I sign away my rights I'll send my business manager to talk it over with you.'

'Do, by all means. That would be Miss Black? I remember her as a first-year student.'

If Professor Barnes was assuming that Laura was still the innocent girl he remembered from five years earlier, he was doomed to disappointment. Laura went to meet the Professor and the university secretary. She came back to the retiring room which Jane shared with two other part-time lecturers, looking smug. 'We get thirty per cent of television revenues worldwide,' she announced. 'We keep all other rights. And they had no idea how to go about selling it to the TV companies, so I'm to undertake it. For an agent's percentage, of course.'

'Of course,' Jane said.

'You don't mind?'

'Of course not. It's about time you made a bob or two.'

Jane was hardly attending to Laura. She was about to give a lecture to second-year students about the relationship between energy consumption and variation of speed, after which she would have to hurry to meet Klinkenhammer's celebrated designer who had at last arrived at a design which he believed would be both champagne-proof and in the height of fashion. Jane was more concerned to find out whether she could don it quickly and modestly.

And another season of racing would soon begin. Others might look on her, variously, as an advertising model, an engineer or a token ornament in a male-dominated activity, but in her own mind she was a serious competitor. She now knew all Henry Two's little quirks and she had got the setting-up down to a fine art and fully tabulated on computer. Also, the honeymoon period was over. She would no longer agonise over the least contact damage. This year, she would prove that she could go. She was going to finish well up in the table, or bust.

Another distraction was making demands on her time and attention. Mr Berkeley was seeking out her society without showing any signs of desiring her body. This for Jane was almost a first. Her older . . . what? Friend? Admirer? Whatever he might be, Julian Berkeley seemed determined never to be alone with her but included her with others in invitations to dinners, the theatre and sporting events. These invitations she accepted whenever she could, usually to find herself partnered by a man nearer to her own age.

On one occasion, when several racing drivers were invited to dinner at Grey Gables, she was paired with Peter Fasque and she thought that she could feel Mr Berkeley's eyes watching her. Peter, she gathered, had now detached himself from his former or any other girlfriend but, although he was still voluble in his gratitude to Jane for the loan of Junior, she found herself wondering what on earth had ever made her think him sexually attractive.

Conversation drifted to the thorny topic of the finances of motor racing. Julian Berkeley bemoaned the grip of accountants on business, strangling otherwise valuable activities for lack of clear-cut profit.

Suddenly there came back to Jane a picture of a younger man at another dinner table, talking with her grandfather. 'You should challenge them on the subject of false accounting,' she said, tongue in cheek. 'Make them tell you how much of their figuring includes costs which would have to be met anyway.'

Mr Berkeley hid his smile but his eyes were alight. 'Very true,' he said. 'I shall have to try it sometime. But tell me one thing, Miss Faraday. You suggested to me once that you have your own solution to the world's transportation problems. Tell us about it.'

Jane was horrified to see her daydreams dragged out into the light of day, but she felt that she had to accept the challenge. 'I don't suppose that I'm being very original,' she said. 'It all seems too obvious. What we have at present is a system which has evolved from the horse and cart. If anybody ever tried to do a rethink, he or she must have been quelled by the accountants or assassinated by road-builders.'

'And your solution?' Mr Berkeley persisted.

'I said that I had an opinion, not a solution,' Jane said. 'First of all, I think it's mad that we're still laying out flat surfaces and building vehicles each of which has to be steered by a fallible human being, relying on the grip of rubber to tarmac, often in circumstances requiring high degrees of skill to survive at all. One sneeze and everybody's dead. Add to which the fact that any system requiring vehicles to carry individual fuel makes the control of pollution impossible. Visitors from outer space would fall about laughing at us. If the same visitors come in two hundred years' time, do you think they'll see the same muddle and compromise? We make a great design fetish of safety, but by that we mean survival of the passenger after the inevitable collision, not making collision impossible — which is well within the scope of modern technology.'

'Go on,' said somebody.

'All right. You've asked for it. The present

alternative to road transport is the railway trains, which are mostly in much too large units and generally useless unless you're going from one city centre to another. Local railways have largely been shut down because of another example of false accounting — the railways have to pay for their own tracks while road transport rides on the public back. And freight clogs up the roads because sending it by rail usually entails too much handling at each end between the user's base and the localised depots.'

'What would you put in its place?' someone asked.

'It seems to me,' Jane said, 'that the time is ripe, socially and technologically, for that rethink. First we have to tackle the problem of pollution from power stations, to make electricity into a preferable option. Then I envisage a total system, possibly overhead monorail, embracing vehicles both large and small. Everything from heavy freight vehicles to personal vehicles for small numbers of people. Mostly publicly owned and called up to be paid for by the hour, but private ownership an option for those who want extra comfort or facilities. Destination keyed in — perhaps the postcode with one more digit — and you go from door to door. Collisions with oncoming traffic become impossible;

and the units are regulated to remain a set distance apart or, when traffic justifies, linked up into trains. I suppose the system might allow smaller vehicles to descend to ground level and be steered for the last, short distance.'

'What would become of the roads?'

'Returned to countryside, mostly.'

'But this is heresy,' one of the drivers said, laughing. 'We all live by or for our motor sport.'

'True,' Jane said. 'But think of the roads that could be made available for it.' She sighed. 'I don't suppose that it will ever happen. Accountants will point to the capital cost and they won't take into account the cost of pollution, hospitalisation and death. But it does seem to me that the first country, or consortium of countries, to grasp this particular nettle will have the rest of the world as its customers for generations to come.'

★ ★ ★

Early in the fresh season it seemed that Jane would live up to her ambitions. Henry Two was meticulously prepared, tuned to a fine pitch and well set-up to suit each circuit. Some of the more experienced competitors had moved on into more senior formulae and their places had been taken by inexperienced newcomers who could be expected to bring up the tail. Remembering her own novice days, Jane was unfailingly kind and helpful to these beginners. These kindnesses were not always correctly interpreted at first, but she took each unsuccessful pass as a compliment and made more friends than enemies.

One newcomer to Formula Ford who was less than welcome to Jane was Rolando Valleja. There was no denying that he was a driver of talent but in all other respects he was generally acknowledged to be a pain in the public posterior. He was an outspoken critic of Jane's every move and of the presence of women among the competitors at all. He collected one or two adherents but in the main Jane was becoming popular and respected enough for such backbiting to be ignored or even to induce angry retorts from some of Jane's friends.

Jane hit an immediate peak of confidence and nerve. She treated each qualifying lap as a sprint aimed at a place near the front of the grid, and having attained a good start position she was prepared to fight off any challenges, seize any chances and go for the lead. She was not invariably successful

— there were too many highly professional teams for that — but in the first five meetings she was in the points three times, with a second and a third to her credit.

Then her luck seemed to turn. At another meeting she was deliberately balked by Valleja and one of his cronies and in trying to outflank the obstructers she went off into the gravel trap. The offenders were given a serious warning by the stewards but that was no comfort to Jane, who had seemed to be heading for another podium finish. At the next meeting Henry Two suffered an oil-pump failure which cost her not only her finish but more money than she cared to part with for a replacement engine.

Worse was to follow. After a heavy day invigilating at exams followed by an early departure from home on the Saturday morning, an electrical problem developed in the camper and they were late arriving at the next venue, dead-heating with a warm front and the onset of steady rain. It was the reverse of her good fortune at the same circuit the previous year. Most competitors had achieved respectable qualifying times in the dry, but the best that Jane could manage put her into the back half of the grid in the provisional, overnight placings.

During the night, a second front moved

through and a storm developed. The wealthier or more generously sponsored competitors slept soundly in their hotel beds or lay listening cosily to the roar of the wind outside. The camper was sheltered enough, tucked against the back wall of the pits, but they heard later that a caravan had been bowled over in the nearby park and an army of contractors' men had been called out to reinforce or take down the marquees.

For the few who depended on the shelter of tents, life became impossible. Ginger was allowed into the camper and he was followed by two brothers, both in the plumbing trade, who were running an even more shoestring operation than Faraday Racing Enterprises. Their soft-topped Land Rover had soon lost its roof and they had given up trying to keep their tent in place and were attempting to bed down in their sleeping-bags in the lee of the pit wall until Laura, wrapped in Ginger's oilskins, braved the storm to offer hospitality.

Conditions were almost impossibly cramped. Jane, as hostess and driver, was allocated one of the bunks by popular acclaim. The two brothers took the front seats while Laura and Ginger managed to curl up at opposite ends of the other bunk. But between the noise of the storm and the comings and goings and the frequent brewings of tea, coffee or cocoa, there was little sleep to be had, and none of it refreshingly deep. In the morning, when the brothers departed with many avowals of lifelong friendship, Jane pronounced herself still exhausted. The wind had blown itself out but the rain persisted.

Jane had little hope of improving her grid position. The times of those ahead of her had been obtained in the dry. But there seemed to be little prospect of the weather improving. She went out for the remaining practice session, not hoping for more than to familiarise herself further with driving the circuit in the wet on grooved tyres and to watch out for places which might drain less quickly than others. She took note of several places where the outside line, where there was less oil on the track, offered the better grip. Then she lay down and slept for an hour. Most drivers seemed similarly to be contenting themselves with a few familiarisation laps.

By race-time the crowd was very thin and made up of the hard-core devotees, but the organisers had decided that the races would go ahead. Jane took her place in the queue and went to the start in a mood of depression. There was small hope of scoring points and she disliked the feel of her wet overalls. Nevertheless, she had tried a few practice starts in the pit lane and when the lights changed she got away smartly, picking up places while others wasted seconds in unprofitable wheelspin.

She found herself in the middle of a compact group. The rain was light now, but the track was wet enough for the cars to throw up fountains of spray. Jane had no experience of driving in the power-hose conditions. Visibility nearly vanished until she raised her visor, allowing spray to run down inside her helmet. It was almost easier to guess the positions of the other cars by the direction of the flying spray than to watch for the cars themselves. The red warning light on the back of each car was next to invisible, despite having been designed for just those conditions. Somehow the first corner was rounded without incident.

If Jane had had a good night's sleep, or had set off in a more cheerful mood, she might have seen or sensed the spinner ahead. But even that is open to doubt. The first that she knew of the multiple crash was a glimpse of a wheel, high above the spray. At the same moment she realised that a car which she had been about to challenge was braking hard and pulling across towards her. Her brakes only induced a slither. She thought that she had room to squeeze past but the car ahead was blasting water onto her face and she misjudged the gap. Her front wheel rode up on the other car's rear wheel.

When the descending tread of one tyre meets the rising surface of another, an enormous upward thrust is generated. Henry Two reared up and flipped. Jane had time to think *Not again!* and then the car was rolling like a barrel onto the grass, over and over, faster than she would have believed possible. She was being shaken as a terrier shakes a rat. Her first fear was that the roll-hoop might collapse or stab into the wet earth and let her head hit the ground. But the roll-hoop did its job and the straps held her in place and the car came to a halt, but upside down. Somewhere along the way she seemed to have switched off the ignition.

At first Jane gave thanks that she was unhurt. Then she realised that she was indeed hurt. She was shaken, pummelled. Her neck was agony and she seemed to have bitten her tongue. She was hanging in the straps but if she released herself she would fall on her head and she knew for certain that her neck would break and her head would roll away across the ground. Blood was running to her head but at least the blood seemed to be staying inside and not leaking out.

She was afraid to touch her nose.

10

There had been other victims of the multiple crash and though she later learned that there had been no serious injuries among them it took time for the first-aiders to establish priorities. It was several minutes before aid reached Jane. Then, under the direction of a paramedic who seemed to have been trained for those exact conditions, the car was rolled very gently, not onto its wheels, for all but one of those had vanished, but at least right-side up. Jane found herself unable to explain with any clarity just what injuries she had suffered. The same hands raised her gently while her spine was explored, then laid her on a stretcher.

She was carried, smoothly but rapidly, to where an ambulance could reach her. Jane was stowed inside and the ambulance set off, making a noise which Jane vaguely thought was almost indecently cheerful, considering the circumstances. A long, low moaning sound would have suited the occasion better.

A halt was made while a doctor climbed aboard, asked questions and shone a torch into her eyes. 'Leave her helmet on,' he told the paramedic. 'It'll act as a neck-brace. Let them remove it at the hospital.'

'I don't want to go to hospital,' she told him thickly.

'Few do,' he said.

'I'm okay. Just let me rest for a minute.'

'Much longer than that. Move your fingers and toes.'

She moved her fingers and toes. 'They tingle,' she said. 'Is my nose all right?'

The doctor nodded. 'It looks fine to me.' He filled a syringe and stooped over her. 'Hospital,' he said. 'Try not to let her roll around.'

★ ★ ★

Jane was received into the Accident and Emergency Department of an unfamiliar hospital in a strange city. She lacked the energy even to ask where she was. For this, the injection may have been partly to blame, but that part of her mind that came and went above the fog had other concerns. Her helmet was removed with great care, she was X-rayed, a neck-brace was fitted to her and a very young doctor examined her for the second or third time, she could not be sure which.

'My legs don't seem to work properly,' she

said. 'And my hands feel funny.'

'But they were all right until now?'

'Just a tingling.'

'That's good. No difficulty breathing?'

'No. Is my nose all right?' She felt that a second opinion was called for.

'Prettiest nose I ever saw. Fine. I can't tell you any more just now. The Professor's coming to see you.'

'Professor Barnes?' she asked, not understanding.

'Who's Professor Barnes? Professor Didcot's coming. Top man in his field. God is one of his lesser patients. I've never heard of him turning out at a weekend for *anybody* before. Old Didcot must fancy you something rotten.'

'I've never even heard of him,' she said. 'As far as I'm concerned, Didcot's where the Williams Formula One team comes from.' She could see that the doctor did not believe her.

She was left for an hour until the Professor arrived, but a nurse looked in every few minutes.

Her experience of professors led her to expect an older man, slightly divorced from reality, but Professor Didcot was not so very much older than herself. He had an undistinguished face compensated by a carefully cultivated mane of black hair. He was dressed for the golf course. He made the same examination, looked at the same X-rays and asked the same questions. Jane found herself describing the crash but the Professor already seemed to know all about it.

'You've been lucky,' the Professor said at last. 'But for your helmet acting as a brace, and the excellent musculature you've built up in your neck and shoulders, it could have been much more serious.'

'Is my nose all right?' *What I tell you three times is true.*

'Wholly admirable.'

'The other doctor said that it was good that I didn't start the symptoms earlier.'

'He was right. If you'd shown signs of paralysis straight away we'd have been dealing with a broken neck. But what you're suffering from is whiplash injury. You'll probably experience a degree of paralysis as the nerves in the spinal column are compressed, but that's only due to bruising. It'll pass.'

'That's something, I suppose.'

He looked at her as though she had gone mad. 'It's everything, surely.' He turned his attention to the younger doctor who had been hovering in the background. 'No need for Intensive Care,' he said. 'And no need for plasterwork, the neck-brace should do it all.

Send her up to a private room. Put a monitor on her, just in case her breathing becomes affected, but I don't expect that. Tell the press, when they call, that she's in no danger.'

The younger doctor smiled. 'The reporters have been phoning already.'

'If they phone again, you'll know what to tell them. Keep me informed. I'll say *au revoir*, then, young lady.'

A man in a brown coat — a porter, she thought — wheeled Jane into a lift.

'How do the press know about this so quickly?' she asked him.

'You were on the telly — in the *News*, no less! We saw it on the set in the waiting room. All you could see at first was one car and a great cloud of spray. Then suddenly a wheel shot out overhead, a car went one way and you came out the other, rolling over and over like I don't know what. And when they said it was you and where you were being taken, and put up your photograph, the phones went mad. Not just the press. You'll be given the messages when they get around to it.'

'That'll make my day!'

'Cheer up. It could be worse.'

'I don't see how,' Jane said. 'I just wrote off my car.'

'You could have written off yourself.'

On balance, Jane was unsure which option

she would have preferred. But there was a more important question. 'Which photograph of me did they show?' she asked.

★ ★ ★

Jane was transferred very carefully to a bed and hooked up to a monitor in a private room which looked, from her limited viewpoint, remarkably luxurious. 'Who's supposed to be paying for all this?' she demanded.

'Don't you have BUPA?' a nurse asked.

'Not a single Boop.'

'If we come back and move you to a bed in a public ward, if there is an empty bed,' said the man in the brown coat cheerfully, 'you'll know that front office has got it wrong again.'

Jane's limbs had become unmanageable. Additionally, she felt limp and exhausted from medication and the aftermath of shock. A sympathetic young nurse helped her to eat. Between them they managed to get most of a meal into Jane without too much going down inside the neck-brace. Jane was cleaned up and left to herself until the nurse returned.

'Your brother's here to see you.'

Jane still had more sense than to say that she did not have a brother. Even a reporter would be better than being left to mope alone. 'Oh good!' she said.

She had difficulty focusing on the visitor, let alone identifying him, washed, shaved and dressed for company. 'You don't mind me saying I was your brother, do you?' he asked anxiously. 'They wouldn't let me in, otherwise.'

Jane recognised him at last as the driving half of the brother plumbers who had shared the camper during the night of storm. He bore a huge bouquet of roses. 'Say what you like,' she said. 'It's Joe, isn't it? I don't even know Joe what.'

'It's Joe Clapper. And please don't say 'That rings a bell,' we get it all the time. We wanted to know how you are.' There was a pause. 'So how are you?'

'My bits don't seem to work, but I'm told that I'll mend.'

'That's good. The rumour went round that you'd broken your neck. There's a lot of sympathy. Dozens of people, mostly the other drivers, said to wish you luck and a good recovery. They had a whip-round and I was told to buy you these. Actually, they said fruit and a bottle of wine, but just you try it on a Sunday evening.'

'Nice of them,' Jane said. 'How's my car?'

'Worse than you are, I'd say. The race was restarted after a bit — the rain had gone off by then — but we helped Ginger and what's-her-name to collect your car. I think we found most of the bits. To be honest, there had been so many cars damaged that it wasn't easy to tell what came off which car, but we made sure that you got four wheels and at least the right number of everything else. Whether they can ever be put together again to make a working car's another matter. They've gone off to take it home but they'll come and visit you tomorrow.'

'I'll be glad to see them,' Jane said. Out of politeness she would have said more, but exhaustion and drugs overcame her and she fell asleep. Joe Clapper, relieved rather than insulted, made his escape.

★ ★ ★

Thanks to the medication, she slept like a log that night. In the morning, numbness lay over her body and mind like snow. Her right side seemed to be receiving none of the messages she was sending it while, on the left, only her forearm and fingers and one toe responded. But everyone seemed determined to assure her that these were signs that she would 'soon be up and about again'. Jane made the replies that she thought they wanted, but she was too dispirited to care very much.

She lay — 'like a pudding', in her own

expression — unable to help except in the most trifling way while she was fed and washed, massaged, given medication and subjected to the most squalid indignities. A physiotherapist visited and, when she found that Jane could not exercise her muscles for herself, applied electric currents to make her muscles jump and twitch.

The next visitor was a hairdresser, an effeminate little man with magic hands. Jane did not have her photographs with her, but he could *quite* see how it was meant to be and *very* sensible too, but if Madam didn't mind he thought that he could get the same easily kept style with just a *little* more flattering effect. Madam didn't give a damn and said so.

Evening visiting brought Laura and Ginger, with flowers to add to the growing collection. Thoughtfully, Laura had brought Jane's make-up case from the camper. Ginger read her the cards and Laura read out the accumulating messages. It seemed that everyone, including many of whom Jane had never heard, were wishing her well.

'We can't do this very often,' Laura warned her. 'It's a six-hour round-trip by car. You can't do it by train at all, not starting from home.'

'Phone me,' Jane said. 'It'll be cheaper.'

With some difficulty, she had raised her head and located a bedside telephone.

'Wait for our calls,' Laura said. 'Hospitals add an enormous percentage oncost to telephone charges. It's how they make up for the government cuts. You'd be cheaper with a mobile.'

'We're not allowed mobiles,' Jane told her. 'They interfere with the monitors.'

'You're sure you don't mind if we limit our visiting? We'll still be thinking about you.'

'No, I don't mind. I don't particularly want anybody to see me in this state. I'll get them to move the phone to where I can reach it.' She called on her reserves of courage and asked the question that had been in her mind since she had hung in her restraining straps. 'Is Henry Two a write-off?'

'You'll have to see it for yourself,' Ginger said, 'but I'm not going to lie to you. That's my guess. Cheaper to buy a new one.'

'Oh, well,' Jane said. 'Poor Harry! But we've had a lot of fun.'

'It may not be over quite yet,' said Laura. 'It depends on you. Money's beginning to trickle in. Your sponsors are coughing up for your recent successes. It's a pity,' she added reflectively, 'that I didn't negotiate a special rate for televised crashes, but at least they won't be able to deny that Henry Two was on television. And that clip's getting repeated over and over.

'Next, your lecture's been bought. I thought that it might go for one of the popular science talks on Beeb Two, but instead ITV want it split into sixteen five-minute talks, one to go out before the broadcast of each Formula One Grand Prix. You get a fee for the extra editing and voice-overs. It'll be something to keep you occupied during your convalescence.

'Then again, orders are coming in from the racing schools for your videos of the circuits. Pierre's begun sending back his videos of the Continental circuits. His voice sounds highly erotic, describing the racing line and technique for getting round it in a hurry, all with that sexy French accent. And finally, I bet you'll get lots of offers of TV appearances when you're out and about again.'

Jane tried to raise her head to look at their faces but the effort was too much. 'That's good. You've done brilliantly. But let's face it, chicks. Racing's over, probably for ever. If some money's coming in, well, goody goody. I'll be able to pay you two and the Dodsons some back wages. But it's coming too late. I wasn't even keeping up with paying back the student loan I had to take out. The mortgage is seriously in arrears. I'd sell the house, but what would become of the Dodsons?'

There was a painful silence. It had been a happy time. They had taken on bigger and much richer teams and had had more success than was usually given to the private entry. But life moved on.

'I've got to be sensible,' Jane said, pleading. 'Don't look at me like that. I'm a big girl now. The time for dreams is over. And motor racing was invented as the most efficient way known to man of getting rid of unwanted money. What's more, it suffers from the same malady as the arts and the other so-called sports — all the rewards go to the top very few.'

The silence came back like a shroud.

'Do I get redundancy money?' Ginger asked suddenly.

'Dream on,' said Laura.

★ ★ ★

She had rather expected a visit from Hugh Waterton, but this never came. During their regular phone calls, Laura was only evasive when Hugh's name came up.

For a week, Jane was numb and almost helpless. Then the tingling began again. It was maddening but it was a sign that she was on the mend. She gritted her teeth and tolerated it. Under the physiotherapist's guidance she exercised, forcing movement into muscle after muscle and joint after joint. She was as weak as a kitten but mobility was coming back and, with it, hope for the future. She was even able to attend to her hair and make-up unaided.

There was a steady trickle of telephoned enquiries after her health. The hospital issued a standard bulletin in reply. This had reached a level of approval roughly equivalent to an MOT certificate when Jane received an unexpected and very welcome visitor.

Julian Berkeley walked into the room. As always, he was well groomed and smartly dressed, this time in a business suit and club tie. She could just manage to smell his aftershave and, even more faintly, a good cigar.

'How lovely to see you!' she exclaimed, without stopping to think. She was suddenly glad that she was sitting up and had managed better than ever before with her face and hair. She wondered if she hadn't been too effusive.

But apparently not. 'Then you forgive me for not coming earlier?' He kissed her chastely on the forehead and took the visitor's chair. 'I wanted to know, before I came, whether or not you were going to make a complete recovery.'

This seemed perfectly reasonable to Jane.

Naturally, anyone with his consideration and manners would wish to know whether he was encouraging a convalescent or cheering up a cripple. 'All my bits are working again,' she said. 'Not very efficiently, but definitely working. Machines do it so much better — you just replace the faulty part and all's well again. But they tell me that I'll be leaping and dancing again by term-time.'

'That's good,' he said gravely. 'I've never seen you leap or dance. When will you be fit to drive again?'

'On the road? Possibly six weeks.'

'I meant competitively.'

'I don't know. The question doesn't arise. I've written off my car and whichever way I think about it, up, down or sideways, I couldn't justify investing in another one even if I had the money, which I haven't. I've started to think like an accountant, which is an awful thing to say about anybody, especially myself. There's no profit in pleasure. It's been a whole lot of fun, but it's over. I made up my mind from the beginning that if, or maybe when, something like this happened, I'd walk away.'

He was nodding slowly. 'I timed my visit carefully,' he said. 'I didn't want to raise false hopes. But I came as soon as the bulletin promised a complete recovery. You see, I think that a Formula Renault team intends to offer you a place.'

'How on earth would you know a thing like that?' she asked.

'I've been checking up on who else has been enquiring after your health — there are ways and means, just don't ask what they are. I don't suppose they intend to pay you, but I can't be sure and you might be tempted. And, of course, there may be others. So I came to get my word in first. How would you like to drive in Formula Three? You probably know that I have an interest in KB Tools, which owns Leopold Engines. You may also know that we run the KB Leopold team, developing the engines and promoting both companies. We've been running two cars and a spare in Formula Three. I've been thinking of a third car, in Alex livery but promoting all three firms, for you to drive.'

He paused and waited. She said nothing and he saw that she was hesitating, caught between hope and wariness. Suddenly he saw the cause of her concern. 'You would be given a contract,' he said, 'and paid a good fee. I assure you, you wouldn't lose by it.'

She felt pleasure like a huge air-bubble run down her body. Her toes curled, even the ones which had so far resisted the efforts of herself and the physiotherapist. Then followed doubt and uncertainty. 'Could I do it?' she asked him.

'Of course you could. I wouldn't have asked you otherwise. We wouldn't be demanding too much at first. If you get into the points, that would be a bonus; but we'll get our investment back in advertising if you just make a showing. I've been watching you since you made your start. You drive with your head as much as your guts, which I appreciate. You finish well and bring the car back safely.'

'Not this time,' she reminded him.

'No. But I've spoken to the driver who was following you. He says that anybody could have been caught that way. He was lucky to come out of it with only a buckled wheel. You've probably earned more respect than you know. But, just by driving, you'll hold the attention of the media and put over the message that you once expressed so eloquently in interview.' He looked into her eyes. 'We would be needing at least one more mechanic. Bring your own with you. He'll know what enables you to give of your best. And now, I've probably given you quite enough to think about. We can hammer out the details later.'

'You can speak to my business manager.'

He smiled wryly. 'If I must. I certainly wouldn't want to play poker with that vixen.'

Jane's mind had been stultified but now it had come alive. 'Have you been paying for all this?' she asked. 'The room and so on?'

'Alex BP is paying for it. The publicity has generated a lot of advertising. As your principal sponsor I felt that we owed it to you.'

'You promise me that it didn't come out of your personal pocket?'

'Why would it matter?'

She never noticed that he had evaded the question. 'I'm not sure that it does,' she said seriously. 'When I come to think, it would have been quite customary if you'd accepted my invitation that evening. Logically, it should be just as acceptable now.' Jane took a deep breath. 'Why *did* you turn me down?'

'Would you expect me to go around seducing the grand-daughters of my late friends?'

'Hardly. But you didn't try to seduce me. I tried to seduce you. Unsuccessfully.'

He smiled ruefully. 'My dear, you'll never know how near you were to success.'

'Easy to say, while I'm stuck here and a nurse may come in at any minute.' She was silent while she wondered how far she dared go in expressing herself. 'Perhaps I should have tried a little harder. Well, the offer remains open without a single string attached to it, but I'll never refer to it again. I always think that the first move should be up to the gentleman, don't you?' He laughed until he choked. 'That's the way that nature intended it,' he said when he had recovered his breath.

★ ★ ★

He left her a basket of fruit and flowers. As soon as the door had closed behind him, she grabbed for the phone. But Laura would be at work and she had no idea of the office number. Instead, she phoned home. Mrs Dodson had called her at least once a day and Jane had kept her abreast of every inch of progress, but she had to spend a few minutes convincing the good lady that she was well on the road to full recovery at last before asking her to get hold of Ginger and Laura and have them phone her, immediately if not much, much sooner.

Relaxation was impossible. She was back in her activity mode. A moment's thought showed that the next priority on her rapidly extending mental list would be the physiotherapist. She dispatched a message by way of the hospital's telephone system and, while she waited, she flexed her muscles and worked her joints and willed the commands of her mind to reach her extremities.

The physiotherapist, whose badge declared her to be a Maureen, had been concerned at Jane's listless uninterest in recovery. She reached Jane's room half an hour later to find her patient transformed. Jane was bright-eyed, already moving better and determined to make immediate and giant progress.

'Do you think you could walk yet?' Maureen asked.

'I shan't know until I try.'

'Hold on while I fetch a Zimmer frame. I'll get one with wheels on the front, so that you'll feel at home.'

With the aid of the frame, Jane hobbled about the room and then, feeling geriatric but pocketing her pride, ventured out into the corridors of the hospital. Maureen, who was a fan of motor racing in general and Jane in particular, hovered anxiously but assured Jane that she was making 'great strides'.

Jane came to a halt. She did not yet feel ready to walk and speak at the same time. 'I'd say that I was making great shuffles, but what's in a word? I want your advice. I want exercises. First to get me back on my feet then back on the track.'

Maureen nodded approvingly. Ambition, even impossible ambition, was a downhill stretch on the road to recovery. 'What in particular?' she asked.

'General fitness. I don't want rippling muscles, that's not the scene at all. I want muscles which can stand strain for long periods. The neck's the most important. It takes a lot of punishment in racing and at the moment mine feels like wet string. Then arms and shoulders. Let's get back to my room. My head's beginning to spin.'

When Jane was back in her bed and undergoing a steel-fingered massage, Maureen said, 'That's more than enough for now. I'll give you some exercises, but mind you build up slowly. You've gone flabby while you've been here, your muscles won't be supporting your joints the way they should and if you try to hurry you'll crock yourself up. I'll write you out a programme.'

'Should I buy some exercise machines?'

'Do you have a health club nearby?'

'Ouch! Yes. Quite a good one.'

'Then I wouldn't bother. A good health club should have more and better machinery than you could find room for. But I'll suggest some exercises you can do in bed for now.'

★ ★ ★

From that day on, Jane's progress was rapid. She was soon allowed home, with the Zimmer frame on loan. Henry came to collect her with the Ford, bringing what Mrs Dodson considered to be suitable clothes for a homecoming invalid. On arrival home Jane went willingly to bed, but that evening a party, restrained but ebullient, germinated in her bedroom. Jane smiled and smiled while stretching and relaxing her muscles secretly under the bedclothes.

Laura attended the party and stayed the night although she had originally come over to report on her preliminary negotiations with Mr Berkeley and representatives of Alex BP, KB Tools and Leopold Engines. 'They're bringing out new cars,' she said. 'The old ones were getting a bit dated. Yours will be the first. They want you to be fit by Christmas and go out to Portugal to do familiarisation and testing, probably until halfway through January. Your fee starts from then. So does Ginger's. He wanted to come and see you this evening but he has a date, too promising to break, with some girl or other. He's over the moon.'

'I'll have to give up my job,' Jane said.

'No, you won't, not yet. Mr Berkeley came with me to see Professor Barnes. The Professor doesn't want to lose you altogether

— recruitment to Applied Science has taken a definite rise since you became a legend in your own lunchtime. They agreed that you could go up to part-time lecturer, not junior any more, and only make yourself useful two days a week in term-time. That won't hamper any of Mr Berkeley's plans for you.'

'Don't I have any say in the matter?' Jane asked.

'No, of course you don't,' Laura said. 'I'm surprised that you even ask such a question. You're just a counter in an economic board game. Lie back and think of England.'

'You're enjoying this,' Jane said accusingly.

'Yes, of course I am. *This is real life and all else is misery or mere endurance.* Who said that?'

'You did. I don't know who said it first.'

For a few days Jane went about the house and garden with the Zimmer frame. Then the frame was sent back to the hospital with gifts of inexpensive wine and chocolates for the staff and Jane got around, first with two sticks and then with one. Finally, the sticks were discarded and serious work could begin at the health club.

During this period of convalescence and until the university term began in October, Jane, when not engaged in her exercises, would have been underoccupied — a state intolerable to one of her energy. It took her only half a day to dictate the new voice-overs for the lecture video. But orders had begun to come steadily for the videotapes of British and European circuits. The agreement negotiated by Laura was that the parent firm of the TV company would produce the copies and Laura would arrange for marketing through the driving schools and by advertisements in the motor-sports magazines, but nobody had given serious consideration to who would receive the orders, make up the sets and post them out. By general agreement, this task fell to Jane.

The work was light. When the weather was fine, much of it could be done in the garden. Most of the orders arrived by telephone. Jane was quite capable of noting down a requirement, an address and a credit card number. But if they happened to find out who they were talking with, most of the callers wanted a chat and Jane found that this passed the time very pleasantly. As she had supposed, many of the orders were from aspiring drivers wanting to familiarise themselves in advance with the circuits they hoped to conquer.

But there were others. One in particular seemed slightly off-beat and she began asking questions. The caller, it turned out, was in a wheelchair. He would never drive anything except perhaps a family car converted to hand controls. He enjoyed watching others do the things he yearned for but which would always be beyond him. In most sports, he could never even pretend to participate. But he had a disused saloon car in his garage and he had rigged up a television set in front of the windscreen and a video machine on the passenger's seat. It was his great pleasure to run the circuit videos and live through the driving in his mind, following the actions insofar as he was able. His feet might nor move on the pedals but in his mind he did it all. Three friends, similarly handicapped, were in the habit of joining him. They were familiar with the British circuits by now and wanted to venture in their imaginations further afield to those on the Continent.

Jane was suddenly overwhelmed by a fellow-feeling and the realisation of how lucky she had been to have recovered from a similar disability. There was only one thing that she could think of to do for these less fortunate men. She recruited Ginger who, as Laura had said, was in a state of euphoria over the promised job and was her slave. The remains of Henry Two were straightened out and welded roughly together. When they bore at least a superficial resemblance to a racing car

301

again, they were presented to the group, for an honourable retirement and to replace the old saloon car. This resulted in delighted letters appearing in the motoring press and a fresh spurt of orders.

* * *

By the start of the university term, Jane had discarded her sticks and was working her way back towards full physical fitness. Some of the teaching staff made it clear that they thought her mad. Most were sympathetic and pleased at her recovery. The students were universally respectful.

By December she was restored in mind and body. The sales side of the video business had been handed over to a professional firm. And the new car was ready.

She flew out to Portugal with Julian Berkeley and the team manager, Phil Sotherby, an elderly man who had once been a star of Formula Two but now found even a journey by air a penance. They left snowbound Britain and arrived in mild, bright weather. Mr Berkeley was at pains to explain that he had come along to treat himself to a holiday, but Jane thought that he might be there to offer moral support. A dual carriageway brought their hired car to Estoril, set among rounded, scrub-covered hills. The smell of pines was all around.

The rest of the team arrived by road. Jane was surprised to see how much gear and how many people had been packed into a single transporter. There would be far more for a race, she was assured, and many times more again for Formula One.

'We'd better get a move on,' Mr Sotheby said on the first morning. 'We've booked for a fortnight. There's another Formula Three team here for the first week. They won't bother us. But a Formula One team arrives during our second week and they usually expect priority. They don't always get it,' he added with a thin smile, 'but they expect it. Certainly, our time-trials may be upset with a Grand Prix car blasting around the place.'

Jane refused to be hurried unduly. The new car was unshipped and she spent most of a morning studying it. She looked under and around it until she could appreciate the design philosophy and make a reasoned guess as to how it would handle. The car looked severe and businesslike in primer, but, as Mr Sotheby said, 'Nobody who matters will set eyes on it just yet and there's no point putting all the embroidery on it when you may be bouncing it off the Armco barriers tomorrow.'

'Thank you very much,' Jane replied.

The wings, the swell of the side-pods and the width of the slick tyres gave it an appearance more akin to a Grand Prix car than anything she had driven before. She fitted herself into it. Her new racing seat was a comfortable fit and she had room for her feet and knees. She spent a long time memorising the unfamiliar gear change.

Nobody had so much as dropped a hint, but she knew that there was a suspicion among the team that she was Julian Berkeley's mistress and not a serious competitor. She did not let that provoke her into being hasty. Only when she felt at home in the car did she don helmet, visor and gloves, strap herself in and give the signal for the car to be started.

She pulled out as soon as the engine had warmed. She had intended to spend several laps in feeling out the car but she came in after the first lap.

The man from the design office hurried to her side. 'Something wrong?'

'The mirrors are vibrating. I shan't be able to see a thing in them.'

'We'll fix that for tomorrow.'

'I'll want the brake pedal moved. Ginger knows how I like it for toe-and-heeling. I can manage for now.'

She went out again. The car came very close to her private predictions but it was subtly different from Henry Two. It was a harder ride but it was faster, more eager, with more grip and a slightly different response. It began to feel like a friend. She came in after twelve more laps and stretched her legs.

'The floor's bottoming at the rear on the bumps at two places on the circuit — the middle of Turn Two and going up the hill at the far corner. A few millimetres raised at the back should do it.'

'No problem.'

'But that will increase the downforce, which feels more than enough already. I'd like to try it with the rear wing angle reduced by one hole.'

'Can do.'

The car was fitted with radio telemetry, far more than would have been fitted in racing conditions. The team could monitor the engine and other working parts. They could also tell a great deal about Jane's manner of driving, but they soon saw that she had charge of the car. They made suggestions, they advised her if out of inexperience she suggested modifications which were unlikely to work, but in general they went by what she said. They tried infinite permutations on the gear ratios.

They were beginning to work as a team.

On the fourth day, becoming more confident, she took the car too far beyond its limit of adhesion and span off into the gravel. There was no damage but the gravel found its way everywhere and the mechanics took an age to remove it. By then the car was good, the set-up suited her and her lap times were becoming respectable.

That evening, Julian Berkeley carried her off for dinner in the town. 'Are you pleased?' she asked him.

'I thought you knew,' he said. 'We're all most impressed. You're approaching Charles's lap times, and he slid off regularly when he clocked them. After only three or four days' acquaintance with the car, your performance has amazed us all.'

'Happy to be giving satisfaction,' she said. The moment the words were out she wanted to call them back. She had been expecting an approach, now that they were far away from those wagging tongues which he seemed to fear. She could see him making up his mind to speak, to invite her up to his room. The sudden passion in his eyes made her knees tremble. She put one finger on the back of his hand. 'I know I said that I wouldn't refer to it again,' she said, 'but I think I must, because I don't want you to feel rebuffed. My invitation remains open, but not now. Not when I'm driving the next day. Relaxed is the last thing I want to be.'

'Relaxed is sometimes fastest,' he said.

'Relaxed is sometimes dead. I want my reactions at their quickest.'

'Before we go home . . . ?'

'That may be quite different.'

'Yes,' he said slowly. 'I can go along with that. I can be patient.'

As the set-up improved and the glitches were eradicated one by one, the sessions became practice and a trial of reliability. Jane was not as fit as she had thought and she found the hours of driving a physical strain at first, but driving a car is the best exercise for driving. Soon, a day spent driving more than the length of a Formula One Grand Prix left her tired but fulfilled. The pile of used tyres beside the transporter was growing large. Estoril is a hard circuit on tyres.

Near the end of their stay, she arrived at the circuit one morning in a thoughtful mood and with her laptop computer under her arm. Two large transporters had arrived late the previous night, but she ignored them. Julian Berkeley was talking with the chief mechanic and the man from the design office. This last was tubby and fair-haired. His mind was as lively as his movements were sluggish. He had become an admirer of Jane. He made frequent use of her still evolving computer program and had contributed material for it. His name was Dennis Yates.

The men broke off politely as she joined them. She devoted a second or two to a polite greeting and then spoke direct to Dennis Yates. 'What is all this downforce *for?*' she asked him.

He looked puzzled. 'To hold the car down,' he said. 'You know it.'

'That's what I thought you'd say,' she said. 'Because it's what every design does. But it's wrong. The reason for holding the car down is to hold the wheels down. Right?'

'Right,' he admitted.

'But in holding the whole car down we're making difficulties for ourselves and we end up with rock-hard suspension. I tell you, the suspension makes my teeth rattle. We've more or less damped out the wheel-patter now, but that's only reducing the problem after we've created it. We could get better roadholding if we could hold the wheels down while we soften the suspension — even a little. Right?'

'I suppose so.'

'I was thinking about it last night. Suppose we introduced a modification to the suspension and the air scoops. We could actually take advantage of the wheel turbulence instead of fighting it. Like this. Give me a notebook and a pencil.' Julian Berkeley obliged and she produced a sketch in a dozen fluid movements. 'This way, the airflow effect presses the wheels down and we could let up a bit on the wings and soften the springs and dampers. Slightly, but even a little would make an improvement.'

'I think it would be considered a breach of the rules,' Dennis said.

The head mechanic looked at him with contempt. 'I don't remember anything in the FIA Yellow Book that says so.'

'It might be worth a try,' Mr Berkeley suggested. 'It could pass as being for additional strength. We could always revert to the original parts if we were ruled against. Let's take the spare assemblies into the town and find a machine-shop. What's the precise shape?'

'Hold on,' Jane said, opening her laptop. 'Let the computer do the work. What's the tensile strength of the alloy?' She sat down on a convenient wall and opened the laptop. For several minutes she tapped the keys and frowned and muttered to herself. Then she said 'Aha!' and keyed some more. An invisible hand began to draw outlines on the screen. 'Here you are. Print this off on your fax machine and you're in business.'

The three men studied the diagrams together. 'Seems clear,' Dennis said. 'I'll get it made up.'

'I'll drive you,' Berkeley said. 'My Portuguese is less than fluent, but it's better than yours. Do you want to come along?' he asked Jane. 'Get lunch in the town?'

'I'll stay here and get in some more practice. I want to try it with slight understeer in the set-up. Brake late, turn in short and accelerate early. I think there's a few tenths of a second to be saved that way.'

A Formula One car had been unloaded from one of the new transporters but nobody seemed to be in a hurry to drive it. Jane settled herself into her car and went out onto the circuit. She knew the way round in her sleep by now and the car was as near perfection as she could make it. To check, she put in a few storming laps and came in again. Lewis, the head mechanic, helped her out of the car. She took off her helmet and shook out her hair.

'Something wrong, Gorgeous? You were going great guns.'

'It's great. We'd better record the perfect set-up before the bosses come back and you have to tear it all apart. These figures will do to start the other cars on as well.'

He nodded. 'You're not as daft as you look,'

he said. 'But who is?'

'You are,' she said quickly. The two had found a rapport but she knew that she had to give as good as she got.

The wintry sun was pleasant. She closed her eyes and leaned on the pit wall to soak it up. After a few minutes she heard somebody approaching and took a look. It was a heavily built man in his fifties, black-haired, blue-chinned and with a look of authority.

'You're Miss Faraday, no?' he asked. He had a faintly Mediterranean accent.

She smiled. 'I am Miss Faraday, yes,' she said. 'And you are Arthur Rosetti, right? I've seen your photograph.'

'Please. I call myself Rossett, now that I too am British. Racing Manager of that rabble over there. But I heard you broke your neck.'

'I mend quickly,' she told him. 'Anyway, it was only whiplash.'

'Aha! You fully mended now?'

'Never better.'

'Certainly I see you going like stink just now. You're test-driving for KB Leopold? Listen, I got a problem. Brand-new Formula One car, just out of the wrapping paper you might say, and I get a fax from my test-driver. He's got a gastric bug, would you believe? He's getting shots today and he'll fly out the day after tomorrow, or maybe the day after that. So here we are, sitting on our hands at God knows how much a day and no driver. You want to break the car in for us? Bring out the first teething troubles, check for leaks and begin the setting-up, no more than that. That way, our driver can get motoring without more time going down the pan. You understand? I've heard good things about you.'

Jane hesitated. All the rules of safety, honesty and fair dealing demanded that she explain immediately that she had never driven a Formula One car or anything to be mentioned in the same breath, that her acquaintance even with Formula Three was so recent that she had never even raced in it. But he had not asked any questions about her experience. He had taken her on trust on the word of others.

Their discussion must have been audible to the mechanics fussing around her car. Ginger left the group and walked towards their transporter. As he brushed close past her, he whispered, 'Go for it.'

Mr Rossett misunderstood her hesitation. 'We don't need much,' he said. 'Mostly just to get a few laps of telemetry to tell us how it's shaking down. There'll be a fee,' he added. He mentioned a figure which, to Jane, seemed enormous for a few hours' work — which she would happily have done for nothing.

'All right,' she said. 'You're on.'

'Just remember, if you spin off, do it where you won't hit anything solid.'

Again, she refused to be hurried. She studied the car with care. The body was arrow-slim. The side-pods, occupied mostly by the cooling systems, were inverted aerofoils. She felt the tyres. The Goodyear slicks were of a different compound from the Avons. She could guess how they would feel when they were hot. She looked at the suspensions, the steering linkages.

The chief mechanic said, 'The set-up should be fairly good. We have a computer program that comes out close. The boss pirated it over the phone off somebody else's computer.'

Jane looked down at the laptop computer in his hand. The tabulation showing on the LCD looked familiar. 'That's my program,' she said.

The man looked appalled. 'Christ!'

Jane chuckled. 'Don't worry about it. I shan't sue. I pirated most of it from others anyway. And don't accept it too wholeheartedly. The ideal racing line's a slightly eccentric parabola and I haven't resolved the geometry of it yet. I'm still working on it.'

Somebody brought her racing seat from the Formula Three car. She sat in the cockpit while the ideal position was marked and then got out for it to be bolted into place. Then she settled herself in and, while they wired her helmet for radio communication, she told herself over and over, *Use the floor clutch to get away from a standstill only. Then steering-wheel changes. Clutch button on left. Right paddle for up, left paddle down. Use left foot for braking. Carbon-fibre brakes, so they work best hot. Brake lightly for a second or two before arriving at braking point. Not too heavy on the throttle and keep it very light in low gears.* The litany went on. By the time all was ready she knew it by heart and thought that it would come to her as it was needed.

She felt hollow and rather breathless, but those sensations were old friends.

The starter was inserted into the gearbox. There were half a dozen men round the car and more standing back. On Jane's nod, she felt the engine being turned over. It fired, and settled into a surprisingly smooth tickover. The nearest faces looked relieved. She went over her litany once more while playing with the throttle to get the feel of its progressive effect. Even with her earplugs and helmet in place the sound of the engine was daunting.

She held the engine to the ideal 4,000 r.p.m. which would maintain steady running without too sudden heating. The head mechanic, watching the temperature on the hand-held telemetry, adjusted the mixture and gave her the nod.

The car had been left with the front wheels turned — possibly as a trap to test her, or so she thought. She was ready to straighten them the moment the car moved so that, when the clutch caught her unawares and the rear wheels span for an instant in a haze of smoke, she instinctively corrected. The car set off with a neat, crabwise flick which could have looked deliberate and highly skilled.

The engine seemed to be misfiring. She was on the point of reporting by radio when she realised that she had not cancelled the pit lane speed controller. A flick of the switch and suddenly it could have been a different car. Jane worked her way up the gears, holding the revs down to a level which she guessed might be about halfway up the power curve. While still on the long straight she twitched the wheel from side to side, ostensibly to warm the tyres but in reality to get more feeling for the steering and grip. Even treading lightly on the throttle the acceleration was breathtaking. It was Jane's first drive with an engine of maximum efficiency. In the lower formulae, the requirements of the rules restricted power output in the interests of economy; in Formula One, money was no object and an engine was seldom expected to last more than one race.

The first turn came at her. When she braked, it was like running into a rubber wall. The car cornered as if on rails. She slowed well down at the second right-hander where there was a bad bump in the middle and where she knew that any car which ran wide would suffer serious damage. Another right-hander. With so much adhesion, the G-forces of cornering and braking and the unimaginable acceleration were enormous and already she was beginning to feel the strain in her neck. The left-handed hairpin was almost a relief. Then it was the bumpy back straight and a left-hander again. The suspension was hard and there was almost nothing to cushion her from every ripple of the road. She had to clamp her jaw to prevent her teeth snapping together.

'Something's not quite right,' she said aloud.

A voice in her ear said, 'Come in.'

When she came out of the tightening last bend and the start-and-finish straight opened up, she worked her way down the gears, found neutral and coasted in with the engine dead.

The car was hardly stopped before she was surrounded by anxious faces. Some, she knew, suspected that she was chickening out. She pushed up her visor. She pressed the button on the steering-wheel to transmit. 'The back end feels different on left- and right-handers,' she said. 'It's not symmetrical. I know it doesn't have to be, but we ought to get the symmetrical set-up right before experimenting with anything fancy. You'd better check the tyres, the shockers, the spring ratings and the height of set-up.'

'There are some funny cambers here,' said the head mechanic.

'I know about the cambers,' she said. 'I've been going round here for the past fortnight until I'm dizzy.' She removed the steering-wheel and her helmet and began to climb out.

'Where you going?' Arthur Rossett demanded.

'I want a pee, while I have a spare moment,' she said. 'Do you mind?' She went back to the KB-Leopold transporter. The mechanics there, idle for the moment, looked at her curiously but she had nothing to say. In the tiny toilet compartment, while she shrugged down her overalls and relieved herself, she reviewed mentally the sensations the car had given her and planned in her mind exactly how she should respond. She gave her neck a massage. Then she went back to the Formula One car.

The head mechanic was smiling. 'One tyre was slightly below pressure,' he said. 'Fancy you noticing that!'

She repeated the routine of settling into the car. This time, she got away cleanly. She was becoming confident along the straights and was feeling her way faster around the bends. Up to the speeds of the Formula Three car she had no problems, but the power combined with the adhesion of the wide slicks beckoned her onward, into unknown territory. The car was good. But not perfect. After four laps, she pressed the button and said aloud, 'I'm getting oversteer.'

'Come in,' said the voice. 'We'll try a little more angle on the rear wing. Two holes, I think, for a start.'

She pulled into the pit lane again. This time, she remained in the car but removed her helmet and rubbed her neck. 'Your injury still troubles you?' Arthur Rossett asked, stooping over her.

'I'm trying to make sure that it doesn't,' she said.

The work only took moments. She went

out again. She found that leaning her head into the bend reduced the strain in her neck, or perhaps it was only that the frequent changes of position helped to keep the cramps at bay. The car was better balanced now and she was getting the corners sorted out at the higher speeds. But she was still taking it cautiously at the bend where she had slid off with the Formula Three car. This was on the slippery left-hander with the bad camber where the new track rejoins the old, as she was reminded each time she came around by the black marks left by a dozen other cars going off before hers. She was acutely conscious of being in charge of a car worth . . . she could only make a guess that she could have bought twenty of Henry Two, brand new, for the same money.

'Push her along a bit,' said the voice in her ear.

Jane had been under the impression that she was 'pushing it along', but she acknowledged the instruction. When she came to tackle each bend more aggressively, braking later and accelerating sooner, she found that the car's adhesion, amplified by ground effect, was more than able to cope. Even at her bugbear, when she tackled it with commitment, the car seemed to dance, threatening to spin, but stayed under control.

She poured on more speed and found that the car had still more to give.

Jane began to sing until she remembered that her thumb was still on the button and every sound was being relayed back to the pits. Suddenly, she was at a pitch of exhilaration she had never known before. She was in command. The car was talking to her, saying that she had reached its limit. She was a Valkyrie. She was a greyhound, a leaping horse. She was flying. She was a singing bird or an angel. She could have walked on water or healed the sick. She was in direct communication with God.

God's voice spoke in her ear. 'Slow down immediately,' it said, 'and come into the pits.'

Immediately, Jane sobered. Had she been committing some unforgivable sin, against which nobody had bothered to warn her? She continued the lap at quarter throttle and turned into the pit lane. As she brought the car to rest she lifted off her helmet and balaclava, instinctively running a hand through her hair.

'What's the matter?' she asked. 'Was I doing something wrong?'

'What's to do wrong?' Arthur Rossett replied. 'You did fine, never ran out of road once. You were quite right not to hurry. Telemetry says a fault develops in the gearbox. Better to fix it quick. Anyway, we got all we need for now from the telemetry. The car will be ready for Carl when he comes out. He can make the next steps. You done your bit. Come to the transporter and I give you a cheque.' He turned away.

The head mechanic helped her out of the car. Her neck was paining her but she was damned if she would let any of these men see it. 'Carl?' she said. 'Would that be Carl Lansdowne?'

'That's the one. And I don't like him much either.'

She forced a smile. 'It shows, does it? He's an arrogant sod. And he did a spin in front of me so that I wrecked my TVR and ever since then he's been trying to make out that it was all my fault.'

'Your own car?'

'My very own.'

He whistled. 'Expensive! Can't blame you for resenting a thing like that.'

'Put itching powder in his helmet, from me.'

'I might just do that.'

Jane walked to the Seat which had been hired for her use. Her neck was on fire and locked solid but she hid her discomfort. Ginger appeared beside her as she got into the car. 'I'm going back to the hotel,' she declared without turning her head. 'Tell Mr Berkeley, would you?'

She headed the car for the tunnel under the track.

★   ★   ★

The staff at the hotel were well accustomed to drivers. Most of them were enthusiasts and always eager to chat with the attractive, red-haired Englishwoman who had suddenly appeared among all the macho, hairy-chested men. But Jane was in no condition for socialising. She walked like an automaton up to her room, took several aspirins without counting them and lowered herself carefully onto her bed, moving cautiously until she had found the least uncomfortable position. When the pain had begun to abate she put up a hand and began, without making any other movement, to massage the long muscles.

Later, when Julian Berkeley arrived and knocked at the door, she was still too tender to rise and let him in. He went to find a maid with a master-key and then she had to satisfy the maid that she was not being intruded on by a ravisher. Finally they were alone.

'What's wrong?' he asked.

'My neck's giving me hell again. I've taken

aspirin, but it's in no hurry to work.'

'I thought that that might be it. If what I've heard is true, that you've been thrashing a GP car round the circuit, then I can't say that I'm surprised.'

She laughed and then groaned as the vibrations disturbed her neck again. 'Arthur Rossett said that I did very well. But he also said that I'd been quite right not to hurry!'

He chuckled. 'Our lads had stopwatches on you. You were getting within five seconds of last year's qualifying time. Not bad, after the first — what? — sixteen or seventeen laps of a strange circuit in a Formula One car. But you were out of your mind to try it, so soon after a bad whiplash injury. I've been watching you like a hawk in case the Formula Three car was too much for you. Now let's see if we can sort you out. Try to rotate on the bed so that your head comes near the foot of it.'

She did as he suggested. But when he began to apply traction she said, 'Do you really know what you're doing?'

'Enough that I know I won't make anything worse.'

'But my neck's coming out of joint.'

'And it's going back in again. I've been around drivers for a long time and this is the commonest injury.' As he spoke, he continued stretching her neck and then relaxing it. 'What's Arthur Rosetti going to think when he finds out he's paid good money to a test driver who'd never driven anything faster than Formula Three — and that for only about ten days?'

'Must he find out?'

'My dear, of course he will. He actually congratulated you. It's far too good a story for anyone of the many who detest him *not* to tell. Now roll over on your face for a proper massage before we try a little manipulation. But first, let's have these overalls off you.'

'I don't have very much on underneath,' she warned.

If she expected him to withdraw like a gentleman, leaving her to struggle out of the overalls as best she could, she was to be disappointed. 'This is no time for modesty,' he said.

'I dare say that you've seen more on the beach,' she agreed.

She raised no further objections as he took off her racing shoes and then undid her overalls, gently helped her to roll onto her face and drew the overalls down and off over her feet. She had one consolation. When, as part of her contract, Klinkenhammer had been persuaded to provide her with a new wardrobe, she had decided that the latest fashions could not be worn over Marks and Spencer undies and had insisted on being supplied with underwear from Verinchy of Paris. She might be shamed but she would not be humiliated.

'I have indeed seen as much or more on the beach,' he said, 'but never so deliciously wrapped.'

He was massaging her back, working up to the shoulders, relaxing the muscles before seeking out the little knots of fibrositis. It was infinitely relaxing. His strong fingers began to dig into the acupuncture points in her neck and she was surprised not to feel any pain. She had no idea how long it had been going on when he rolled her onto her back and applied traction again, but this time he was rotating her head gently from side to side.

'If this still hurts,' he said, 'tell me and we'll get you to a hospital.'

'I'll tell you, sure enough,' she said. But there was no pain. He moved her neck through every possible angle, then slipped a low pillow under her head. 'Now for the last part of the relaxation therapy,' he said.

Now that the pain was gone, she had found her state of euphoria again. This had been a day of days. She relived in her mind her ecstatic affair with the Formula One car. And now the relief of delightful massage. She was half asleep when she realised that the massage had finished. Instead, he seemed to be working his way over her whole body with little kisses, determined not to miss a single inch.

'You'd better help me into the shower,' she said. 'I must stink of sweat.'

'Nothing of the sort,' he said. 'As always, you smell like a beautiful dream.'

She was surprised to notice that he had removed his clothes, but it seemed too late to protest. This man, she decided, could outpoint Pierre in the romancing stakes.

★ ★ ★

'You may care to know,' he said as they drove to the circuit in the morning, 'that you have made a happy man very old.'

'You didn't seem very old last night.'

The new suspension fittings were in place. She went out to try them. There was activity around the Formula One transporters but nobody seemed to be paying her any attention beyond the usual professional interest.

The new fittings certainly had an effect. But for some reason Jane's lap times were, if anything, slightly down on her best and it was decided to revert to the original design.

Many potentially valuable ideas fail to see the light of day for reasons quite unconnected with the merit of the original inspiration.

11

As soon as Mr Berkeley's chauffeur deposited her at home, Jane phoned the hospital. Maureen, the physiotherapist, gave her the address and a recommendation to a colleague, only a mile or two from Jane's home, who took private patients.

The new physiotherapist was a stout lady who had once been pretty. According to her card she was Elizabeth Cotton but, 'Call me Eliza,' she said. 'Everyone else does.' She had had male racing-drivers for clients and she quite appreciated Jane's problem.

She ran sensitive fingers over Jane's joints and muscles. 'That was a nasty whiplash,' she said, 'and frankly, dear, you were mad to make such demands on your neck before it was absolutely, totally and without a shadow of a doubt all better. Never mind. We can sort it out. When do you drive again?'

'April, I think.'

Eliza tutted. 'Couldn't you change to something that doesn't pull your head sideways?'

'I suppose I could switch to motorbikes.'

'No, don't do that, dear. Nasty, dangerous things.'

'I was joking,' Jane explained. 'Anyway, I'll only be driving Formula Three. That doesn't put as much strain on the neck as Formula One cars do and the races are shorter. That Grand Prix car was a one-off.'

'Well, all right,' Eliza said doubtfully. 'We'll just have to repair the damage, build up the muscles and hope for the best. But we don't have very long.'

Jane suddenly pictured one of the female body-builders that she had seen on the television. 'I don't want a neck like a tree trunk, mind. I'm also supposed to look sexy. It goes with the job.'

'Don't worry about it, dear. There's muscles and muscles. We'll have to build your neck up a bit, but if you grow your hair a little longer nobody'll ever notice.'

So Jane's fitness routine was enlarged to include a special muscle-building programme for the neck and arms. Alex BP was engaged in serious discussions with an up-market hairdressing chain with a view to taking over, and Jane was introduced to their most talented stylist, now much too senior to see ordinary clients personally. A longer style, but still falling naturally into place, was created and photographed.

At about that time, Jane was smitten with another of her inspirations. She retired to the garage with Henry. A racing driver in approved gear is covered with flame-proofed material from top to toe. But a vulnerable point where flames can enter is at the neck. In some designs this is closed by an extra collar. Jane set about replacing this with an inflatable collar below her helmet. This she could inflate through a thin, flexible tube inside her helmet. The helmet and collar together would then give her neck extra support from her shoulder. The collar was as easily deflated again but, as Jane pointed out to Laura and others, when she was driving she needed to move her eyes but very small head movements were enough.

★ ★ ★

The Formula Three championship series began early in April. The lecture programme was running down as syllabuses were completed, but during the run-up to exam-time tutorials were more frequent. Professor Barnes, no doubt encouraged by Julian Berkeley, was helpful in allowing Jane to cram a fortnight's commitments into one week, leaving the alternate week available for racing and all the allied activities.

For Jane, it was a new experience to arrive as a member of a team, a driver backed by mechanics and an organisation. Now she felt entitled to stroll among the pavilions, no longer an interloper on the scrounge. Food was provided on demand. (As she told Laura, 'All I have to say is 'Give us a quiche . . . ' ')

The media had not overlooked the return from her 'brush with death' of 'Racy Lady Jane Faraday', as the tabloids had dubbed her. (This sobriquet gave rise to misunderstandings. Once, on being introduced to a hostess who was punctilious about protocol, she was asked, 'Is it Lady Jane or Lady Faraday?')

To the occasional irritation of more significant competitors, Jane was much in demand at press conferences and her autograph was sought after at 'Meet The Public' sessions, but she took it all so modestly that this attention was little resented.

Some of Jane's former rivals had graduated into this more senior class, but in general the faces were again strange and the competition ferocious. Very few dilettantes, racing only for fun or status, appeared in Formula Three. Most of the drivers were deadly serious competitors, battling to make it into Formula Three Thousand (or the Japanese equivalent,

Formula Nippon) or Indycars, en route for the golden goal of Formula One. No quarter was given.

One familiar face was that of Peter Fasque, driving for one of the better-funded teams and again fully equipped with a girlfriend, this time a fiancée. Peter, remembering the loan of Junior which had enabled him to win the Formula Vauxhall Junior Championship, was ready to fall at Jane's feet — a readiness rightly resented by his fiancée, a pretty but vulnerable youngster by the name of Gail.

Gail's jealousy became so extreme that she could hardly bear to see her fiancé in the same group as Jane without hurrying to join them. Jane eventually had to take her aside. 'You're making an ass of yourself,' she said sternly, 'and you'd better cut it out before you become a laughing stock and lose him altogether.'

The possibility of losing her beloved only increased Gail's hostility. 'I know you're carrying on behind my back,' she said. 'He proposed to you once on television. A friend told me.'

Jane sighed. 'Whoever told you that certainly wasn't your friend. He was joking. I'd lent him my car, he'd won the race and the championship with it and they were interviewing us. He had another girlfriend at the time — I've forgotten her name and so, probably, has he. We were joking with the reporters and interviewers and we'd been making inroads into somebody's bottle of champagne. He pretended to propose to me and I turned him down flat. Big laugh. End of story.'

'Is that true? Really? I'm sorry,' Gail said miserably. 'I've been making an ass of myself, just as you said. It's just that . . . just that . . .'

'It's all right. I understand. I have a love of my own now,' Jane said.

'Really? Who?'

'Never you mind. It's a secret.'

The idea of Jane being embroiled in a torrid, secret affair so intrigued Gail that she forgot to be jealous. Instead, she was determined to find out the identity of Jane's secret love and coupled her in her imagination with almost every driver in turn.

Julian Berkeley attended every meeting at which his Formula Three cars were to run. She was never sure whether he would have done so without the prospect of her overnight companionship. She still resolutely refused any amorous proposals while driving was still in prospect, but as soon as the race was over and the car was in the transporter they made their separate ways to whichever hotel they were both patronising. There, they would dine openly and innocently together, retiring late towards their separate rooms but both ending up in one or the other. So discreet were they that even Gail never suspected the passion that linked them.

If Julian had ever been a randy and impetuous youth, those days were gone. He needed, as he explained, both time and stimulus. He loved to undress her as if he were undoing a gift-wrapped present of great value. He took pleasure in every caress and in giving her pleasure in turn. When at last he entered her, his movements until the last seconds were leisurely and luxurious. All this, for Jane, was very good. Her few previous adventures had been pleasant but not nearly so rewarding. She had reached orgasm on a number of occasions but never such mind-blowing and repeated climaxes as these. She returned to the university after each such weekend feeling as though she *on honeydew has fed and drunk the milk of Paradise.*

If Jane's life away from the track had taken on a new bloom, the signs that her racing would be similarly blessed were at first unfulfilled. She knew the car, which was handsomely prepared in the familiar lilac colour and carried the decals of Alex, Klinkenhammer, KB Tools, Leopold Engines and other firms whose names were less familiar. She knew the circuits. Her neck bothered her very little and very rarely and was improving week by week. She now had the reassurance of driving somebody else's car at somebody else's risk and expense and she found that the broad back of a large organisation and the availability of a spare car went a long way to removing her last inhibitions. She could now drive on the limit without any fear of financial consequences, but this on its own was not enough to ensure results.

In the first race of the year, at Silverstone, she qualified quite respectably for the sixth row only to break a universal joint when the lights changed and be left on the line, nearly being wiped out by the cars from behind. Two weeks later, at Thruxton, she earned a slightly better place on the grid, to have one rear-wheel assembly removed after three laps of the race by a driver who thought, wrongly, that he could bully her into letting him through on the inside. The other driver received a two-race suspension, but this was no comfort to Jane or the team. At Donington, while lying sixth and making an impression on the leaders, she hit a patch of oil and ended up in the gravel.

But Julian Berkeley pronounced himself

satisfied. Jane was getting publicity which was rubbing off on the sponsors. Jane, however, was not so easily pleased. She was not interested in publicity for being unlucky or female, but only for being a successful driver.

Then things began to improve. At Brands Hatch she managed to finish, though in twelfth place. At Oulton Park, the car was perfect and Jane suddenly recovered form to qualify in the fourth row and finish sixth — in the points at last. At Donington, she was just squeezed out of the points into seventh place but then, back at Silverstone, with the Formula Three race one of the curtain-raisers to the British Grand Prix, she fought her way out of the ruck, beat off a determined challenge from Peter Fasque (who had no intention of letting past favours affect his will to win) and she stole third place at the last corner. A podium finish at last! She endeared herself to the team by bringing back the presentation champagne unopened and adding to it a second bottle which she had been bringing in readiness for such an occasion, just to be sure the supply would go round.

Two weeks later it was Thruxton again. This time it was Jane's turn to challenge Peter Fasque for a place in the points. She stole the inside line to a sharp bend and was alongside him before the apex. He sat on her tail along the straight but vanished from her mirrors at the next bend. On the next lap she saw his car. It was damaged, but Peter himself, who was being attended by a pair of first-aiders, was obviously walking wounded.

She could make a guess at the scene in the pits. She swung into the pit lane, passed the KB-Leopold pit to the obvious consternation of the occupants and braked to a halt at the alien pit of Peter Fasque's team. She had been telling herself that she would look the world's biggest idiot if the girl was waiting calmly for definitive news but, as she had supposed, Gail had given way to hysteria. She was struggling with two mechanics, who were each both embarrassed and quite worried enough on their own account without having to deal with a driver's girlfriend. But it was clear that Gail, if released, was quite prepared to run to the scene of the accident, even if it meant crossing or running along the middle of the track to do so.

Jane detached her steering-wheel, climbed hastily out of her car and shed her helmet and gloves. 'It's all right,' she said loudly. 'He's up on his feet.'

Everyone in the pit gave a sigh of relief but she had to repeat the message several times before it got through to Gail. Then the other girl sagged, nearly fainted, burst into tears and when the mechanics thankfully released her she fell into Jane's arms and howled. Ever after, Jane could only think of her as 'Howling Gail'.

Any thought of rejoining the race forgotten, Jane patted Gail's back and waited. The howls became hiccups and Gail said over and over that she was sorry, so sorry.

'But,' she said at last, 'he'll have to stop driving. I couldn't go through this again.'

Jane wanted to dash back to her pit and apologise to everybody, but there seemed to be a prior claim to her attention. She pulled Gail out of everyone's way to where they could find seats and a degree of privacy. 'Don't do it,' she said. 'You'll lose him if you try.'

'If he doesn't love me enough . . .'

'The point is,' Jane said, 'do you love him enough? If so, worrying is a small price to pay. You could be one of the lucky ones.'

'I don't know what you mean.'

'Then I'll tell you. You might, just might, be able to persuade Peter to retire. But then you'd be like another Peter, Peter Moran and his wife. I bought my first racing car from him and later we were both driving in Formula Ford. That Peter always said that he was only trying to make it in racing for the money that he could earn if he got to the top, but it was untrue. It was his life, the excitement, the challenge. When the baby came along, Maud made him retire. It was the end of love and the end of their marriage. If your Peter retired to please you, he would resent it and you'd be in the divorce courts within two or three years. As it is, he loves you dearly. If you can accept the worry, you can have the happiness.'

'But if he's killed . . . '

'That's very unlikely these days. You get more frights on the open road.'

'But it could happen,' Gail persisted tearfully.

'Then you'll have had time together. Isn't that better than parting now and not having any time at all?'

Gaul bit her lip. 'Perhaps. I don't know.'

'You'll think about what I've said?'

'I promise.'

Jane left her there. The car had already been collected. She walked back to the transporter to face the wrath of Julian Berkeley. But it was soon clear that Julian was delighted. Television had captured the entire episode, including the drama in the pits. The human interest would guarantee maximum exposure, far outweighing a championship point or two, and much of the warmth would attach to Alex Beauty Products.

Peter Fasque's injuries were very slight and the car was rebuildable. He was back racing two weeks later, and regularly finishing just ahead of Jane — to her chagrin. 'Sometimes,' she told Ginger, 'I wish I'd let Gail talk him into retiring.'

Jane's fortunes continued to improve. She was regularly in the points. But podium places were few and far between. 'The trouble is,' she told Julian over dinner, 'that I know I'm as good as the other drivers, but as a female I'm disadvantaged. I don't mean physically. I mean that women know that they're essential to the continuation of the human race. Men, whether they know it or not, recognise that they're expendable. So they're always prepared to go that little bit further into danger territory.'

'You seem to be straying further and further into that territory yourself,' Julian said. 'I'm trying very hard not to be the sort of person who says, 'Do be careful,' which is a fatuous thing to say in the circumstances. But do, all the same.'

Jane thought it over for as long as it took

340

the waiter to serve the main course. 'I don't think I'm knowingly wandering into danger,' she said at last. 'Of course, there always is danger. Somebody can do something stupid or some component can break. But I hold myself back until I know that, barring unforeseens like that, I can do what I intend to do. If I'm looking for the last tiny fraction, I look for it first where there's a lot of safe run-off and only apply what I've learned where there isn't, later on if at all.'

'Nobody ever asked you for wins,' Julian pointed out. 'You're delivering the goods already. The media follow you around, gasping for photographs of you and the car. The advertising is paying off handsomely. If you become Formula Three champion, I doubt if it would bring in any extra returns. Conversely, do you know how much all this is costing?'

'No, I don't,' Jane said. 'And please don't tell me. I don't want to know. More than that, I very much want *not* to know.'

'Don't let it worry you. But the point I'm trying to make is that, barring interference, you always bring the car back more or less in one piece. That saves a great deal of money and makes the whole exercise viable. I won't worry you by telling you what major damage to the car might cost — '

'It might attract some extra publicity,' Jane said, tongue in cheek.

'Only if you emerged still looking fit for a calendar, which isn't what happened last time. Yes, I know,' he added quickly. 'You did that one at your own expense. Well, I don't want you to have the next one on me. In fact, I don't want you to have it at all. I've got used to having you around. What I'm saying is that I want you to go on racing and getting respectable results, but even more I want you to go on coming back safe. After all, the next two drivers above you in the championship league table are your team colleagues in the KB-Leopold cars. The fact that you're all together suggests that you're getting the best out of the cars; and they're promoting Leopold Engines instead of glamour, so I don't want them knocked off their pedestals.

'Having said that,' Julian went on, 'I may as well tell you that I've had an approach from Simon Vanderveldt. He's the man at the back of Impala, which as you may know —'

' — is the Formula One team whose car I stole a free drive in,' Jane finished for him.

'He wants you to do some more testing.'

'Over Arthur Rossett's dead body. I'm told that he was calling down all sorts of damnations on my head after Estoril.'

'That's partly why he's been replaced. He'd

recommended Carl Lansdowne for a place on the team and as test-driver. Lansdowne turned up after we left. He did seven laps and then virtually wrote the car off.'

'At Turn Two, I suppose?'

'As a matter of fact, yes.'

'Nasty place.'

'So he discovered. He put himself into hospital. The next Impala car wasn't ready yet, so the whole costly exercise produced exactly nothing.

'As you might expect, Lansdowne from his hospital bed tried to blame your setting-up, but it was pointed out to him by everybody concerned that he hadn't even got down to your best lap times before he fell off the road. Vanderveldt called for printouts of the radio telemetry, yours and Lansdowne's, and he decided that he liked yours much better. He got Felidas hired for what development time was left to them but they're having a poor result this season and they want to change engines and partly redesign the car.'

Jane plucked the least important of several messages out of this speech. 'Felidas?' she said. 'Colombian? Raymon Felidas?'

'Yes. You know him?'

'He was one of my lodgers when we were both students.'

'He's been doing the European Formula

Three Thousand circuit, but he looks set to get a Formula One drive soon. But that's by the way. Rossett's been replaced as team manager by his assistant and they want you to go back to Portugal this winter and test for them. You could be available to us between times.'

'What engine are they changing to?'

He grinned. 'Ours. Leopold. They want us to develop a new engine for Formula One. That's why, if you agree, I'm prepared to lend your services. You keep any fee. Before speaking to you, I took the liberty of speaking to Professor Barnes. He's prepared to juggle things to suit you again, so you can hang onto your university connection.' He looked at her seriously. 'This could open doors for you.'

'I'll have to think about it,' Jane said. 'I'll talk it over with Laura.'

'That brings me to the next item on the agenda,' Julian said. 'Phil Sotheby's been a great asset in his day, and what he doesn't know about motor racing management isn't worth knowing, but he's getting past it. He's forgetting things. You and the others are covering up for him — don't think I don't know it.'

'He's such a nice old boy. You're not thinking of getting rid of him?'

'I'm thinking that he needs an assistant to

learn the job. Do you think that manager of yours — Laura, is it? — do you think she'd be interested?'

'I could ask her.'

'Do that small thing.' He signed the bill. 'And now, you're looking tired. You've had a hard day. Shall I escort you to your room?'

'Do that small thing,' Jane said. She yawned ostentatiously.

★ ★ ★

When Laura received Jane's phone call, she drove over the same evening. They both took chairs out on the lawn in what had once been their favourite place. They could hear the golfers topping and cursing beyond the hedge but the garden was a haven of peace.

'This feels like the first time I've sat down for a fortnight,' Jane said, 'except in a racing car, of course.'

'It probably is. So what's this news you have for me?'

Jane explained about the failure of Phil Sotheby to withstand the ageing process. She fished inside her dress and produced a slightly crumpled envelope. 'I was to ask you whether you'd be interested in a job, understudying him — implicitly with a view to inheriting the post when Phil finally succumbs to senility or something. The terms are all spelled out in this letter. But, of course, you may be committed to your dad's firm.'

Laura scanned the letter quickly. 'Could I do the job?'

'Now you sound like me. It's almost exactly what you've been doing for me except there are three cars instead of one but on the other hand you don't have to worry about where the money's coming from. And you'd have to lay on some entertainment for important clients instead of scrounging it so that we can eat.'

'It's manna from heaven,' Laura said. 'To be honest, I don't think lawyers like being managed. I've set up the systems and they use them or ignore them, just as they feel inclined at the time. No doubt they'll go on doing so after I leave. The ways were going to have to part, whatever happened. But Jane, one question. Would Hugh Waterton go with the job?'

'Now, this may be the rub,' Jane said. 'I've hardly set eyes on Hugh. Mr Berkeley has been coming along to do the sponsor-liaison bit.'

'You couldn't suggest that perhaps he's a little too senior to waste his time on such trivialities?'

346

'No,' Jane said. 'I couldn't.'

Jane was convinced that Laura had extra-sensory perception when it came to affairs of the heart or other organs. Laura sat up and looked at her friend. 'Hullo! What's this?'

'Nothing.'

'You've got a thing for the boss. The question is, does he have a thing for you? Have you been sleeping together?'

'None of your damn business.'

'So you have, then! I told you all along that you should.'

'You did nothing of the sort,' Jane snapped. 'You told me not to set my cap at him because he was already entangled with a horsy blonde — who turned out to be his cousin, by the way, and married to a farmer nearby. We've been keeping it pretty quiet. We're both sensitive on the subject. I don't want to be thought to be after his money and he doesn't want to be seen as an elderly roué leading young girls up the garden path.'

'You'd better tell him you're pregnant,' Laura suggested. 'He's just the type to marry you.'

'He wouldn't believe it, after all the precautions I've insisted on.'

'Mistake. Definitely a mistake. Never mind, I'll think of a solution for you later. What are managers for? But first, let me make my own decision.' She read the letter aloud. 'So, what do you think?'

'For Christ's sake,' said a voice from beyond the hedge, 'at that money, I'll do it.'

★ ★ ★

The racing season ended conveniently just before the start of the new academic year. Jane had not won any trophies, but to finish eighth in the Formula Three championship table was no disgrace.

Professor Barnes had been as good as his word to Julian Berkeley. Jane's programme had been rearranged so that she could honour most of her commitments during the autumn term, thus allowing one of her colleagues to go on a research trip to Japan. In turn, this would free Jane for almost all the remainder of the academic year.

Despite a heavy lecturing schedule, Jane managed to accept Julian's invitation to visit the Leopold Engines works near Swindon. He also suggested that she should bring her computer.

'Oho!' was Jane's only comment.

At the works, she saw the main production line where engines were being assembled for a new design of taxi. Smaller production lines were producing other engines down to one for a famous lawnmower, while a huge diesel engine was being fabricated as a one-off order, to power a tunnel-boring machine.

Across a yard was an office block housing, in addition to the secretariat, the design department and the pattern shop. In a small room adjoining the pattern shop, a man in a grey linen coat was engaged in debate with another man, this one in a brown coat. The room was airtight, dust-proof, more like an operating theatre than a workshop. The man in grey was introduced to Jane as Steven Jenkinson, one of the senior designers. Above a pleasantly undistinguished face he had a remarkable shock of curly, white hair — an unusual combination, Jane thought, on one who could not have been more than thirty. The thought triggered a recollection.

'I've seen you before, somewhere,' she told him.

Jenkinson nodded. 'And I've seen you, but never for very long at a time. I was looking after the telemetry while you did your tests on the Impala. Rossett had already fallen out with the old engine-builders and talks were in hand with us. Any time you care to go over the telemetry records with me, I think you could pick up some valuable clues. Like where you may be late in starting to accelerate out of a corner. You don't mind my saying that?'

'Not in the least,' Jane said. 'I may be getting old, but not too old to learn.'

Steven paused. 'This is the new Formula One engine, or supposed to be.'

'May I take a good look?'

'I suppose so.'

'Well,' Jane said, 'after all, it's what I was invited here to see.'

'Yes, of course.' He stepped out of her way. 'We're not getting the performance it's designed for . . . yet.'

A partly dismantled ten-cylinder V-engine sat in a cradle. A pair of cylinder heads rested on the adjacent bench alongside the wooden patterns from which the lost-wax mouldings would be taken. Further along the bench was a complex exhaust manifold. Drawings were fastened to the wall above. Jane stood, contemplating the design and mentally reassembling the components. 'Are you planning on a mechanical throttle linkage?' she asked at last.

'Heavens, no! Fly-by-wire. The linkage you see is only the final connection to the fuel-injection system.'

'I'll tell you one thing for nothing,' Jane said. 'You'll have to alter that throttle linkage.'

He drew himself up. 'Why?'

Jane had been much too interested in her surroundings to take note of his stiffness of manner. 'Give me a pencil and paper.' She drew a slanting curve. 'This is a typical power curve. Now, *this* is roughly the relationship between throttle opening and power. Put the two together and you have something like this curve for the ratio between pedal movement and power. In other words, with that linkage most of the pedal movement occurs where power is least. The difference between half and full power, which is where you want to feel your way gently, would be about five millimetres at the pedal. At Estoril, for example, which is the one Grand Prix circuit we both know, there's a deadly hairpin where you need to put just the right amount of power on the road. With no margin between half and full power it would be . . . death or glory.'

There was a pause. 'Point taken,' Steven Jenkinson said at last. 'Thank you. That may be helpful.' The acknowledgement seemed to be dragged out of him.

'Now, let's have a look at your cylinder-heads.' Their two principals and the pattern-maker had retired tactfully out of earshot. Men had been coming and going but all traffic stopped. Word had gone round. No highly skilled engineer wants to be set right by a girl, especially within earshot of his colleagues. Steven's face was registering excessive patience. But Jane never noticed. She pored for some time over the wooden pattern on the bench. 'Yes,' she said at last.

'Yes?' Steven's tone was of cautious interest.

'What ignition advance do you need?'

Steven's expression might have seemed familiar to his dentist. 'Forty-eight degrees. All right,' he added quickly, 'so there's a combustion problem. The BMEPs are unsatisfactory.'

There was another long wait but Steven was showing more genuine patience. The girl seemed to know what she was talking about. She might even stumble on the magic solution. She stirred at last.

'Yes?' he said again.

'I think so. We can make some improvement to the gas flow, but . . . Could you reverse the porting at the second and fourth cylinders, both sides? You'd have to redesign your manifolds and camshafts, of course.'

'That wouldn't matter, if we were getting the power output we've been aiming for.' He began to sound interested.

'Then you could get identical distances over the lengths of the exhausts, without your exhaust manifold looking quite so much like a demented octopus. Same on the inlet side. Fine-tuning then becomes possible instead of a pipe dream. And I suggest that we try it with the valves less deeply set in and compensating with slots in the heads of the pistons. At what revs are you aiming for peak power?' She opened her computer.

'This could last for hours,' Julian Berkeley said to the Leopold manager. 'The boy looks stunned. We may as well go for lunch. By the time we come back, one will have killed and eaten the other, or else they'll be talking marriage.'

'You wouldn't care to have a bet as to which?' the manager asked.

Julian grinned. 'No, I would not. But if I did, it would be that he was talking marriage right up until she killed and ate him. Believe me, under that sweet exterior is a very tough young lady.'

★ ★ ★

It went against the grain for Steven Jenkinson to admit it, even to himself, but the girl was good. She had a habit of making comments which he suddenly saw were revelations rather than mere truths. He moved from resentment through grudging acceptance to

353

delighted welcome. Jane became a fairly regular visitor to the Leopold works. When the new cylinder-heads had been cast, polished and installed, she spent a delightful day with Steven Jenkinson and the Leopold dynamometer which, she noticed, was almost as good as the one at the university.

'Well, that's very satisfactory,' Steven said at last, pushing up his ear protectors.

Jane was poring over graphic printouts. 'There's still a slight flat spot,' she said wistfully.

'Not enough to notice. I'll check the timings again tomorrow. I'd invite you for a drink except that I was warned not to make a pass at you.'

'You can make a pass,' Jane said. 'It won't get you anywhere but, if a free drink comes with it, make it anyway. Will you be coming to Estoril?'

'With a little luck.'

The working day had finished long before. They left the now silent works and crossed the road to an unmodernised pub. They found a small lounge which they had to themselves. Jane, who had an hour's drive ahead of her, settled for a small shandy.

Steven dug into a bulging inside pocket and produced two folded lengths of translucent computer paper. 'You can have these to keep, if you like,' he said. 'This one's a copy of the telemetry for your best lap of Estoril in the Impala last January. I've coloured in your braking and acceleration to make it clearer. The other gives the same information for a similar lap by the then world champion the year before. I'm not saying where I got it from and you didn't get it from me.'

Jane opened the papers out, laid one on top of the other and studied them until she could extract their meanings. 'He was about seven seconds a lap faster than me,' she said.

'But look where.'

'Interesting . . . ' She folded the papers up again and stowed them in a plain leather handbag. 'Steven, could I get a look inside one of the Formula Three engines?'

'It'd be as much as my life's worth. The F-Three engine was and still is my immediate boss's personal baby. Can you imagine a mother's feelings if somebody practised vivisection on the apple of her eye?'

★　★　★

Julian Berkeley seemed to be in an endless series of meetings. It was several days before Jane could get him on the phone.

'I want a look inside the Formula Three engine,' she said.

355

'Difficult.'

'I know all about its being what's-his-name's — '

'Mark Denby.'

'Mark Denby's personal baby and the great man being a prima donna and all that jazz — '

'Can a man be a prima donna? And I don't think your grandfather would have approved of the word jazz in the same sentence.'

' — but you took me over there in the hope that I'd be able to help. Right?'

'Confidence rather than hope. Otherwise, quite true, my dear.'

'And I dug them out of a hole, didn't I?'

'I believe everyone's most impressed. And relieved. The F-One engine looked like being an expensive white elephant.'

'Right,' Jane said. 'I've been taking the Formula Three engine for granted, but now that I've seen the sort of elementary errors that might creep in — '

'They may be elementary to you, my dear, but not everybody sees it that way. After all, your speciality is and always has been gas flow.'

'Which is the main conditioner of engine performance. But never mind that,' she said earnestly. 'Our cars corner as well as anyone else's. Your other drivers are top-notch. We

356

should have been further up the champion-ship table. I want to look inside the engine and see if I can see why we're not.'

Over the phone line, she heard him sigh. 'If you put it like that, how can I refuse? Leave it with me. I'll call you back in a day or two.'

'And, Julian, don't let the big cheese — '

'Mark Denby,' he said patiently.

'Don't let him take it out on Steven. This is my idea and mine alone.'

12

Jane flew out to Lisbon first class, on a scheduled flight with a party from Leopold Engines and Impala Racing. The Formula Three car and team from KB Tools would follow later. Julian Berkeley was to join them as soon as he could get away, but he made no promises. Hired cars whisked the party along the dual carriageway to Estoril. The staff at the hotel welcomed her as an old friend.

The two transporters from Impala were waiting at the circuit next morning.

On this occasion, three other Formula One teams had arrived to test new cars or new engines. No amount of bench testing or computer simulation can replace testing on the road, nor the 'feel' of a skilled driver. But there was to be no racing. It was generally agreed that whenever more than one car was out at a time they would aim to set off spaced apart and to stay like that. The smaller-engined Formula Three car, when it arrived, would have to fit in as best it could.

Such agreements, Jane found, were easily entered but very difficult to keep. The Impala car was waiting for her in the pits on the first morning in its full livery of sponsor's colours and advertisements. The new engine being similar in weight and dimensions to the old, it had not been deemed necessary to build a wholly new car. Jane, settling herself into her racing seat and strapping herself in, had a comfortable sensation of *déjà vu*, but when she moved out onto the track she found that this was a beast of quite another colour. The extra power, which she and Steven Jenkinson had managed to coax out of it, was the least of her worries. The slight shift of balance had, in theory, been compensated within the available adjustments built into the car, but the car handled, as she said shortly afterwards, 'like steering a cow by the tail'. The setting-up had to begin again almost from scratch. Jane had taken the car onto the circuit shortly after the other car out at the time had passed by, but it was only a few laps before it was in her mirrors. She gave the other driver ample room to pass and pulled into the pits again.

Estoril is popular for out-of-season testing because there is at least a fifty-fifty chance of good weather, but that year, as they told each other, they might just as well have stayed in Britain. Heavy rain fell, and nearly always at the very moment when testing under fair conditions was most wanted. After five days, however, they had reached a point which they would usually have reached in two and by the middle of the following week the Impala was handling well.

The weather faired. It was now time to check reliability by prolonged driving while at the same time perfecting the set-up. Jane was happy to discover that her neck was much less troublesome than before, thanks in part to the attentions of a Portuguese masseuse who had been engaged to attend to her twice a day and partly to her inflatable neck support.

Two other Formula One cars were present, but one of these had suffered damage and was awaiting parts from Britain while the guilty driver hung his head and tried to stay out of sight. The other car, still anonymous in grey primer, was lapping, but it was known, in the way that knowledge passes magically from team to team, that all was not well. The other team was using a standard transponder to send signals to the timing equipment. A surreptitious glance at their timing monitor soon confirmed that it was lapping a full ten seconds below par. Jane, being Jane, sneaked a good look at the suspension before the other team could get the cover over the car.

A satisfactory setting-up had been achieved. Jane had recovered her touch with the car and become used to the slightly changed feel and the increased power. She had also realised, from study of the telemetry printouts furnished by Steven Jenkinson, that her speeds on the straights and through the faster curves were well up to standard; it was on the slower corners that tenths of a second could still be shaved away. Armed with this knowledge, Jane was returning lap times that would have put her well up the starting grid. The sensation was even better than it had been the previous year. She no longer felt akin to someone riding a monocycle across a high wire while juggling several sharp knives and a running chainsaw. She and the car were becoming one entity. In perfect harmony they were following the perfect racing line, swooping from verge to apex to verge again, right at the limit of adhesion and yet fully controlled. This was as near to Heaven as Jane ever expected to get.

The grey car was up ahead. She had overtaken it several times already that morning. The other driver, who was circulating apparently in the hope that something would run in or heal up, or that his team would pluck inspiration out of the telemetry, had kept out of her way. Again he slowed and raised a finger to beckon her by, but Jane had a sudden impulse. She slowed and fell in behind the grey car. The other driver accepted the gesture and moved on.

Jane watched the car ahead intently as she followed it through the lefts and rights of Turns Eight to Twelve. It seemed to shiver on braking and again on acceleration. It was difficult to arrive at a positive judgement while both cars were moving. Her observation was more of a hunch based on her quick study of the suspension and yet she was becoming ever more sure of her diagnosis.

She pressed the Transmit button and spoke aloud. 'His rear wheel tracking is varying. He's getting more than normal toe-in on acceleration and toe-out on braking. There must be some flexion in his chassis or suspension that he doesn't know about.'

'He's the opposition,' said the voice.

'Don't tell him if you don't want to,' Jane said. 'But if he gets a fatigue fracture, crashes and dies, I'll tell the world that you decided to keep the news to yourself. And don't forget that we may need a favour some day.' She pulled out to overtake.

Twenty minutes later, she was called in. Fuel was running short and they had found out all that they were going to learn that day. She pulled up behind the transporter, from where it would be easiest to put the car to bed for the night. She took off her helmet, shook out her hair, stretched and went through the process of removing the steering-wheel, unbuckling her safety straps and climbing out. There was only the slightest crick in her neck but she rubbed it anyway and did some loosening exercises. The KB engineer and Steven Jenkinson had their heads down over the telemetry, no doubt searching for other areas in which they might be able to skin off another hundredth of a second.

Around the other car was a huddle of engineers, all poking and prodding and measuring the rear suspension mountings.

The other driver was a familiar face from the hotel and she had seen him around the British circuits. Tim Makepeace was a round-faced, curly-headed man of about her own age though looking younger — far too young to drive a car at all, let alone a Formula One monster. Like herself, he was a test-driver for Formula One, but he had very nearly carried off the Formula Three Thousand championship.

'You were absolutely right,' he said. 'The one place they hadn't got around to fitting sensors. But how did you know?'

Jane decided to let the other team's engineers save face. 'I was the only person who's been in a position to see while the car

363

was in motion. That makes all the difference.'

His forehead creased, giving him the look of a petulant toddler. 'But you couldn't have seen. Not while the cars were both in motion. The movement would have been too small.'

She thought about it. 'All I can say is that it looked as if that was what was happening,' she said. 'Does that make sense?'

'I suppose so.'

'Have I given you egg on your face?'

'I don't think so. Probably the reverse. Anyway, now I'll get the chance to show them what I can do with a car that doesn't waggle its arse whenever I put my foot down.' He paused and was overcome with bashfulness. 'I say, I'm sorry. Have I offended you?'

She smiled. 'I have heard the word before.'

He smiled in reply. 'You're a cracker. What's more, you're a damn good driver. May I take you out for a meal tonight?'

'I don't drink more than a low-alcohol lager when I'm driving the next day,' she said, 'and I don't sleep with anyone at all. If you still want to invite me out to dinner, ask me again.'

He bowed. 'Madam, may I take you for a meal tonight? I have a fiancée of my own back in Britain. All I ask is that you stay off the lobster. It's a hell of a price, considering that we're not far from the sea.'

The arrival of a new British-made racing engine would be news. The prospect of cars of wholly British manufacture figuring in the Grands Prix would attract journalists, whose interest would in turn publicise Leopold Engines, racing and otherwise.

The period of testing was to conclude with a presentation to the media. Motoring journalists and cameramen would be flown in from Britain and elsewhere, entertained in the lavish fashion to which they were becoming addicted and treated to an inspection of the exterior of the new engine and the sight of a few fast laps by the Impala cars in the hands of their appointed drivers. As a preliminary appetiser, the Formula Three Alex-Leopold car was to be driven by Jane. The second Impala car had been brought to Estoril. With the setting-up already established on the first car, little more than a day's work was needed for the other to be readied.

For a day, transport shuttled to and fro, bringing journalists from the Lisbon airport. Julian Berkeley, free at last from his business commitments, arrived, looking tired. Laura, who had already taken up her new post and had been assisting with the organising from the British end, came with him. Jane stole a surreptitious look at the pair but decided that nothing untoward had been going on.

The weather was merciful and the whole tightly organised event rolled cheerfully on its way. The journalists were scattered through several hotels but were brought together that evening for a dinner and brief speeches. In the morning, those who were not too hung-over were lifted to the circuit where a highly polished engine was on display. Most elected to watch the cars from a conveniently positioned bar, but some photographers moved round the circuit to positions which they considered visually advantageous.

Jane did her few allotted laps. She was pleasantly relaxed after a night in the arms of her Julian but, as she had said when the suggestion was made, 'The car knows its own way round by now. After hammering round and round that track for the past three weeks, I'm due for a little TLC.' On her last lap, she was accompanied by the two Formula One cars, treating it as a warming-up lap. Back in the main straight, they pulled out and roared away in an impressive surge of acceleration. Jane finished the lap and pulled into the pits. Several high-tech video cameras were trained on her as she did her quick-change act, transforming herself within a few seconds from a brightly coloured space traveller into a glamorous young lady, but without offering the hoped-for glimpse of underwear.

The drivers, the design teams and the managers were to face the journalists and cameras, but drinks were again provided and the throng was slow to settle. Heading for her place on the rostrum, Jane found herself sandwiched between the other two drivers. She had not seen Carl Lansdowne since the fracas in the Motor Club though during the intervening years the motoring press had kept her informed of his progress.

It seemed that the Canadian still bore a grudge. 'Your setting-up was crap,' he said. 'I could hardly control the car and I'm going to tell them so.'

'My setting-up must have been brilliant,' Jane retorted. 'You managed to stay on the road this time.'

Lansdowne's team-mate, a German with a high reputation and some excellent finishes to his credit, gave a short bark of laughter. 'Setting-up was ver' good,' he said, 'and if anyone says different I tell these people so. Also I tell them what you both just said.'

The Canadian pursed his lips. 'I believe you would, you fat-arsed Kraut,' he snapped.

'As you say, you better believe it. And keep

your voice down. There are ears all around you.'

The media session got under way. The journalists wanted to get back to their partying but they also wanted some questions and answers to justify the time spent on their brief escape from the British winter. Questions followed one another quickly. The new engine received only token attention. More than her fair share were directed at Jane, but by now she was well practised at fielding them and had her answers off pat. Carl Lansdowne still looked thunderous, but this could be taken for his normal expression. He said nothing about the setting-up.

The formal session petered out. There was still an hour before the hired coaches would start to ferry the visitors back to Lisbon.

Polly Parsons, the only woman among the journalists, a hard-faced ex-rallyist now working for one of the tabloids, got to Jane first. 'Let's grab a drink and get out of this pandemonium,' she said. 'I'd like to ask a few questions on behalf of your women fans.'

Jane was amenable. Now that she had finished driving for the moment, a glass of the *vino verde* which all the others were pouring down their throats would be welcome. They carried their drinks outside and found a quiet spot sheltered from the mild breeze.

'Fire away,' Jane said.

'You mind if I tape this?'

'Not at all.'

Polly Parsons produced a miniature tape-recorder from her handbag and clipped it to the front of her imitation leopard-skin coat. Her make-up looked ferocious in the flat sunshine. 'Tell me, Miss Faraday — it *is* Miss? Tell me. Why do you change into ordinary clothes the moment you're finished driving?'

'I'm an employee, the same as everyone else,' Jane said. 'I'm employed by Alex Beauty Products to make their products look good, by driving racing-cars and still managing to step out looking glamorous. You'll notice that I very rarely touch my make-up after getting out of the car.'

'And is it a successful advertising approach?'

'I'm told that they're satisfied. The figures aren't my concern.'

'You don't think that racing overalls would add to the glamour, by contrast?'

'No, I don't,' Jane said. 'The tomboy image isn't what they want. You don't show luxury goods against a background of sacking.'

'But you were already driving racing-cars before they hired you,' Ms Parsons said. 'You must enjoy it.'

'I do. It's the greatest fun in the world. But Alex BP were giving me some sponsorship from the beginning or I could never have afforded it. It's a damned expensive business. Only advertising keeps it going, though almost every formula below Formula One has rules framed to keep the costs down, like requiring some kind of restrictor on the engine. Otherwise, engines would be worked to the limit and virtually discarded after a race or two, as happens in Formula One. The deepest pocket would always win.'

'Very interesting . . . ' There was a pause. Ms Parsons seemed to be considering her next question. 'How long have you known Julian Berkeley?' she asked suddenly.

Jane felt a sudden flicker of apprehension. But the truthful answer was perfectly innocent. 'I first met him at my grandfather's house, when I was — I think — seventeen.'

'Rather young, don't you think?'

Jane looked sharply at the other woman and saw a faint, triumphant smile. 'What are you getting at?' Jane asked.

'Rather young for being — what did you call yourself? 'Luxury goods'. Surely you're not going to deny that you're sleeping together? Perhaps I should warn you that I've already spread some money around in your

370

hotel. You shared a room there last year and again last night.'

Jane thought frantically. 'Why do you want to know?' she asked. 'That sort of thing doesn't raise eyebrows any more.'

Ms Parson's smile was meant to be sympathetic but to Jane it looked distinctly unfriendly. 'It depends who's doing it, a cabinet minister or Joe Bloggs. Julian Berkeley has been on the list of Britain's Ten Most Eligible Male Singles for several years — two places ahead of Prince Charles, if I remember rightly. And your face has become public property. The fact that the two of you are humping like stoats should fire the imaginations of our readers. Are you quite sure that you'd reached the age of consent?'

Jane felt stunned. She felt the blood rush to her face. Her ears were burning. She tried to fall back on her logic, but logic no longer seemed to apply. 'He was a guest at my grandfather's table,' she said. 'That was all. I never set eyes on him again until I started racing. Even then, nothing happened . . . '

'Until? Remember, we already know.'

'This time last year was the very first, and that's the honest-to-God truth.'

'Are you going to marry him?'

'I don't know. We've never even discussed it.'

'Thank you.' Ms Parsons snapped the tape-recorder off, unclipped it and dropped it into her handbag.

'For God's sake, don't print any of this,' Jane said desperately. 'We've been keeping it quiet because of the way it would look.'

'What way is that?'

'I would look like a gold-digger and he'd look like a . . . an old man who fancies young women.'

'That's true. Well, we'll just have to wait and see how my editor feels about it.' Ms Parsons turned away.

Jane hurried in search of Julian Berkeley. He was with a group of men. Rather than break in, she looked for Laura and found her in what seemed to be amorous discussion with Hugh Waterton. Without explaining, she persuaded Hugh to go and detach Julian from his companions.

'What on earth's wrong?' Laura asked anxiously. 'As deputy team manager, I'm entitled to know.'

'Polly Parsons has found out that Julian and I are lovers.'

Laura looked puzzled. 'That's no reason to look as though the world's coming to an end,' she said. 'Everybody does it, or the human race would die out. It isn't news any more. On TV, people refer to a 'partner'.'

'I tried to tell her that. But we're a bit sensitive about the subject.'

'Well, I don't see why.' Laura's sex-life, centering around Hugh Waterton, was so satisfactory that she would have liked the whole world to know about it.

'Just take it for a fact,' said Jane.

Jane could see the top of Julian's head approaching through the crush. She pushed to meet him and led him outside, to where she and Ms Parsons had stood.

'Polly Parsons knows that we've been sleeping together.'

He froze, then, 'Tell me everything,' he said.

She repeated her conversation with the journalist, word for word. 'I was wondering,' she finished. 'Do you think money . . . '

He shook his head roughly. 'Any of the others, but not her. By reputation, she lives for her work. And she's very well paid. We'll just have to tough it out. But whatever were you thinking about?'

'I was thinking about our reputations,' she said weakly.

'And you claim to be the one with the logic! You've made a real hash of it, haven't you? Not only letting her bluff you into admitting everything but putting it on tape.' He paused and looked at her with hooded eyes. 'I've never known you to be so naive. I suppose this isn't some subtle ploy? Telling the world, so as to stake your claim?'

Jane felt as though she had been punched. 'That's a *bloody* thing to say.'

She saw his face change. 'You're quite right,' he said quickly. 'I'm sorry. I think I know you better than that.'

'I never want to see you again.' She wanted very much to call the words back but it was too late.

He pursed his lips. 'If that's the way you want it.'

Some devil inside her was driving her on. 'You can do your own driving.'

'You're under contract,' he said, 'and don't you forget it. You drive, to the utmost of your ability, or you fetch up in court. Hugh can do the liaison from now on.'

He turned and left her. He only looked back once.

★ ★ ★

All the way home, Jane waited for a chance to speak to him. She knew that he was aware of her, but he always seemed to be in discussion with other men. Jane was left with the company of Laura, who seemed a little too unaware that anything was wrong. She

374

wanted to catch him alone, to call back her words, to beg forgiveness, even to grovel.

She could not even reach him by phone. It seemed that he must have left instructions that she was not to be put through to him. Then she thought of his mobile number. He answered, but as soon as she identified herself he said, 'I'm sorry, but you're right. I would always be wondering.' And he disconnected.

The media made bad worse. Polly Parson's editor presumably liked the touch of scandal, because the paper's gossip columns flaunted the story which was then taken up by the other tabloids. Facts were soon discarded in favour of fiction. All the rules of grammar, discretion and taste were abandoned. Racy Lady Jane Faraday was credited with amazing antics along with her wealthy lover. The same old photograph of her standing in the back of the open car and showing a lot of leg was resurrected. Aided by an air-brush, her skirt was blown ever higher.

Life had to go on. There was always work. Even without a contract hanging over her, she would have hated to abandon racing. She returned to her duties at the university and also prepared for the coming season, but she was not at her best and she knew it. There was a numb void where once there had been warmth and love and she knew that there was giggling behind her back. She could not remember ever having cried since she was twelve except when the Wingco died, but sometimes, at night, she cried very quietly to herself.

One very slight compensation was that money was no longer a problem. She was well paid by Alex BP and less so by the university. The racing-circuit videos were selling well. She thought of honouring her promise to herself and buying a really good camper, but the recent publicity seemed to have convinced all the more predatory males that she was easy meat. If she slept alone in a camper she might be at their mercy. She would certainly confirm her unearned reputation. When the meetings were a long way from home she let Laura book her into hotels, specifying only that they should not be the hotels where the other drivers tended to congregate.

The first Formula Three race of Jane's second season was again set at Silverstone in mid-April. Jane approached it in a mood of depression, but when she went out for first practice she found that driving a well-engineered car still had the power to lift her heart, for the moment at least. The two KB-Leopold and the Alex-Leopold cars were meticulously prepared and, thanks at least in part to Jane's efforts, were faster than ever before.

And Jane had one new advantage over all rivals. It suddenly occurred to her that she didn't give a damn whether she lived or died. The world had mistreated her — so why should she cling to it? She had no intention of wrecking the car, her respect for great machinery was too deeply ingrained for that. But she took the car closer to the absolute limit of its performance, stealing every tiny fragment of a second by trusting the car and her own skills to balance on the knife-edge of disaster. She qualified to start from the front row.

From the moment the lights changed and the race began, those in the pit knew that something special was in train. Jane lost a fraction of a second in starting and arrived at Turn One in second place. But the leader, last year's champion, found that he was being pursued by a fury. He was slipstreamed and harassed. Ten times a lap, the lilac car feinted or made a serious attempt to get by until, inevitably, the leader left the door open for a moment too long. Jane snatched the lead and dealt ruthlessly with any challengers, coming home to her first win in Formula Three. The two KB-Leopold cars were in the points at fourth and sixth.

She put on her champagne-proof skirt and hooded jacket in the *parc fermé*. But she might have been breathing fire and glaring thunderbolts. Her auburn hair looked scarlet in the sunshine. There went before her a general recognition that she was not to be trifled with. The other two drivers on the podium squirted each other and the bystanders half-heartedly with champagne but never dared to send a drop in her direction. During the succeeding interviews, where in previous years she would have expected a little friendly leg-pulling, she was treated with cautious courtesy. She escaped as soon as she could. She carried her unopened bottle of champagne back to the transporters in the paddock. The team drank her health and Laura made a speech, but Jane's mood had communicated itself and there was not the exuberance that would usually have followed such a good, early result.

The following morning brought a stiff little note of congratulation on Alex BP notepaper. It was signed J. Berkeley (Chairman).

★　★　★

The early promise was almost fulfilled. The win was followed by a third place and then a second. The motoring press began to whisper

Jane's name in connection with the championship.

Two days before Jane was due at Oulton Park to practise for the fourth race of the season she was alone, preparing some exam questions in the retiring room which she shared with two other part-time lecturers, when Laura's head came round the door.

'Come in,' Jane said absently. 'Come along in. Unless you'd care to fetch a couple of coffees out of the Machine From Hell?'

Dutifully, Laura fetched two coffees and then settled into a spare chair and sat in silence.

Jane, her concentration broken, was inclined to be peevish. 'You may as well tell me what you can do for me, or else buzz off,' she said.

'I was wondering whether anyone had told you about Mr Berkeley,' Laura said.

Jane looked at her. Laura was looking very unhappy. Jane tried to say, 'What?'

Laura moistened her lips. 'He had a heart attack yesterday.'

'My God! He's not — '

'I believe he's doing very well. He's in the private hospital at Didsbury. I thought I'd better tell you, in case you saw it in the papers or something. I say, are you all right?'

Jane pushed her chair back and put her

head down on her knees until the faintness went away. She was still white when she looked up. 'If I go to see him, will you come with me?'

'When?'

'Now. This very minute.'

'Jane, I can't.'

'All right. I'll pick you up as usual for Oulton. So long.'

'I'd come if I could, but I'm due at a meeting of the Logistics Group in about ten minutes time and fifty miles away. I'll have to drive like you do to get — '

But Jane was gone.

* * *

Jane had taken the good magistrate's words to heart and had never again broken the speed limit by more than an acceptable margin. But this, she considered, was an occasion outside normal rules. She wanted, she needed, she *must* get to Julian quickly. If he . . . fell off the perch (she could not bring herself even to *think* the words 'die' or 'death') before she had told him that she had been a fool and was sorry and loved him to desperation she would never, ever forgive herself. Fortunately, her shortest route was by secondary roads. She had earned her earlier prosecution on secondary roads but she told herself that lightning never struck twice in the same place. The aphorism is not always to be trusted but on this occasion it proved to hold a vestige of truth. Jane entered the private hospital in less than an hour, leaving the Ford muttering to itself in the doctors' car park.

The reception area was more like that of a good hotel than a hospital. A notice invited all visitors to call at the desk but Jane could not be sure that either the hospital or Julian would welcome her visit. She walked straight across the hallway and took to the stairs. One advantage of having a known but not famous face is that strangers have a recollection of having seen it before. The staff, seeing her purposeful stride and realising that they seemed to know her face, assumed that she was a regular visitor, perhaps a therapist, and ignored her.

Jane was fit enough to run up the stairs without losing breath. The levels were clearly posted. On the third landing a sign pointed out the Cardiac Care Unit, which seemed to be the place to start.

Jane accosted a young nurse. 'I'm looking for Mr Berkeley. Julian Berkeley.'

The nurse was more suspicious than the staff at Reception. 'Are you a relative?' she asked.

Jane was not going to be balked now, and by a chit no older than herself. She advanced her nose to within a few inches of the other's and glared, eyeball to eyeball. 'I'm . . . his . . . bloody . . . *mother*,' she said through gritted teeth.

The nurse, demoralised, swallowed and capitulated. She pointed to one of the many doors and then fled.

Jane opened the door. Julian Berkeley, in striped pyjamas and looking suddenly older, was half propped up in bed. Wires connected him to a cardiograph. Something was draining from a bag above his head into a catheter in his elbow.

On the journey, Jane had rehearsed many fine phrases, but they had all deserted her. So also had her mood of ascendancy. She closed the door gently, stumbled forward and then fell on his chest. 'I'm sorry,' she wailed and repeated the words over and over again. 'I'm sorry.'

'This may not be the best treatment for a damaged heart,' he said gently. Then, as she began to pull back, he added, 'On the other hand, perhaps it is after all. Anyway, don't move. You can't know how I've longed to say those words. I'm the one who has to be sorry.'

She moved until her lips were almost

against his ear. 'No,' she whispered. 'You had every right to be suspicious. But I promise you, I did try to keep our secret, for your sake. If I blew it, put it down to stupidity.'

'No, you're not stupid. And when I came to think it over, I realised that I only wanted to keep our affair secret because I would be afraid that you'd be thought a gold-digger. And then I almost accused you of the very same thing. I must have been mad. Has all the ballyhoo been too hurtful?'

'I can survive. I was offered a huge sum for the story, by one of the tabloids. If I was really a gold-digger, I'd have taken it.'

'I know, I know. If it isn't too late, if you can forgive me for going off at half-cock, some good may come out of it yet. We needn't be secretive any more. In fact, there's nothing to stop you moving into Grey Gables if you want to. Do you? Please do.'

Jane was not yet quite ready for such a sudden and total commitment. 'Some day, when we're both ready. Julian, please tell me that I didn't cause your heart attack.'

She felt him chuckle. 'Heavens, no! I've just been trying to do too much, instead of delegating as a good chairman should. Alex Beauty Products is moving into Europe and I had the foolish idea that I had to spearhead the invasion.'

'And you're going to be all right?'

'I'm told that I'll have to take life easier. But, nowadays, a heart attack is thought of as little more than a warning. With a little care and the right medicines, one can live for many more years and die of old age.'

'I'm so thankful!'

'I'm rather pleased, myself. But, for now, I think you should move. You're getting my face all wet. What's more, I'm not supposed to get excited.'

'Are you getting excited?'

'I am, rather.'

'That's good,' she said. 'The day I can cry all over your chest without getting you excited, I'll start to worry.' But she began to get up. Immediately, a warning note began to sound at the electro-cardiograph, there was an electronic scream from the corridor and the line which had traced his heartbeats became straight. 'My God!' she said. 'Have I killed you?'

'The reverse. You've given me something to live for. But you've pulled off one of these damned terminals.'

In the corridor, there came the sound of hurrying feet.

★   ★   ★

Jane was summarily ejected from the hospital and given to understand that she would not be a welcome visitor, but she drove homeward singing at the top of her never very musical voice.

She returned to her usual lifestyle, but this was now illumined with a rosy glow. Friends and colleagues, who for the last few weeks had recoiled from her air of being undecided whether to bite or to dissolve in tears, were now repelled by the singing and other signs of almost indecently excessive happiness.

She was brought down to earth with a bump at Oulton Park. She was aware of her own capabilities and saw no contradiction in her determination to stay out of trouble, now that life once again had so much to offer. As a result, she qualified only for the hindmost row on the grid, a position which she had not occupied for several years. She pulled herself together and saved face by making some microscopic adjustments to the set-up, but during the race itself she was still only too well aware of places where a careless or unlucky driver might be in serious danger and she managed to carve her way up the field only as far as an ignoble fourteenth place.

Julian went home from hospital a few days later. It was made clear to him that sex was definitely off the agenda for several more weeks so, after a dangerously passionate visit from Jane, they agreed that it would be better not to see each other again until that embargo was lifted.

At the next three meetings, Jane did better — twice in the points and once just outside. Then, in time for the meeting at Snetterton, Julian phoned to say that he had now been told to resume all aspects of his former life. 'They assure me,' he said, 'that my body will tell me what I can and can't do; and just at the moment what do you think it's telling me to do?'

Jane uttered what she thought of as her dirty laugh. 'Me?' she said.

'You've got it.'

Jane wished that he could see the evil messages that she was sending with her eyebrows. 'Not yet, I haven't,' she said. 'How about Snetterton?'

Julian's chauffeur brought him to Snetterton on race-day, only for Jane to misjudge a manoeuvre and slide wide, inflicting some minor damage to the car and putting herself out of contention. But the day was not to be wholly a loss. They settled in a small hotel on the road home, and there they accomplished a most satisfactory union, with Jane, to be on the safe side, putting out most of the physical effort.

Jane put off making any decision about moving into Grey Gables. She spent many nights there, but never just before racing. The season passed by. Jane never hit the peak that she had found at the beginning of the season, but she was never far out of contention.

Then, out of the blue, he said, 'How would you like to move to the top of the ladder?'

They were lying in at Grey Gables after a night well spent and Jane was thinking about nothing in particular. 'As long as I don't go down the snake. Like what?' she said.

'Like Formula One. Listen. Impala have been running two cars and a spare, but one of them was written off at Hockenheim. You probably heard? They've also lost their sponsorship — the tobacco firms aren't as rich as they used to be and more countries are to ban tobacco advertising. Simon Vanderveldt can't afford to replace the written-off car and the whole thing has become a millstone round his neck. The whole organisation is on the market at less than cost. It would give us one car to run, plus a spare. At the same time, the Alex group of companies is aiming to expand through Europe, offering everything the fashionable woman could want but at a price her husband can afford, whether he knows it or not. Now would be the perfect time . . . '

Jane stopped yawning and sat upright. She came straight to the point. 'Could your heart stand the strain?'

'I'm sure of it. I wouldn't do the hard work myself. And I trust you. I can watch you racing without having palpitations. Anyway, if I have to live wrapped in cotton wool, I . . . '

'Don't want to live?'

'Don't put words into my mouth. I'll word it another way. You're one of the most reliable of the drivers, and Formula One has become incredibly safe, considering what it is. But if by any chance you should be in a really bad smash . . . '

'Yes?'

'I wouldn't want to live without you. So let's both live dangerously.'

So satisfactory was that answer that it was some little time before the discussion was resumed. Then, 'I'm not very experienced. Would they let me race in Formula One?'

'I don't see why not. You've been showing up well in Formula Three and you've served two periods as a test-driver on Formula One cars, so they should issue a 'super licence' without quibbling. And, just at the moment, they've been so worried about poor entries in Formula One races that they're on the point of inviting teams to enter three cars instead of two. I don't see them turning any competent driver away.'

'I'll need a little time to think about it. I'll want to talk it over with Laura.'

'So will I. She's going to have to take on more responsibility if we go ahead.'

13

The Formula One season begins in March and visits a different country, on average, every fortnight. It would clearly be impossible for Jane to attend the university, except occasionally and then only as a visiting lecturer. By arrangement with the Professor she finished her commitments by mid-December and then resigned. Only later did she realise that she had worked, part-time, nearly four academic years for the university and been paid for three.

If Jane's racing career had already attracted the attention of the media, her arrival in Formula One drove them near to a feeding frenzy, but she had already learned how to cope. She stayed calm and modest, submitted to interviews and photo sessions and went her own way.

Her first season went by in a blaze of colour and noise and excitement, yet somehow the driving seemed to be a lesser component of it than before. The circuits, all but Silverstone and Estoril, were strange to her and although she came to the car as to an old friend she had no experience of handling it under race conditions.

Previously it had been her habit, while waiting for confidence to surface, to qualify deliberately for a place at the back of the grid; but in Formula One, the rule was that only those cars qualifying in 107 per cent of the time of the car in pole position might run. This sensible rule, designed to prevent slow cars entering and endangering the traffic, would have turned any such caution into brinkmanship. She drove her qualifying laps flat out, never failing to qualify and usually starting from somewhere near the middle of the grid. She tried not to lose places but made little attempt to gain them in the pandemonium of the start, where cars were packed tightly and jockeying for position, preferring to slot herself carefully into the fast-moving queue of cars for the outside of the first bend and pay no attention to those who might slip by on the inside. Once the traffic had strung out, she would pick up places as and when she could.

At Monaco, she was hit from behind and put out on the first lap. At Hockenheim the car for once let her down. Apart from those two races she always finished, usually quite respectably. She even had two points to her credit as they arrived at the last race of the season.

But in retrospect, she could remember only incidents from the races. Mostly, they were a blur of noise and effort, the smells of hot metal and burned fuel and smoking rubber, of holding the racing line, fending off the car behind and always thinking how to get by the car in front, while calculating tactics, trying to keep the pit informed and responding to instructions. She remembered also the strain on her neck in the magnified G-forces, but with her specially designed collar and the attentions of a local masseur wherever they went she never again suffered unduly.

These factors were only magnified variants of all that had gone before. It was off the circuit that the changes were most noticeable.

It requires not less than seventeen people to carry out a refuel and wheel change on a Grand Prix car. This is a skilled exercise by which races may very easily be won or lost. Provided the pit-stops are separated, that number of mechanics can maintain two cars. With only one car to service, the team could aim for perfection and yet have an occasional let-up in the usual sometimes frantic pace. One consequence was that the car could be prepared to an exceptionally high standard, with a reward reaped in reliability. The mechanics were usually in holiday mood and adopted Jane as a favourite sister. Even the early realisation that they were required to wear lilac overalls to match the Alex-Leopold car had occasioned no more than half a day's go-slow before the team even left Britain, although anyone from another pit daring to comment was risking serious assault. It is customary for a car to bear its driver's name beside the cockpit, but the legend on Jane's car read RACY LADY. It provoked only smiles.

Laura had been brought along as assistant manager of the new team. Three races into the season, the former manager, from Impala days, decided that his loyalties lay elsewhere and resigned. Before a replacement could be found, Laura had taken over and showed such competence that she was left in place. She was hard put to it at first to manage the logistics and finances for this huge family but common sense and a methodical approach saw her through.

Julian Berkeley attended every Grand Prix in Europe but jibbed at travelling further afield. Jane missed his company but had little time for regrets. Life at the top of the ladder was hectic. Formula One attracts far more public attention and media hype than all the others put together. There were briefing meetings and press conferences and meet-the-public sessions and events somewhere in the overlapping areas of socialising and public relations, and invitations to appear on chat-shows and serious discussion panels. Jane signed autographs and smiled her way through the ballyhoo.

Among all this seething activity there was remarkably little time for gaining more than a superficial acquaintance with other drivers. But that year there were many Brits in the Formula One ranks and several old friends (and others) made sometimes surprising appearances. Raymon Felidas, her Colombian friend and lodger, had arrived in Formula One by way of Formula Three Thousand and a brief testing contract with Impala. Rolando Valleja had come from Formula Three (European) the previous year, and was still spitting venom; but the stories that he tried to spread about Jane were so obviously exaggerated that only the very credulous paid any attention. Joe Clapper arrived suddenly, following two successful seasons in sports supercars, to replace a driver who had quarrelled irretrievably with his team owner. Tim Makepeace, who she had last seen testing in Estoril, greeted her with cries of affection and also with pats on the bottom until she squeezed his hand, bringing tears to his eyes. Her long hours of exercise had given Jane a formidable grip.

The season usually begins and ends with those races closest to or below the equator. That year, the last race of the season was in Japan, at Suzuka. Jane stretched herself and the car to the limit and finished third. Her appearance on the podium after her quick-change act was welcomed by a roar of approval.

She went through the concluding interviews and appearances in a daze and hurried to catch the first available plane home. In the comparative luxury of first class she managed to sleep during much of the long flight. Julian Berkeley's chauffeur met her at Heathrow and she reached Grey Gables comparatively fresh.

Julian, on the other hand, was looking drawn. Jane offered him only a cheek to peck. 'I must have a bath,' she said. 'I can hardly bear to live with myself any longer. After that, you're going to tell me all about what's bothering you.'

'Treat yourself to some sleep as well. You must be jet-lagged to hell and back.'

She shook her head. 'Jet-lag never bothers me much and I slept along the way. Give me an hour.'

She kept several changes of clothes at Grey

Gables. She was back downstairs within the hour, as fresh as ever. This time they kissed with their old ardour. They settled in Julian's study, as he referred to it, although it more resembled a modern office, with filing cabinets instead of bookshelves and a run of desk occupied by a computer, a photocopier, several telephones and a fax machine, but the severity was relieved by several comfortable chairs and a coffee table.

'Now,' she said. 'Fire away.'

'You can read me like a book,' he said. 'What a secretary you'd have made. You know that I resigned as chairman of Alex after my heart attack?'

'I knew that you were thinking about it. I agreed that you should. It was too much for your heart.'

'Maybe. The point is that I'm just one shareholder now and an ordinary member of the board. We had to float an issue of shares to finance the recent expansions and most of them were taken up by pension funds, unit trusts and insurance companies. Sir Adrian Harcourt, of Allied Investors, was voted into the chair.'

'I met him once, didn't I, at one of your dinners? I thought him rather feeble.'

'You've summed him up. A straw going every way the wind blows. I suspect that

that's why he was nominated. There's been a board meeting called for tomorrow. The only item on the agenda is whether to continue supporting a Formula One effort.'

The silence in the room was so complete that Jane could hear the call of a woodpigeon in the trees a hundred yards behind the stables. 'I'll be sorry to give up now,' Jane said at last. 'This was my learning year. I'd have liked one more year, so that I can go out knowing what I can really do. But I suppose it's a matter for the board.'

'I *want* you to have at least one more year,' he said. 'I'll tell them so tomorrow. But I don't know if they'll listen. I'm convinced that you've been good value for money. But how can I prove that we wouldn't have had the same results without the publicity that's been following you around?'

'Including the glamour of being a rich man's mistress?' She kneeled down beside his chair and set her cheek against his. 'Don't worry about it on my account. If I don't get another Formula One contract, I might buy another Formula Ford car. Thanks to Alex BP, I could afford it now. Or I might go back to lecturing.'

'It may not come to that. Let's relax and enjoy tonight. Or are you too tired?'

'I'm never too tired,' she said. 'But this

time you're the one who shouldn't be too relaxed tomorrow.'

They went to bed together that night, but they were both sleepy and they had the whole winter to come. Like an old married couple they slept entwined after sharing no more than a cuddle and a friendly kiss.

In the early morning, Jane woke. Something was wrong but it took her several minutes of sensory exploration to decide what it was. Then she realised that Julian's breathing had changed. He was awake but trying not to let her know that he was in pain.

'Is it angina again?' she asked.

He sighed. 'There's no fooling you. Yes, and it's a bad one. But I don't think it's another attack.'

She switched on a bedside lamp and saw that he was nursing his chest and left arm. He was subject, she knew, to the headaches that glyceryl trinitrate can bring and so could not use a mouth spray but was limited to pills for dissolving under the tongue and which could, at least, be spat out at the headache's onset. She gave him a pill. It helped, but the angina returned half an hour later and when he risked a second pill he was smitten immediately by the headache which, he sometimes maintained, was worse than the angina.

She nursed him in her arms. 'One thing's for certain,' she said at last. 'You can't go up to London in this state.'

'I may be all right in a little while.'

'When this happens, it takes more than a little while. And when the pains go away, you're knackered until you've had a long sleep. Can't somebody else put the case for you?'

'Is Laura Black in Britain?'

'She was going to stay on in Japan to see everything on its way.'

'Then you'll have to do it.'

'Me? How could I possibly?'

Despite the pains, he produced a hoarse chuckle. 'You've risen to every other challenge I've given you. This is just one more. In my briefcase, on the desk, are some notes of what I intended to say. There's a paper by the Financial Director, Aubrey Kinnell, spelling out the reasons why he thinks that involvement with racing should stop. Watch out for him — he's a clever accountant but he's a petty-minded back-stabber. I always kept him on a tight rein but he seems to have got loose. There's also a set of the audited accounts. Look through them. You may spot something I've missed — I really haven't been fit to give it my full attention. I'll phone later and tell the Chairman that you have authority to address the board on my behalf.'

'Shall I call the doctor?'

'Not yet. He won't be able to do anything except dispense comforting words and there's no point everybody losing sleep. I'll have him called later.'

She dressed and went downstairs. When the staff awoke, they found her deep in a study of the papers. She ate a light breakfast and the chauffeur drove her to the station. In the London train, she studied the papers again.

A taxi brought her to Alex House. The meeting was almost due to begin but she was left to kick her heels in an ante-room. She supposed that they were arguing over whether she was to be allowed to speak at all. It gave her time for a third look at the papers and to make two phone calls on her mobile.

A secretary brought her a cup of tea and later escorted her to the boardroom before taking a seat at a side-table. The Chairman, Sir Adrian Harcourt, at the head of the long table, was a stout man with watery eyes. Six or seven men sat on either side of the table. Not one of them was less than fifty years old and nearly all were bald. Three of them stood politely as Jane crossed the soft carpet. The Chairman was not among them. She was shown to a seat at the foot of the table. The men, for the most part, were regarding her curiously as if examining some strange animal. She supposed that the media inventions were responsible.

'The purpose of this meeting — ' the Chairman began.

One of the three who had stood up broke in. 'Mr Chairman,' he said. He had a north-country accent. 'Julian Berkeley has made a lifetime's contribution to this group of companies. If he's unable to attend this meeting because of ill health, it would not be seemly to start without asking how he is.'

The Chairman looked flustered. 'Of course,' he said. 'Of course. Miss Faraday —?'

'I saw him this morning,' Jane said, firmly and quite truthfully. 'He was recovering from a very painful angina attack which had kept him awake for most of the night. He sent his apologies but asked me to speak for him.'

'I'm sure,' said the Chairman, 'that we all send him our good wishes. And now — '

'Mr Chairman,' said the man who had spoken earlier, 'in fairness to all concerned, perhaps we should postpone this discussion until Mr Berkeley can be with us in person.'

'I understand that the matter has some urgency attached to it,' said the Chairman. He looked helplessly at a thin-faced man at his right hand. 'Mr Kinnell?'

So this was the Finance Director. 'It does,' he said. 'If we are to cancel, we must do it now before next season's commitments become firm and while we still have time to commission other publicity.'

'Well, then . . . ' The Chairman sounded relieved. 'We are met to consider the paper by Mr Kinnell, proposing that we abandon our commitment to motor racing and resume a more normal advertising programme. Miss Faraday, you have a copy of that paper?'

'I do,' Jane said.

'Mr Kinnell?'

'Thank you, Mr Chairman.' The Finance Director paused until he was sure that he had their full attention. 'My paper was designed to draw attention to the very considerable expenditure which has been made on this racing venture and the savings which could be made by reverting to a conventional programme of advertising. The figures in the summary speak for themselves. They do not need me to speak for them, but if they are in any way unclear I will be happy to answer any questions.'

'That's admirably brief,' said the Chairman. 'Are there any questions?'

The men looked down at the table or across at each other, in silence.

'I have one or two questions,' Jane said, 'but perhaps I might incorporate them while I make a few points on Mr Berkeley's behalf?'

'Very well,' said the Chairman. His tone suggested that if Miss Faraday really insisted on wasting their valuable time there was nothing that he could do about it.

'First,' Jane said bravely, 'Mr Berkeley asked me to draw to your attention the growth of business during the past year. It is not the volume of turnover but the growth which should be considered against this expenditure and he submits that the growth has been exceptional. No, more than exceptional, phenomenal. He attributes this to the huge amount of publicity which has been generated by what Mr Kinnell refers to as 'this racing venture'.'

The Finance Director leaned forward to look down the table. 'He would never be able to prove that the increase in sales was a result of the publicity.'

'Nor would anyone be able to prove that it wasn't,' said the man who had spoken earlier. 'It's easy to say we'd save money by changing our publicity. We could save more by stopping it altogether. But what would that do to sales? Let the lass have her say.' There was a murmur of assent.

'Thank you,' Jane said. 'Mr Berkeley has

had these figures for some time whereas you'll appreciate that I only returned from Japan some sixteen hours ago. But he took the trouble to find out the turnovers and the expenditures on advertising of seven large cosmetics and similar companies. And please bear in mind that these companies were not expanding at anything like the rate of this group, yet the ratio of advertising to turnover is not dissimilar. This is a highly competitive field in which the end cost is less important than the fight for a market share. Here are the figures.' She read them out. Several members jotted them down.

'While I was waiting to be admitted to this meeting,' Jane said, 'I had time to make one or two phone calls. I already had the impression that the figure allowed in Mr Kinnell's paper for the assets of the racing operation would barely cover the value of the premises they occupy. The capital value of two Formula One cars with a large volume of spares, tools and machinery is very large. Depressing this figure naturally very much increases the figure put against expenditure and amortisation for the year.'

Mr Kinnell leaned forward again. 'Are you by any chance accusing me of tampering with the figures?'

'The words that Mr Berkeley used,' Jane

said bravely, 'and I have them here in his own handwriting, were 'creative accounting'.' Some of the board members chuckled.

Mr Kinnell flushed. 'Mr Chairman, I resent that.'

The man with the north-country accent spoke again. 'Mr Chairman, I suggest that we note Mr Kinnell's resentment and get on with the meeting. Has Miss Faraday anything else to say?'

'I have,' said Jane. Her lips had gone very dry. She was venturing out of her own field and might well be making a fool of herself. But — 'Mr Kinnell did offer to answer questions,' she said, 'and I would like to ask them now. In his paper, I see that Mr Kinnell put an oncost of nine per cent against the costs of the racing operation.'

'That is a standard oncost,' the Finance Director said angrily. 'All of our operations carry that share of the overheads required for headquarters staff, premises, maintenance, electricity and so on.'

'The premises occupied by the racing team are included in that oncost?' Jane asked.

'Of course.'

'But,' Jane said, 'I see that a separate charge for the cost of premises is put against the racing operation. I'm not an accountant, I'm only a mathematician, but — '

Mr Kinnell was frowning. 'What is your question?'

'My question is, do these figures represent real money?'

The frown became a glare. 'Of course they're real money. What are you getting at?'

A thin man who had not spoken before cleared his throat. He was totally bald and looked a thousand years old, but Jane could see that his wits were still very much alive. 'Mr Chairman,' he said, 'if Mr Kinnell is unable to see the young lady's point, I will spell it out for him. In Mr Kinnell's paper, he has charged oncost on oncost. I will elucidate further if Mr Kinnell or anyone else is unable to understand.'

'You needn't explain them to me,' said the north-countryman. 'Mr Chairman, I've lost faith in this document. It seems to me that there's no call to change our methods while we're in the middle of the expansion programme. Everything's going to plan. And I'll tell you another thing. My good lady stayed up half the night to watch Miss Faraday on the TV and do you know what she said? No, you couldn't know. But she woke me up coming to bed and she said to me, 'That must be good stuff you make, Ben, if she can get out of that car after racing for two hours and beating all the men and still look that good. Maybe if I get some of it I'll look just as pretty.' Well, that's what she said and we can always live in hope, I'm not holding my breath, but I'll take her home a package of our products tonight and I'll be satisfied if they make her look half as good. I propose that we postpone any decision until next summer and then consider the matter after getting an audited report from independent accountants.'

'Those in favour?' said the Chairman. It looked to Jane as if only Mr Kinnell failed to raise a hand.

★ ★ ★

While away from the race-track, Jane sometimes wondered at the other Jane, the one who did such extraordinary things with cars and then faced up to the resulting hype with apparent *sangfroid*. But once back behind the wheel she found herself at home. She had a quick mind and quicker reactions. She was very fit. The complex equations of line and grip solved themselves in her mind as easily and as instantly as walking or hitting a tennis ball. Had it not been for the jolting and the enormous G-forces, she could sometimes have believed that the car was still and the rest of the world in motion. If at any

407

time she became more than subconsciously aware of the precarious balance between speed and control, then something was dangerously wrong. She viewed the approach of another season anxiously yet with the certainty that total confidence would return.

Polly Parsons wrote:

With the retirement of the three most experienced drivers (deadly rivals who, I believe, were each only hanging on rather than leave a clear field for the others) and the arrival of a number of new recruits, the Formula One prospects for the coming season look wide open, all the more so because the fastest cars are not necessarily paired with the fastest drivers. Nevertheless, although the imminent Australian Grand Prix in Melbourne may provide us with some useful pointers, your editor has asked me to stick my poor old neck out and make some advance predictions, with particular regard to the Driver's World Championship.

So here goes.

To judge from last year's form and the winter testing results which have so far been leaked, the two American newcomers, team-mates Jenkins and Grundheim, seem to have a slight edge. Their cars are as fast as any others and the two have had very successful seasons in Indycars. They are tearaway drivers, happy to drive on the very threshold of disaster. If they can refrain from crossing that threshold, which they have not always managed in the past, either of them could triumph.

Canadian Carl Lansdowne rejoins Formula One after a season in Formula Nipon. He blames his poor showing in his previous visit to F1 on the car. He may be right. Given the right car, he can get out of his own way. His team-mate, Rolando Valleja, made a good début in F1 last year, and I'm told that the cars will be much improved this year.

There is no doubt in my mind that Raymon Felidas is among the more talented drivers. Unfortunately for his aspirations, the car, though fast, proved unreliable last year and may or may not have been improved.

Of last year's recruits, Jane Faraday ('Racy Lady') is worth watching. Don't be fooled by the cover-girl looks — any woman who can make it into the ranks of the Grand Prix drivers must have something on the ball and a physique of spring steel to go with it. She has what may be the fastest car of all this year, the Alex-Leopold mechanics and technicians have no other car to distract them and Jane is a slow learner. While she was working her way up the more junior formulae, she would put in an indifferent first year only to show surprising form in the second. It may be so again. She is noted as a reliable finisher. Whether this will be enough, I beg leave to wonder; but no doubt her backer, millionaire Julian Berkeley of Alex Beauty Products and Leopold Engines, will be completely satisfied.

Largely unknown quantities among recent arrivals are Britons Harry Appleby, Peter Fasque and Joe Clapper; also Pierre Duclos, the new addition to the French team . . .

Jane flew out from a dank and windy Britain to find Melbourne cradled in warm autumn sunshine.

Almost the first person she met in the airport was Peter Fasque, lanky and fit-looking as ever and still recalling with gratitude the loan of Junior. 'If you hadn't helped me out,' he said, 'I wouldn't be here. I'd probably be slaving in my father's office.'

Jane was embarrassed by such lasting gratitude, largely because she had made up her mind never to be such a soft touch again.

She searched for a change of subject. 'Are you married yet?' she asked him.

He beamed. 'At Christmas,' he confirmed.

'And how is . . . ' She was tired after the long flight. To her horror she could not remember his fiancée's name. Then it came back to her by way of a sort of inverted Pelmanism. 'Howling Gail?' Only when she saw him looking at her oddly did she realise that she had said it aloud. 'I'm sorry,' she added quickly. 'I shouldn't have said that.'

'Say what you like,' he said. 'Gail ran off with a stockbroker. I married my father's secretary.'

'I hope you'll be very happy,' Jane said feebly. They were arriving at the baggage carousels. Another man nodded to Jane and attempted a smile. His face was faintly familiar but Jane, unable to place him, thought that she associated his face with something less than pleasant and was suddenly nervous of making another *faux pas*. She returned his nod and turned away. Jeremy Francis looked daggers at her back But Jane was quite unaware of his animosity.

★　★　★

411

It seemed at first that Ms Parsons's predictions might turn out to be remarkably accurate.

When the teams arrived in San Marino after the first three races the two Americans had almost wiped the board, with three wins, two second places and a third between them. But in San Marino the open car which they were sharing to make an almost royal procession from their hotel to the circuit, vanished under an out-of-control juggernaut. Miraculously, nobody was killed, but Grundheim and Jenkins were both hospitalised and it was soon clear that neither would be back at the wheel before the end of the season.

That mishap brought Carl Lansdowne and Rolando Valleja to the fore, with fifteen and sixteen points respectively. Jane, who had been making a fifth place finish all her own, was faint but pursuing with six.

The two new leaders, who were soon making themselves unpopular by assuming an air suggesting that there were no other contenders for the championship, were brought down to earth at San Marino. Raymon Felidas, without a point to his name so far, found the Imola circuit, despite its several blind crests, very much to his liking and the car for once kept going to the end. He suddenly found form and made the right tactical decisions. He took pole position and romped home in the lead, hotly pursued by Valleja and Lansdowne. Jane moved up to fourth.

At Monaco, Jane moved up again. By putting in a storming qualifying lap while she had the circuit almost to herself, she earned a place on the front row of the grid. After the start, she was in second place at Ste-Devote, the first bend, and by making her single stop early and driving a defensive race she held that place almost throughout and finished second to Tim Makepiece. Lansdowne and Valleja finished third and fourth, but their cars were deemed to have contravened a regulation, were disqualified and suspended for another race. It was generally supposed that the scrutineers were being unusually severe because the pair were incurring universal dislike.

In Canada, Jane dropped back again to fifth. The other points went to drivers who had not previously scored.

From then on, the old pattern re-established itself. Harry Appleby found form and managed two wins before lapsing again into comparative obscurity, but Valleja and Lansdowne each collected three more wins and other points. After the penultimate race of the season, before wildly enthusiastic

413

crowds at Jerez in Spain, the safest circuit of all and the pleasantest to drive, Lansdowne had amassed sixty-five points and Valleja sixty-four. Even when closer scrutiny of the scoreboard showed that Jane, who had only failed to finish once and had otherwise never been out of the points, had gathered a remarkable fifty-six, it seemed inevitable that Lansdowne or Valleja would become World Champion, but if neither of them finished in Suzuka and Jane managed to take her first win in Formula One, she could in theory still take the title.

★   ★   ★

Most of the drivers flew from Spain directly to Japan and had a respite before the last race of the season. But Jane had received a phone call which worried her. She resigned herself to extra hours spent in aeroplanes and airports and flew home.

Back at Grey Gables, she found Julian Berkeley looking older than his years. What had been taken for a second heart attack was now believed to have been a very severe angina, but his heart was giving cause for concern. An appointment had been made for a bypass operation.

'I'm going to stay with you,' Jane said.

'You are not.'

'I can't leave you at a time like this.'

Julian took her wrist although there was little strength in his grip. 'If you stay here,' he said, 'you'll be one more person whose feelings I have to spare. The doctors can do more for me than you can. While I'm under the knife, I won't even know that you are there. And you would be letting down all those who've backed you from the beginning.'

'You've always said that I'd have done my bit if I made a showing,' Jane pointed out. 'Well, I've made my showing for this year.'

'Do you think your mechanics see it that way? Or the Leopold Engines team? You've had luck riding with you. You'll never be so well placed again.'

'I don't have a hope in hell of the title. Even if I won the race, one of those two yobs would be bound to pick up a couple of points and scrape home.'

'You don't know that. But even if it turns out to be true, would you want to have gone down without a fight? More to the point, do you want me to live for the rest of my life, long or short as it may be, knowing that I cost you your one chance of reaching the absolute summit? I thought you were more of a fighter than that.'

They had nearly a week together before

they parted, Jane to Japan and Julian to hospital. There was a special passion in their farewells which neither of them could have explained.

In Japan, Jane found the atmosphere fairly crackling with electricity. Complete strangers stopped her to wish her luck. When she expressed surprise at this, Laura asked her if she was daft. 'You've got all the feminists rooting for you,' she said, 'most of the other women, nearly all the Brits and everybody whose back's ever been put up by Rolando or Carl. Between them that must be nine-tenths of the human race and probably quite a lot of animals as well. I'll bet you Carl Lansdowne would rather kick a dog out of the way than step over it.'

Race-day approached and arrived amid a more than usually carnival atmosphere. The Constructor's Championship was already decided and only Rolando Valleja, Carl Lansdowne and, just possibly, Jane could aspire to the Driver's Championship. For the rest, it was as if the all too brief winter respite had already begun. School was almost Out.

The Japanese are passionate and knowledgeable devotees of motor racing. Jane submitted to the attention of the fans and the razzmatazz and ballyhoo of the run-up, patiently but absently. She felt unsettled.

Ginger had told her that he was to be married and introduced his fiancée, a dark, plump girl as unlike Jane as it was possible to be. Jane had no designs on Ginger and she had a love of her own, yet somehow she felt betrayed. Ginger had been in the background since the beginning, faithful and admiring. Life without his support outside the racing game as well as within, would not be the same.

She gave her attention to the briefing meeting and made polite answers at the media conference and meet-the-public sessions. She qualified for a place on the sixth row, a lowly position for her and one which caused the members of her team to look at each other with pursed lips and attack the set-up of the car with a new ferocity. Hope is the life-blood of motor racing and the team was determined that Jane should have her chance.

Before getting into the car, while she should have been summoning the adrenaline, she took a phone call which failed to settle her down. Waiting on the grid to start the warm-up lap, she ran over in her mind what would almost certainly be her last season. Leaving aside other factors, she could see for herself that the expansion of the Alex group of companies was almost complete, its market share established. Now would be the time to cut back on advertising and reap the rewards. It had been a good time, a marvellous time, a time such as was given to very few, but it was almost over.

It had been a season without a single win, but she had earned four second places, four thirds, three fourths, three fifths and a sixth place. (The sixth, to her disappointment, had been the British GP at Silverstone, where she had desperately wanted to shine.) A perfectly creditable year's performance. And yet Julian's words kept struggling to the front of her mind . . . *that I cost you your one chance.* And . . . *I thought that you were more of a fighter than that.*

The cockpit for once seemed an alien environment. She checked that the radio was receiving and not transmitting. 'Goddam,' she said aloud, and 'Thost!'

She began, belatedly, to summon up the mood. They set off on the warming-up lap, strictly retaining order for fear of a time penalty. By the time they were back in their places on the grid she was halfway psyched up.

The lights changed before she was ready for them.

Up ahead, a car had stalled on the line and was hit by the car behind. A similar accident might easily have involved Jane. The driver in front of her, a Swede, also stalled, but Jane was concentrating on not being penalised for jumping the start on the awkward downhill slope and so she was getting away late and had time to take avoiding action. In the long run to the first corner she sorted herself out and realised that she had picked up three places already without trying.

There is only one perfect line through the first bend at Suzuka and two cars competed for it. One, the Japanese driver, was forced to run wide and was out, to the despair of the local crowd.

Two drivers, both Italian, had been caught out by the down-slope at the start and were adjudged to have jumped the lights. They were black-flagged and given a time penalty. Without overtaking a single car, Jane had made up half of her deficit.

Most drivers enjoy Suzuka. Jane made up her mind to enjoy her last race and in doing so she picked up seconds a lap.

Cars began to come in for fuel and a wheel-change. Two drivers exceeded the pit lane speed limit and were given time penalties for jumping the start. Faster cars were soon lapping slower ones, or being held up. Jane had as usual chosen a one-stop strategy. Two or even three stops might be faster in the computer, but that approach entailed more overtaking and so more risk of holdup or damage. Stubbornly defensive driving by a rival could undo the best-laid plans. Jane's pit-stop, refined by hours of practice and analysis, was among the quickest. It gained her another place and nobody stole an advantage from her.

With ten laps to go, six cars had developed faults and been retired. Jane had fought her way past others and into third place. But ahead of her and still out of sight, Lansdowne and Valleja were still fighting it out. Team-mates they might be, but there were no team orders. Whichever came in first would take the championship, the kudos and the benefits that went with it.

Lansdowne was in the lead entering The Spoon and intended to stay there. But the back straight which follows would be Valleja's best chance to challenge. He arrived as fast as he dared, in fourth gear, and put the power on too early while exiting. He started to run wide. He would certainly spin off if he lifted his foot. He had a slightly better percentage chance if he kept the power on, but not this time. The car went off at speed and hit the tyre wall. Valleja counted himself lucky to walk away. But his chance of the championship was gone. He stamped back through the pedestrian underpass, hating everybody.

As the in-car radios immediately con-firmed, Lansdowne had only to finish. Even if Jane won the race, he would need only two points for a fifth place for the championship to be his.

But the long, fierce duel with his team-mate had placed great strain on the car. The engine, in particular, had suffered. Time after time, Lansdowne had taken the revs to the absolute limit, searching for that last ounce of power. The technician on the telemetry could read the signs and he warned the team manager, who used the radio to warn the driver. Lansdowne nursed his engine but, four laps from the end, the television monitors showed an ominous puff of blue smoke.

Jane's car was still running as sweetly as a Mozart aria. She had no cause for caution any more and was shaving her margins to the bone. She had Lansdowne in her view and was coming up fast. His radio warned him, but he had already seen her in his mirrors through a cloud of his own smoke. He only needed to finish fifth to become World Champion, but on the subject of Jane he was no longer quite rational. It would have been against his instinct to let her go by. He speeded up as much as he dared. There was a different beat to the engine now. He knew through his fingertips that the car was about to fail.

The cars swept right-handed into the start/finish straight. Jane saw her chance and went to sweep by. Lansdowne moved over to 'shut the door'. Jane found room. He twitched the wheel. Jane went by but she felt him nudge her back wheel.

Lansdowne's engine failed with a crunch. He coasted to the side of the track.

Nobody was in any doubt as to what had happened. It had taken place in front of much of the crowd and in full view of the television cameras. Rightly or wrongly, it was taken for a deliberate side-swipe. Lansdowne set off to walk to the pits through a barrage of reproof, screwed-up programmes, empty drinks cans and orange peel.

Jane found herself in the lead at last but there was a serious vibration from that rear wheel. The telemetry picked it up. 'Slow down,' said the voice in her ear urgently. She slowed by about 40 k.p.h. The vibration stopped. 'You don't have time to come in,' said the voice. (Jane could have told him that.) 'Our best guess is that you can keep going if you stay below the critical speed where that vibration starts.'

Jane pressed the Transmit button. 'At this speed, who can catch me before the end?'

There was a short pause while the lap-charts were consulted. 'Almost everybody,' said the voice dully. 'Just keep going. The age of miracles is not yet past.'

* * *

Back in the pits there was consternation and fury. But for the discipline imposed by their chief, war might have broken out between Jane's mechanics and those of Lansdowne, doing terrible things to each other with air-hoses.

Laura was more practical. 'Answer Jane's question,' she screamed at the racing manager.

He shrugged and consulted the lap-charts again. 'Pierre Duclos is coming up fast,' he said into the radio. 'Then it's mostly Brits. Tim Makepeace, Peter Fasque, Joe Clapper, Harry Appleby, Jeremy Francis. Anyone further back has more chance of becoming Pope than of catching you, if you can keep going as you are.'

Laura found Ginger beside her, swearing imaginatively under his breath. 'Do something useful,' she said. 'You heard that?'

'I heard.'

'You go that way,' she said, pointing. 'I'll go the other. Tell each pit — '

She was interrupted by a sweating technician from Tim Makepeace's pit. 'We told Tim what happened,' he said. 'He's furious. He says he won't overtake the Racy Lady if nobody else does.'

'Great!' Laura said. 'Help spread the word.' She did a quick sum in her head. 'Tell them that we won't let anybody lose financially. Everybody must stay in the same order, or there'll be mayhem.'

'Right.'

They scattered. Along the line of pits there was much gabbling and waving of hands but Lasdowne was universally loathed and the message was passed.

★   ★   ★

Pierre came up behind Jane and slowed. He was thinking, *I could win this race. It would not be my first and probably not my last. But the memory of Jane in bed will always be with me. Mon Dieu, but we were good together. Formidable! I will settle for a place on the podium.* He fought with the car. A Formula One car does not handle easily at reduced speed.

Tim Makepeace also slowed. He thought, *She didn't have to tell the opposition what she saw, testing at Estoril. I could have got*

424

egg all over my face. I could have been killed.

Peter Fasque came within a second of Tim Makepeace and then lifted his foot. He thought, *If Jane hadn't lent me her Formula Vauxhall Junior car, I wouldn't be here. And then she pulled out of a race to reassure my girl-friend. The woman's a saint. Which makes Lansdowne the devil.*

Joe Clapper listened to his radio and slowed immediately. He thought, *I could say that I'd spent the night with her — and her business manager. It would almost be true. They took us in out of the storm — two luscious birds. If she hadn't been exhausted because of that, she mightn't have wrecked her car.*

Harry Appleby was closing on Joe Clapper. He thought, *I'm buggered if I do! The bitch asked me if I was in the male menopause. And then pretended that she didn't remember me.*

Joe saw Appleby coming in his mirror and coming fast. This one was not going to take any prisoners. Joe knew that there had been some tension between Appleby and Jane. *Probably a lover's tiff,* he thought. *Either that, or he's too greedy to be generous and he'll let Snot-face have the championship just to pick up points for himself. And — what the hell? — I'll be driving for a new, Mickey Mouse outfit next season because these bastards aren't renewing my contract. I don't owe them a damn thing. Here goes. Greater love hath no man than this, and similar daft bloody expressions.*

He led Appleby down to the final chicane, slowing further. Appleby pulled out to thrust by and Joe, at the crucial moment, turned on the power. There was no way that two cars could go through side by side at that speed or anything like it. The two cars slid wide, locked together like lovers.

Jane and Pierre were on the last lap. Suddenly, on the back straight, Pierre pulled out and shot ahead. TV cameras caught it, commentators raised their voices, the crowd hushed. Carl Lansdowne began to believe in God. If Jane came in second, he had it made.

Jane slowed further. There was no point in breaking down now.

The chicane was empty. Joe Clapper and Harry Appleby had slid clear of the track and were now out of the cars and engaging in a shouting match in front of the delighted spectators. Pierre braked late and came out with the car dancing. Up ahead, the chequered flag was waiting. He slowed to a halt, turning his front wheels in to the high kerb.

Jane came out of the chicane for the last time. Pierre had removed his wheel and was climbing out of his car. As a Frenchman, he might be less than magnificent in bed but he could be trusted to make the grand gesture. As Jane went by to take the chequered flag, he bowed low.

At that moment, his car's uncertain tickover faltered and the engine stopped. Another car was coming. Pierre's second place was in danger. So were his chances of third. Even a miserable point or two were at risk. He threw himself at the car to push it over the line, but the front wheels were angled towards the low kerb, and the slight slope, combined with the toeing of the wheels, defeated his efforts to haul it backwards. Any assistance from marshals would result in disqualification.

Tim Makepeace exited the chicane. An excited running commentary over his radio had kept him in touch. He took in the new situation at a glance. *Well*, he thought, *after all, I did once make a promise.* As the photographers converged on the spot, he braked hard, crawled up to the rear of Pierre's car and very gently, wing to tail, nudged it over the line. The car began to run away on the down-slope with the Frenchman running in furious pursuit.

14

Jane, out of overalls as was her custom, took top place on the podium, gravely accepting the trophies and the wave after wave of applause. As usual, she carried the champagne back for her team. For once, she proved unavailable for the customary interviews. She avoided those journalists who tried to intercept her and she missed the traditional drinks and karaoke celebration afterwards in the Suzuka Circuit Hotel. Instead, she managed to get a seat on an early plane home. The cabin crew recognised her and wondered why she did not look elated by her triumph.

Two days later, Jane was present by invitation at the board of the Alex BP group of companies. This time, she was not kept waiting but was admitted to the room before the formal session began and while coffee was still on the table. She was even invited to take a cup, but declined. The men all stood as she entered and there was even a modest patter of applause. She was amused to note that Mr Kinnell, the Director of Finance, had been replaced — by his former deputy, she learned.

Sir Adrian, the Chairman, cleared his throat to request silence. 'First,' he said, 'I think that we owe Miss Faraday our most sincere congratulations. Her success would have been remarkable for a man. For a woman it is unprecedented. The resultant publicity has been amazing, and it has had a measurable effect on business.'

There was a murmur of agreement and smiles round the table.

'Thank you, gentlemen,' Jane said quietly. 'I was lucky.'

'We make our own luck,' said the north-countryman who had supported her a year earlier. He seemed to have put on at least another stone since then. 'You made yours by being popular with your fellow competitors. If they'd liked you a bit less — '

'Or liked Carl Lansdowne a little more,' Jane said. She smiled for the first time in what felt like several weeks. 'Point taken. It was a strange sort of a day.'

'Aye, lass. It must've been.'

The Chairman decided to recapture, if he could, his control of the discussion. 'We asked you to meet us today,' he began, 'to learn your plans for the future and to tell you ours.'

Nobody was meeting her eye. Jane decided to cut short any embarrassment. 'Let me say straight away that I would not expect you to go on supporting a Formula One team for another year. I can quite see that it has served its purpose and that the high cost could no longer be justified.'

She could almost smell the relief round the table.

'Exactly,' said the Chairman. 'And, in fact, it happens that we've had an excellent offer for the team, plant, premises and cars as a going concern. But the offer comes from one of the biggest manufacturers of men's sporting equipment and clothing.'

Jane nodded. 'The very last concern to want the image of a woman driver,' she suggested.

'Exactly. We were wondering whether you've had an offer yet from some other team?'

'I had one approach,' Jane said. 'I turned it down flat.'

'You'll get others,' said the north-countryman. 'Bound to.'

'Whether I do or not,' Jane said, 'I am now retired and going to stay that way.'

'Oh. We had hoped,' said the Chairman, 'that you might be given a contract by another team. In which case we would certainly have bought space on the car for a major decal, or whatever the term is.'

'You shouldn't retire yet,' the new Financial Director said seriously. 'Now is the time when you can command the really enormous fees.'

Jane smiled at the grave faces. 'You have already been quite generous,' she said, 'and I have more than enough money for my needs. The fact is that I am pregnant.'

There was a moment of total silence, as if the sound had been switched off. Then a man with an aged but kindly face leaned forward. 'May we assume that this is a matter for congratulation?' he asked.

'Certainly.'

'Then we extend our congratulations and good wishes. But, if you'll indulge an old man's curiosity, did you know of your interesting condition before starting in the Japanese Grand Prix?'

'As a matter of fact,' Jane said, 'yes. Only the day before. I almost made up my mind to withdraw. But one of the last things Mr Berkeley said to me before I left was that he wanted me to go on. Then I decided to run but to go gently and not take any risks. I rather forgot that good resolution as the race went on. And that turned out to be one occasion on which the fates were determined to see me through.'

'And when did you hear that Julian

Berkeley had failed to come out of the anaesthetic?'

Jane nearly made a sharp answer. But the question, though intrusive, was kindly meant and these men had supported her to good effect in the past. She owed them a little tolerance. 'I had a phone call just before getting into the car for the warming-up lap,' Jane said. She blinked. She was determined not to let these men see tears. 'But his expressed wish was that he would not want to be the cause of my not achieving all my ambitions.'

'You are a woman of great resolve. So, no more driving except on the roads?'

Jane managed to smile. 'Probably not even that,' she said. 'I seem to have collected no less than three chauffeurs. But I hope that one of them will stay with the team as a mechanic.'

The Chairman blinked but decided not to pursue that provocative line. 'I think it only remains,' he said, 'to wish you every happiness at the conclusion of an association which has been very satisfactory for all parties.'

'Not quite the conclusion,' Jane said. 'I have been waiting for the proper moment to tell you that Mr Berkeley and I were married several weeks ago, at which time he made a new will. I now hold all his shares in the Alex group of companies. At the next general meeting I shall offer myself for election to the board.'

There was a stirring around the table but none of the faces was hostile.

'You'll have my vote,' said the north-countryman. 'For the last two years we've benefited from your beauty. Now let's have the benefit of your brains. What else do you intend to do with the time . . . and the money? Just be a mother?'

'That, of course, back in my family home. But I'd like to do a little more than that. I may go back to lecturing, part-time. And I'm thinking, in memory of my late husband, of using his house and money to fund a department in my old faculty, to study ground-surface transport and determine which way it should be going in the very long term.'

The Director of Finance was frowning. 'You may find that an expensive undertaking, beyond even Mr Berkeley's purse.'

'I could see retirement approaching,' Jane said, 'so I have been taking soundings for several months. The university has been promised a grant from the lottery fund and two European universities hope to become partners, with the help of EU grants. An engineering consortium is also interested.'

'In road transport?' a voice said doubtfully.

'Roads are not the answer,' Jane said firmly. 'Vehicles with individual drivers pouring along a flat surface. Somebody sneezes and everybody dies . . . ?

'You're not wrong,' said the north-countryman. 'Have you spoken to Leopold Engineering?'

'They're in the consortium,' Jane said.

She made a polite farewell and left a few minutes later. Several pairs of eyes followed her exit, speculatively.

'A woman of character,' said the Chairman. 'And now, to business.'

THE END

Other titles in the
Ulverscroft Large Print Series:

STRANGER IN THE PLACE

Anne Doughty

Elizabeth Stewart, a Belfast student and only daughter of hardline Protestant parents, sets out on a study visit to the remote west coast of Ireland. Delighted as she is by the beauty of her new surroundings and the small community which welcomes her, she soon discovers she has more to learn than the details of the old country way of life. She comes to reappraise so much that is slighted and dismissed by her family — not least in regard to herself. But it is her relationship with a much older, Catholic man, Patrick Delargy, which compels her to decide what kind of life she really wants.

A FANCY TO KILL FOR

Hilary Bonner

Richard Corrington is rich, handsome and a household name. But is he sane . . . ? When journalist Joyce Carter is murdered only a few miles from Richard's west country home, his wife suspects he has been having an affair with her, and forensics implicate him in the killing. But Detective Chief Inspector Todd Mallett believes that Joyce's murder is part of something much more sinister and complex. There have been other deaths; the senseless killing of a young woman on a Cornish beach, another in a grim London subway . . . And somewhere on the Exmoor hills a killer waits. Stalking his prey. Ready to strike again . . .

RUN WILD MY HEART

Maureen Child

For beautiful Margaret Allen, travelling alone across the western plains was her only escape from a loveless marriage — a marriage secretly arranged by her father as part of a heartless business scheme. In a fury, she left her quiet, unassuming life behind and ventured out on her own . . . Cheyenne Boder set out to claim a cash reward for finding Margaret and bringing her home. But the handsome frontiersman found a promise of love in her sweet smile and vowed to unearth the hidden passions that made her a bold, proud woman of the west!

SECRET OF WERE

Susan Clitheroe

Blessed with wealth and beauty, Miss Sylvestra Harvey makes her debut in the spring of 1812, and she seems destined to take London society by storm. Sylvestra, however, has other ideas; she is set upon marrying her childhood friend, Perry Maynard. What better way, then, to cool the ardour of her admirers than to nurture rumours of a scandalous liaison between herself and the dangerous Marquis of Derwent? This daring plan is to lead Sylvestra into mortal danger before she finally discovers the secrets of her own heart.

ONE BRIGHT CHILD

Patricia Cumper

1936: Leaving behind her favourite perch in the family mango tree in Kingston, Jamaica, little Gloria Carter is sent to a girls' school in England, to receive the finest education money can buy. Gloria discovers two things — one, that in mainly white England she will always need to be twice as good as everyone else in order to be considered half as good; and two, that her ambition is to become a barrister and right the wrongs of her own people. Ahead lies struggle — and joy. The road stretches to Cambridge University, to academic triumph and a controversial mixed marriage. Based on a real-life story.